Praise for the novels of Cassie Edwards

"Cassie Edwards has created an intriguing heroine. . . . There are many threads and subplots tying the story together, but at the heart of this novel are unique characters who put differences aside." —*Romantic Times*

"Cassie Edwards pens simply satisfying Indian romances. . . . High adventure and a surprise season this Indian romance." —*Affaire de Coeur*

"A fast-paced adventure story centering on forbidden love. . . . Cassie Edwards continues to write classic Indian romances that have captivated readers for over a decade. Attuned to what readers want . . . this is Ms. Edwards's genius, and her continued success proves that many readers still crave a good old-fashioned read." —*Romantic Times*

continued on next page . . .

"As always, Cassie Edwards writes with compassion and sensitivity of the Native American struggles to find peace in a world torn asunder by hatred and war."
—*Romantic Times*

"Heartwarming, very descriptive, the story will make you think. Clearly essential for your fall reading list!"
—*Rendezvous*

"Intense . . . readers will enjoy [Edwards's] masterful touch with the symbolic and sensual elements of Indian romance." —*Romantic Times*

"A fine writer . . . accurate . . . Indian history and language keep readers interested." —*Tribune*, Greeley, CO

"Edwards puts an emphasis on placing authentic customs and language in each book. Her Indian books have generated much interest throughout the country, and elsewhere." — *Journal Gazette*, Mattoon, IL

Also by Cassie Edwards

Silver Wing
Lone Eagle
Bold Wolf
Flaming Arrow
White Fire
Rolling Thunder
Wild Whispers
Wild Thunder
Wild Bliss
Wild Abandon
Wild Desire
Wild Splendor
Wild Embrace
Wild Rapture
Wild Ecstasy

THUNDER HEART

Cassie Edwards

SIGNET
Published by New American Library, a division of
Penguin Putnam Inc., 375 Hudson Street,
New York, New York 10014, U.S.A.
Penguin Books Ltd, 27 Wrights Lane,
London W8 5TZ, England
Penguin Books Australia Ltd,
Ringwood, Victoria, Australia
Penguin Books Canada Ltd, 10 Alcorn Avenue,
Toronto, Ontario, Canada M4V 3B2
Penguin Books (N.Z.) Ltd, 182–190 Wairau Road,
Auckland 10, New Zealand

Penguin Books Ltd, Registered Offices:
Harmondsworth, Middlesex, England

First published by Signet, an imprint of New American Library, a division of
Penguin Putnam Inc.

First Printing, December 1999
10 9 8 7 6 5 4 3 2 1

The poem on page ix appears by permission of Patricia McCalpin

Printed in the United States of America

With much love and pride I dedicate Thunder Heart *to my dear son Brian Edwards, and also to sweet Tiffany Schrock.*

Love,

Mom

The Indians walked for thousands of miles,
And we never once thought of their hardships and trials,
Along the way their loved ones died.
And we never listened to their pleas and cries.
All they wanted was to be left in peace.
And all we did was give them grief.
The trail they trod so long ago
Is now a trail well traveled and old.
But as we take the path through the years,
Let us not forget their
Fears and tears.

—PATRICIA MCCALPIN, *Poet and Romance Reader*

PROLOGUE

Tell me not, in mournful numbers,
Life is but an empty dream!

—Henry Wadsworth Longfellow
(1807–1882)

The Black Hills—South Dakota, 1877

The sky was blue, deep, and flawless. The green foothills lifted to the mountains. The winds were warm and pleasant as smoke spiraled slowly from the Ponca people's conical lodges.

Also adrift in the air was the sweet laughter of small children at play, dogs yapping as they joined the fun this early morning.

His bare bronze chest swollen with pride, his waist-length black hair fluttering down his back, and his breechclout lifting from his long muscled legs in the gentle breeze, Thunder Heart looked out across the land that had been set aside for his people's large garden. He was glad that winter was behind them. The women and older children of his village were planting the crops that would, when harvested, sustain them through the next long winter.

Their corn was always planted, in a ritual, soon after the frost had left the ground. A planter removed a sod from the ground to form a *magdage,* or corn hill. Then he made a "buffalo track" with his hand, dropped a few seeds into this, and covered and smoothed out the hill of dirt.

Thunder Heart recalled the very first time he had joined his people during the planting season, and smiled at the way his mother had explained to him how to make the buffalo track by forming a fist with his right hand, the first and second fingers extended and bent at the first joint.

Following his mother's teaching, Thunder Heart had pressed his fist into the soft earth, making a depression that very much resembled a bison's hoofprint.

"My *wizige,* my son, you are lost in deep thought."

The voice of Seven Drums, his chieftain father, brought Thunder Heart out of his deep reverie. He turned and gazed with much affection at the patriarch, who wore a wreath of sage about his head. His graying hair hung loose and fell way past his shoulders. He also wore a brilliantly designed blanket around his thin frame.

Thunder Heart could not help but be concerned about how his father's face had become so gaunt of late. And the winter had been hard not only on him but on most all of the villagers who were growing into the twilight years of their lives.

"*Indadi,* my father, I am glad that winter and its woes are behind our Ponca people," Thunder Heart said, placing a gentle hand on his father's shoulder. "Now there is the blessing of the sun and what it brings from the earth to think about and be thankful for. The land has been good to us in the past. So shall it be this growing season."

As Thunder Heart withdrew his hand, Chief Seven Drums stepped closer to him.

Then Seven Drums too looked at those of his people who were dropping corn into the mounds that had been opened in the soil. He too could envision a bountiful harvest. This land *had* been good to his people, but only he knew that they would not be there to harvest it in late summer. A few days ago a white pony soldier had brought word to him of his people's impending removal by the white government.

So badly wanting it to be false, Seven Drums had ignored the message and had encouraged his people to plant their crops as usual. He had thought that as long as they went on with their normal lives, perhaps they could continue living as they had for generations.

"*Indadi,* you look at your people, yet I sense you do not truly see them," Thunder Heart said, as he studied his father's eyes closely. In them he saw a strange sort of haunting, a sadness unfamiliar to the son of this great Ponca chief.

"I am just tired," Seven Drums said in a subdued voice.

Seven Drums was only now aware of how he had lowered his eyes to the ground, which, had he caught himself in time, he would never have done in the presence of his son.

But he felt defeated. Although he had placed his mark on what were called treaty papers, which should have saved his people from banishment from their precious land, it was not to be so. Like other tribes, his people had been tricked.

And now all his people would have to pay for this old man's stupidity and ignorance!

He looked over at Thunder Heart, who was next in line to be chief for their Wasabe (Grizzly Bear) Clan. He could not have asked for a son who gave him more pride. He was not only intelligent and brave, a born leader, he was a man of thick muscle, broad shoulders, and a chiseled face of nobility and intelligence.

Chief Seven Drums now realized the wrong in not having allowed his son to sit in on the treaty meetings with the United States Government people.

But it had not been out of wanting all of the glory himself that he had sat alone with the white men in their blue uniforms.

It was because he was afraid of what might come from the meeting—the trickery that he now knew to be true, and that he did not want his son to carry with him, on his shoulders and inside his heart, for the rest of his life.

If anyone was to be blamed now, it would be Seven Drums . . . only Seven Drums!

He was old and could live with the shame of it for the few years that he had left on this earth.

"*Indadi*, please tell me what is heavy on your heart today," Thunder Heart persisted, sensing a battle within his father's soul by the way he had hung his head in a shameful gesture of defeat and seeing, before his father had lowered his head, the pain in his eyes.

"Is not the sun warm and a blessing today on your face?" Thunder Heart asked with an ease he did not feel. "Do not our people hum and sing as they plant the seeds that will bring forth their rich crops?"

He swung around and with a hand motioned toward the happy children. "Does our children's laughter not fill your soul with gladness, pride, and warmth?" he asked, smiling as one of the young braves turned and gave him a smile and a wave.

Thunder Heart returned the wave, then placed a gentle hand on his father's shoulder again. "Does not my wife, Pretty Eagle, carry your first grandchild in her belly?" he said thickly.

Thunder Heart smiled to himself remembering the very moment Pretty Eagle had revealed such wondrous news to a husband who was eager to have a *wizige*, a son. Never had Thunder Heart been as proud, or as happy!

That happiness was now being threatened, as was everything that he did to make life good for his beloved wife.

Chief Seven Drums nodded. "Yes, that is all true, but, *wizige,* son . . ."

Seven Drums did not get out the words that he had hoped might ease the tension. The sound of many horses approaching interrupted, and he knew that it was the white pony soldiers arriving now with the news that would devastate his people's hearts and lives.

Removal. Their removal from their precious land!

And how could his people stand this? The Black Hills had always been their home. They knew no other!

Generations of children had been born and raised here. The graves of a dozen generations were here.

"Who comes, *Indadi*?" Thunder Heart asked. He turned and placed a hand above his eyes to shield them from the sun as he looked into the distance.

When he saw the thick cloud of dust rising into the sky, his insides tightened. Scarcely did anyone come to his village in such great numbers, not unless it was . . .

He looked quickly over at his father. When he saw the chief's wavering eyes and then his bowed head, which kept him from looking directly into his son's eyes, Thunder Heart's insides splashed cold with a dread he knew was too real to deny. It had not been that long ago when his father had sat with the treaty papers and the white eyes.

His father alone had signed the papers!

And when his father had returned to their village with a deep despair in his eyes, instead of the happy victory that should have been there, Thunder Heart knew that things had not gone as planned for his chieftain *indadi.*

Since he didn't really want to know the worst of it and realized that nothing he could do would change it, Thunder Heart had not pressed his father for answers. He had just gone about his business, trying to pretend that all was well. But deep inside his heart he knew it was not so. The change in his father's behavior from that day forward had convinced Thunder Heart that nothing would ever be the same for his people again.

The planting of the crops had just been a way to pretend for a while longer.

"They tricked us, did they not, *Indadi*?" Thunder Heart blurted out, the question like a sword being thrust into his belly.

When his father only looked up at him slowly and nodded, his eyes filled with sorrowful tears, Thunder Heart knew the answer without actually hearing the words.

The first thing Thunder Heart thought about was his wife and unborn child.

He glanced toward his conical lodge, where Pretty Eagle with her swollen belly was preparing their evening meal, her time in the fields shortened because of her pregnancy.

"My wife . . ." he whispered, then turned and

glared at the pony soldiers in their fancy uniforms with the shining brass buttons. They were now inside the perimeter of his village, the pounding of their steeds' hooves like thunder, sending children scattering and screaming in fear.

"My *wizige,* take what is said today by the pony soldiers without too much anger toward your *indadi,*" Chief Seven Drums said just as the horses stopped and were drawn up into a tight line before him and Thunder Heart.

"Chief Seven Drums, President Ulysses S. Grant has ordered me to bring you these papers of removal," General Steele said as he handed a leather folder to Seven Drums. "You know what is written on the papers without me having to take the time to read them to you. You and your people have no choice but to leave. The white president in the large white house in Washington has spoken."

Thunder Heart placed a hand between his father and the leather folder. "*Indadi,* you need not take the papers and the insult they bring with them," he said. He glared up at General Steele. "White man, take the papers back to your president. Tell him that the Ponca people are not going from their land. Treaties were made to prevent such atrocities against the red man."

"Treaties?" General Steele said. He threw his head back in a fit of laughter.

He then locked his eyes on Thunder Heart's. "The treaties signed by *all* Ponca, not only by your clan, but by the others also, are null and void," he said dryly. "Now, do as I say. Prepare your people to move at once to Indian Territory in Nebraska."

One by one, the soldiers and their horses inched closer to Thunder Heart and his people, who had now gathered on all sides, their eyes wary, their shoulders slumped. One by one the soldiers drew their swords and brandished them in the air for all redskins to see.

"Savages, you have your orders," General Steele said between clenched teeth as he glared at Thunder Heart and then at his chieftain father. He threw the leather folder on the ground before them. "Here's the papers. They are yours. Read them if you can, then prepare yourselves to git. If you don't obey, your people will pay. I have it in my power to kill you all, one by one, if you don't comply with the orders sent directly from the president."

"*Wizige*, we must do what he says," Seven Drums said. He gently placed a hand on Thunder Heart's arm. "Can you not see? The white pony soldiers are many. Our warriors who are old enough to fight are few."

Seven Drums lowered his arm to his side and faced his people. "We must all do as we are told," he said, his voice breaking. "Or . . ."

He didn't finish his statement.

He didn't have to.

He knew that his people understood too well what had happened here and that they had no choice but to follow the orders laid down by the white president in Washington. They understood too well the consequences of not obeying.

"We will be leaving now, but many soldiers will return soon to escort you to Nebraska," General Steele said, his eyes locking once again in silent battle with Thunder Heart's.

Then he wheeled his horse and rode off with the other soldiers.

Sad and disillusioned, the Ponca people walked away, forgetting their mounds of freshly planted corn. The harvest would not be theirs. They must ready themselves and their families for the long march that lay before them.

Even Chief Seven Drums walked away from Thunder Heart, his head low, his walk slow and somewhat unsteady.

Thunder Heart stayed behind long enough to grind his moccasined heel into the leather folder on the ground. Then with his coyote pup, which he had only recently found abandoned by its mother, he left the village and went to Wind Cave to pray for guidance and the courage that would be required during the many weeks and months ahead.

Always a place of solace and privacy, Wind Cave had been found by the Ponca. Intrigued by how the wind behaved there, they had named it *Pah-hah-wah-tha-hu-ni*, Hill That Sucked In, or Hill That Swallowed.

Holding Ista-Duba, or Four Eyes, the name given to the coyote because just above its eyes were two tan spots, Thunder Heart knelt at the very entrance of Wind Cave and began his prayers.

His sorrow was deep. His longing for his homeland was already an ache in his heart, and he had not yet even said his good-bye.

He knew that the Ponca had no choice but to leave this sacred and beloved land. If they did not, they would die!

"Why?" he cried as he gazed up at the peaceful blue sky, wondering where his Great Spirit was now when blessings were needed the most.

CHAPTER ONE

Heaven is not gained at a single bound,
But we build the ladder by which we rise
From the lowly earth to the vaulted skies;
And we mount to its summit, round by round.
—Josiah Gilbert Holland
(1819–1881)

Several Months Later—Missouri

Thunder Heart could not believe how life could continue to be so cruel to his people, when their hearts were filled with nothing but goodness.

He stood outside his tepee and looked at his people's new village, which was set up in a *hudaga,* circle, beside the Mississippi River.

Thunder Heart's insides ached as he listened to the moans and cries of his people who lay ill, some dying. The remorseful songs of others tore at the very core of his being.

When his small clan of Ponca had arrived at their destination several sunrises ago, they had discovered that they had been lied to again. Without the Ponca being aware of it—since all clans did not live with each other but had been spread across the

Black Hills—the United States government had divided them into two separate bands.

One was led to Nebraska and became known as Osni-Ponca, meaning "Cold Ponca."

Thunder Heart's band was named Masti-Ponca, meaning "Warm Ponca," because instead of leading his people to Indian Country in Nebraska, the white soldiers had taken them to a place called Missouri, where there was nothing but hills and rocks.

None of his people liked Missouri. The moist climate was vastly different from the dry, bracing air of their homeland.

It was hot today, and it was humid, the close kind of humidity that didn't go away when a breeze wafted across the land.

The climate of Missouri had brought on much sickness among the Ponca. When they had arrived, many were already ragged and nearly starved from the long, grueling journey.

But now something else had hit their camp. A white trader had established a temporary post close by and had brought a virulent stomach ailment to Thunder Heart's clan. Shortly after his arrival, the trader had died. Now, one by one, Thunder Heart's people were dying.

His chieftain father was critically ill. Until his father's recovery—if he did recover—Thunder Heart was acting as chief. But being chief did not make things magically right for his people. He had helplessly watched the number of graves increasing outside the new village, and resentment toward all whites was growing like wildfire inside his heart.

Because of the white eyes he had lost too much already. On the long march Thunder Heart had lost his wife, his unborn child, and his mother to a fever called malaria.

And now, was he going to lose everything else that was dear to him? His father, and his people?

Their shaman, Lightning Eyes, had prescribed medicines, but they had failed to help his people. Chokeberry bark and fruit concoctions used for diarrhea had hot helped.

Nor had the oak and red elm bark boiled in water that usually helped stop the vomiting.

Thunder Heart had never felt so helpless. But he had to be strong. If he were not, all would be lost. He was their leader, the one they looked to for guidance . . . for their very existence!

"What more can I do?" he thought dejectedly to himself. He hung his head as a sob lodged in his throat.

CHAPTER TWO

Sing, and the hills will answer;
Sigh, it is lost on the air.
The echoes bound to a joyful sound
But shrink from voicing care.

—Ella Wheeler Wilcox
(1850–1919)

"Mama, the wind sounds funny today," Johnny Martin said. He gave his mother a quizzical look as she stood at the dinner table shelling peas from the garden for supper. "It sounds like it's moaning and crying."

Dorothy, known as Dede by her friends and relatives, stopped her shelling to look out the open kitchen window. On its sill sat a steaming freshly baked apple pie, a simple gesture of a life that was comfortable and sweet.

Past the windowsill, and beyond, stood an Indian village where crying and wailing lifted into the air, sounds of lives that were filled with suffering.

The eeriness of the sorrowful cries sent goose bumps up and down Dede's spine.

Sometimes, mingled with the wails and cries,

Dede heard voices singing such mournful songs that she could not help but feel their pain clean inside her heart.

"Mama, what is it?" Johnny asked as he continued to stare at his mother, a softly beautiful, tiny-boned woman of medium height, with waist-length blond hair and blue eyes. Today she wore a plain cotton dress and apron, but even attired so simply she looked like a princess from one of his storybooks.

"Mama, you suddenly look so sad," Johnny said.

Wiping her hands on her apron, Dede went to the window, took the pie from the sill, and set it on the counter beneath the window.

She took time to look outside at the beautiful summer day. From her window she could see rainbow-colored flowers of all the different prairie plants growing wild and scattered everywhere. Beautiful deep-blue flowers, in patches here and there, were the most pronounced.

The grass and trees seemed plusher and greener this year than she could remember them having been in the past. And the nearby forest was thick with beech and maple trees. The maples were big and tall and straight, with few low limbs. All their leaves were concentrated at the top, where the sunlight was. There were tulip trees, too, themselves tall and straight.

The air smelled crisp and clean. Birds sang in the trees, and squirrels, chattering like magpies, hopped and jumped from limb to limb.

But even though Dede enjoyed having her window open to the loveliness of the out-of-doors, today she had no choice but to shut it out.

Determinedly, she closed the window, though she knew it wouldn't permanently block out the sound of the Ponca's lamentations.

But at least, for a while, it would keep the sad sounds from Johnny, who, as a healthy ten-year-old, was sometimes too curious for his own good.

Because of his father's violent murder, Johnny had already experienced the injustices of life. And he would learn more soon enough, especially about how people's prejudices made them do things they would otherwise never do. Dede couldn't protect him from the world outside of the safe cocoon of "home."

It was enough that Johnny had lost his father and his precious grandparents. He didn't need to learn so soon the ugly side of life that held prejudice in its clutches like some evil seed that grew inside one's soul.

The Civil War had been fought over the enslavement of blacks. But no wars had been fought, or probably ever would be, over the wrongs done to the red-skinned people of America. They were viewed as "savages," not as humans.

"Johnny, do you think you can finish shelling these peas for me?" Dede asked, reaching around to untie her apron. "I . . . I need to talk to Bill."

"But he has several men in his study," Johnny said, again questioning Dede with his dark eyes, which he had inherited from his father. "You know that he has told us both never to disturb him while he's discussing things with his men friends."

"Yes, I know, but they've been here for quite a spell now and should be leaving soon," Dede said. She draped her apron over the back of a chair.

She then went to Johnny and tousled his thick, shoulder-length black hair. "And, son, as for what you heard today, what you thought were wind sounds?"

She stopped short of explaining about what both she and Johnny had heard. She didn't think it was wise to talk about the nearby Indians and why they were dying . . . because of an illness brought to them by whites!

Such a subject just wasn't something you would discuss with your ten-year-old son. He would, in turn, want more answers—answers that Dede did not have, for she knew very little about Indians, especially why they were treated so unjustly by whites.

Yet she didn't make it a habit of lying to her son about anything, except for her living arrangement with Bill Martin. Neither Johnny nor anyone else knew that she wasn't truly Bill Martin's wife, that they pretended to be married in order to make her living with a man who was not her husband seem decent and legitimate.

In truth, Bill was just a friend who had cared enough for her and Johnny to give them a comfortable home after Dede's father had died of a heart attack two years ago.

When Dede had been widowed, Johnny was only two, and she had moved in with her father, who was a widower himself. Then tragedy struck again in her family, and she and Johnny would have been left almost penniless, had her father's best friend, William Martin, not taken them under his wing.

Even though neither of them had a true attraction for the other that would have made them comfortable being man and wife, Bill suggested they tell everyone they were married to prevent gossip.

It was a lie that had worked. Everyone considered them legally married. But never in the two years that they'd been together had they shared a bed . . . only a close friendship and an intense love for Johnny.

"Mama, there you go again, lost in another world," Johnny said, drawing Dede's thoughts back to the present. He plopped down on a chair at the kitchen table and began shelling the garden peas into a ceramic crock. He gave Dede a sideways smile. "And you don't have to go on with telling me about those sounds we've been hearing this morning. I know what they are. I know it's not the wind. I wish it was, though. I hate knowing the Indians are ailing."

Dede's eyes widened and her heart skipped a beat. "Johnny," she gasped, "how on earth could you know that? And if you knew, why did you pretend otherwise?"

"I went and hid behind some bushes close to the Indian village the other day," Johnny said, wincing when he saw that telling his mother such a truth caused the color to leave her face. "You know, Mama, the day I tried out the new pony that Bill gave me?"

"Johnny, you were told to stay in the pasture on your pony," Dede said. She went to him and placed a hand beneath his chin. She lifted it so that his eyes looked directly into hers. "Son, you've been told never to go farther than where Bill's horses graze. We explained the dangers to you."

"Mama, I'd never go so far that I'd get lost," Johnny said, his eyes pleading with her. "That was what you were afraid of, wasn't it? You truly aren't afraid of the Ponca Indians, are you? They aren't the reason you warned me time and again to stay within our property line?"

"Johnny, you know that I warned you about straying too far way before the Ponca set up their village close to Bill's land," Dede murmured.

"Mama, why do you always call this property Bill's? Isn't it also yours?" Johnny asked softly, that question causing Dede's heart to lurch and her hand to drop away from her son's chin.

"Why, yes, Johnny, it is," Dede said, feeling suddenly caught in a trap. "It's just that it was Bill's for so long before he married me I . . . I . . . still look to it as his."

"Bill told me that it would all be mine one day," Johnny said, now focusing his attention on shelling the peas again. "But before that ever happens, he has said more than once to me that he wants me to go to law school." He dropped a row of peas from its shell into the bowl, then gazed up at Dede again. "Is that what you want for me, Mama? For me to be a lawyer like my true father was?"

"If that's what you want," Dede said. Tears burned in the corners of her eyes as she thought about her beloved Ross, whose life had centered around his family and his law practice, until the day he had gotten in the way of two men who were too drunk to know what they were doing.

She shuddered as she thought again, as she had so often since that fateful day, about how her husband had died . . . how her husband had been actually gunned down in the city of St. Genevieve.

Ross had been casually walking along the board sidewalk, headed for his law office, when suddenly two men burst out of a saloon shooting at one another. Ross had gotten caught in the cross fire.

He had not lived long enough to tell his wife and son good-bye.

"Johnny," Dede quickly added, "you know that your father would have been proud of you should you have the same love for the law that he did. But, son, he would also want you to follow your heart, not just do something because someone else wants it of you. It's a mite too soon for those kinds of decisions, anyway, isn't it, sweetie?"

"Maybe not. I've been thinkin' on it pretty seriously these past several days," Johnny said in a teasing fashion, trying to change the subject since he saw that discussing his father brought back too many painful memories for his mother.

"You've been thinkin' on it?" Dede said, then laughed softly. "Well, don't think too hard. You've still got a few years left to figure it all out."

The sound of raucous laughter drifting into the kitchen from Bill's study brought Dede back to the seriousness of life.

And after thinking about it, she knew that she truly couldn't go to Bill and ask him to help the Ponca. He had his own reasons for hating men whose skin was red. When he had been in the cavalry many years ago, stationed at a fort near the Black Hills, he had taken his new bride to live at the fort with him. Soon she was with child.

Unwisely, she had gone horseback riding alone one day outside the fort's walls. The horse had returned without her. An eagle feather had been tied within the dangling reins, a mark of the way an Indian bragged about stealing one of the white pony soldiers' wives.

Bill and the cavalry searched for her for many days and never found her. But they left a trail of blood behind them in the Indian villages to feed Bill's hunger for vengeance against the redskins.

When Bill retired from the cavalry he returned to his home in Missouri, some miles outside of St. Genevieve, and buried himself in building up his vast estate, which included many Guernsey cows and prize horseflesh. He had since amassed a great fortune and was now one of the wealthiest men in the St. Genevieve area.

Bill had told Dede about what had happened to his wife only once, then had never spoken of it again. But Dede knew that he carried the hurt and anger inside him like a sore that would never heal. That was the real reason Bill didn't want to marry Dede, and she didn't object to it.

He was a lonely man, but he still loved his wife too much to speak vows with another woman, or even to make love. He had told Dede that he had never touched a woman sexually since the disappearance of his wife. His needs, his hunger of the flesh, seemed to have died the same day he lost her. In his heart she was still alive.

After moving in with Bill, Dede had the opportunity to hire maids and servants. But she had always lived a simple life. Her husband had spent every cent of his money attending law school and had not had the chance to rebuild his finances before he died. And then she had lived with her father, a doctor who rarely accepted monetary payment for his services, instead taking a pig, or a chicken, or canned foods from those who were too poor to pay him in cash.

Dede had enjoyed baking, cleaning, and all that went along with doing for those she loved. And now she did the same for Bill, and she knew he was grateful.

But they had agreed on one thing between them: If either of them ever found someone they wanted to spend their lives with in marriage, each of them would be free to go and do so. They would make it look as though their separation was legally done, and they would tell people they'd gotten a divorce.

Yet Dede doubted she would ever need to leave Bill. Although she had accepted her husband's death long ago, she didn't see how she could ever find anyone who could replace him. As for Bill, he had always sworn that he would never marry again.

Dede had pretended to be Bill's wife for so long now it seemed to her that she was—except at night when they went to their own separate rooms and slept in their own separate beds. It was hard now for her to see herself in any other sort of life with any other man.

"Mama, aren't you going to go and talk to Bill?" Johnny asked, again coaxing a row of round green peas out of their shell and into the crock.

"I don't believe I will, after all," Dede said, sighing heavily. She saw how Johnny seemed to be enjoying his little chore, and it gave her time to do other things. "But I will go and gather up the laundry for tomorrow's washing."

"Take your time," Johnny said, picking up another pea pod. "This is fun. It's kinda like playing with miniature green marbles."

Laughing, Dede left the kitchen and walked down the long corridor toward the bedroom area of the large, one-story house. But just as she was about to pass Bill's study, what was being said behind the closed door drew her to a quick halt.

Tiptoeing closer to the door, she listened. She had wondered what had brought so many ranchers to Bill's home to meet with him.

And now she knew.

Bill was talking about the Ponca Indians and how the government had given them a parcel of land that ran too close to the ranchers' properties.

Everyone took turns to speak up, and all agreed with Bill about wanting the Ponca gone. None of them trusted redskins.

Dede recognized the voice of one of the men. He was a man who seemed as gentle as a priest, yet when she heard what he was saying, she saw him as a different man and stiffened.

"The time is ripe to take action against the Ponca. The Injuns are too ill to do much about anything right now," Abner Dunn said in his slow drawl. "Some sort of stomach ailment is wiping them out, one by one."

"That makes it a perfect time to truly weaken the savages," Bill growled out in a tone of voice that was totally unfamiliar to Dede. Normally he spoke kindly to everyone—but mainly he did usually avoid talking about Indians.

But today? Indians were the reason the meeting had been called, and this meeting was bringing out the worst in everyone, to Dede's way of thinking.

"Bill, what do you have in mind?" Abner asked eagerly.

"We ranchers can go and take all of the redskins' horses and weapons," Bill said dryly. "That will render them totally helpless. And if they try to stop us, or say that they are going to tell people about what we did, we can warn them by saying we'll slaughter them as though they were no more than worthless cattle."

He laughed, then said, "We can tell the savages that the law is always on the side of white people, that no one in this area, not even the law, would care if the savages lived or died, that they have become a thorn in the sides of all whites by their mere presence on land that was wrongly allotted to them."

The more Dede heard, the worse she felt. The men's attitudes toward the Ponca, and what they were planning to do, were making her physically ill.

Yet she couldn't move. It was as though her feet were frozen to the floor. So she stood there listening, seeing this new side of a man she had admired for so long.

Yes, she had always known that his hatred of Indians ran deep, but . . . this deep?

"If we do this, I hope the Ponca don't find a way to get back at us," Abner said, his voice revealing the apprehension he felt. "I've heard them called Pa-mase, or 'head cutters' . . . that they scalp and cut off the heads of enemies and throw them away."

Bill laughed. "I wouldn't put it past them, but, no, the Ponca are known for their gentle ways and peaceful nature," he said. "The fire within them has been extinguished by the white man's rifles. It'll be easy to overthrow them."

"When do you want to do this?" one of the other men asked.

"Let's make plans to go tomorrow," Bill said. "We will surround the Indians' village and take their horses and weapons as they watch, too weak to do anything about it. Don't you see? Without horses and weapons they will be totally helpless. Without a means to hunt they will starve. They will begin dropping like flies!"

Dede was even more mortified by this. She had a strong urge to go and warn the Ponca. She had heard that even though the tribe had lost so much because of the white people, they weren't hostile toward them. They *did* want peace. But if Bill and the ranchers did what they were planning, it could be the last straw for the Ponca. They might find a way to get more weapons and horses. They could retaliate and kill many people in the area, including Bill and his cohorts.

Dede went into the parlor and began to pace. She was torn over what to do. She tried to understand Bill's motives for doing such a horrendous thing to the Ponca. Of course it was because of how his wife had been abducted by Indians and had surely died while with them. But that didn't make what Bill was planning to do right. He had to be stopped!

But how? She knew better than to even try and talk some sense into Bill's head. Although he treated her kindly, he made no bones about how he felt about all women—they should keep their opinions to themselves and understand it was a man's world.

And for certain he had his mind made up!

That left only one thing for Dede to do. She would ride into St. Genevieve and meet with the sheriff. She would tell him about the plan so that he could stop Bill and the others before they made the mistake of going to the Ponca village.

But there was a flaw in that plan.

Johnny.

His future could be threatened. If Bill got angry enough with Dede over her interference and ordered her and Johnny out of his house, that would mean the end of Johnny's opportunities to go to law school and become an attorney.

"Oh, Johnny, I don't even know if you want to be an attorney," she whispered.

She went to the parlor window, parted the sheer curtains, and slowly raised the sash, allowing the Ponca's mournful wailing to enter her heart again.

"I must do what I must do," she whispered, feeling deeply for a people whose lives had already been altered too much by the white man and were now being shortened by a terrible disease.

She spun on her heel and stamped out into the corridor. As she listened to the raucous laughter coming from Bill's study and imagined the men laughing about the fate of the Ponca, she was more determined than ever to do what she could for the Indians.

All she could do after she went to the sheriff would be to hope and pray that should Bill discover her actions, he would not be so judgmental that he would ruin her son's life as payment.

Dede hurried to the kitchen. Just as she got there, she heard the men leaving. She watched them all ride away, Bill among them.

She turned to Johnny. "Son, I've got to leave for a while," she murmured. "I'll go next door and ask Frannie to come and sit with you until I return."

"I'm no baby," Johnny said, shoving the filled bowl of peas away from him. "I can stay by myself."

He went over to Dede and took her hand. "Mama, you look so worried," he said softly. "What about?"

"I'm all right," Dede said, falling to her knees to hug him. "Just stay in the house until I return. Your pal Joel will probably come with his mother. Pop some corn, then maybe play a game or two of Chinese checkers with Joel while I'm gone."

"Why can't I go with you?" Johnny asked, easing out of her arms.

"Just because," Dede said, her usual way of getting past such a question from her son. "Now go on to your room. Get the checkerboard and marbles. Joel'll be here in a minute."

She bent over and gave Johnny a kiss on his brow, then hurried out of the house to get her horse and buggy. She prayed that the sheriff would agree with her that the Indians had suffered enough injustice already!

She prayed that Bill would understand what drove her to do what she had to do today . . . her deep feelings for humanity, for everyone, no matter the color of their skin.

CHAPTER THREE

To me alone there came a thought of grief,
A timely utterance that thought gave relief,
And I again am strong.

—William Wordsworth
(1770–1850)

With Four Eyes tagging along behind him, Thunder Heart, clad in only breechclout and moccasins, trotted out of his village toward a butte that overlooked his home and the vast Mississippi River. Here he went to fast and pray for his people's welfare, especially for his ailing father.

The heads of each family also left the village on foot to have their own private time with the Great Spirit in their own chosen, secret places. They had faith that if they all combined their prayers with their chief's fasting, things would turn around . . . that the killing disease would leave their beloved people and their strength would return, so that they could once again live normal lives before the cold clutches of winter came.

Thunder Heart's time alone with the One Above

would keep him away from his people for four days and nights. The other warriors would also leave the village to pray those four days, but each day they would return, for without their presence their people were too vulnerable.

On the bluff, Four Eyes settled down on the hard rock beside his master, and Thunder Heart knelt, raising his hands heavenward. As he gazed into the clouds he began his sorrowful prayers, while below him the wailing and chanting of those in mourning continued.

He prayed that the illness would leave his village.

He prayed that there would be no more burials.

He prayed that his father might become strong again and be able to move among his people to give them comfort, to resume his role as chief.

He prayed to the One Above to give him, Thunder Heart, the courage to go on in the face of the unknown.

Four Eyes whined and nestled closer to Thunder Heart, who looked down and paused in his prayers long enough to stroke the coyote's fur, glad that his pet was no longer a pup. He was strong and muscled now and had come with Thunder Heart to be a part of the fasting and the prayers. He had left his cherished bones behind for as long as Thunder Heart himself would be fasting.

"You are as one with me, are you not, my coyote friend?" Thunder Heart said, smiling into the animal's soft gray eyes. Four Eyes seemed to know what Thunder Heart said and answered in his silent way, with his eyes and a lift of his paw.

Thunder Heart leaned down and gave the coyote an affectionate hug and then again raised his eyes and voice to the heavens. He had only just begun his fast but was already somewhat weak, for these past several days he had worked tirelessly to comfort those who were ill, neglecting himself and his own need to eat and conserve his strength.

Even now he ignored the gnawing emptiness in his stomach and continued to pray.

CHAPTER FOUR

By a route obscure and lonely,
Haunted by ill angels only,
Where an eidolon, named Night,
On a black throne reigns upright.

—Edgar Allan Poe
(1809–1849)

After looping her reins around a hitching rail, Dede walked away from her horse and buggy toward the sheriff's office that sat flush with the boardwalk, its false front looming high over her with the bold black word "Sheriff" painted on top.

Hoping that Bill wasn't anywhere near, and glad that thus far she hadn't seen his horse reined in before any of the town's stores, Dede stopped long enough to glance from side to side before stepping inside.

When she still saw no signs of Bill, nor his steed, she looked over her shoulder at her own horse and buggy. All that Bill would have to do would be to ride down this street and he would know that she was there, for he had only a year ago bought her the grand black buggy.

And he had only recently given her the beautiful black horse, knowing that horseback riding was her greatest passion, next to her love for Johnny.

"I can't let myself worry about Bill seeing me," she whispered.

Besides, she knew that in time Bill would know what she had done. Even if the sheriff agreed not to tell Bill where he had gotten his information about the raid on the Indians, she knew men and how they couldn't keep secrets about anything when they gathered, smoking their fat cigars and playing poker, several glasses of whiskey loosening not only their inhibitions but their tongues as well.

Sighing deeply, and knowing that she must try to save a few innocent lives at the Indian village, Dede opened the door and stepped into a smoky, dingy room, where sunlight struggled to get through the dirty glass of the one window.

"Dede? Dede Martin?"

The voice of the sheriff drew Dede around to face him as he stood up behind a cluttered oak desk. He was a tall, lean man whose face was covered with coils of orange-red whiskers, his hair hanging in greasy wisps to his shoulders.

His deep-brown eyes were friendly as he came around from behind the desk and smiled, reaching his arms out for her. "Dede, what's brought you to my office?" he asked. He gave her a gentle hug, then stepped back to gaze down at her from his six-foot-four-inch height.

His smile faded when he saw the seriousness of

Dede's expression. "Lord, no," he gasped. "Something has happened to Bill, hasn't it? You've come to give me the terrible news."

"No, nothing has happened to Bill," Dede said, realizing now that she was there, face-to-face with the sheriff, just how hard it was to do something that she knew Bill would abhor. If Bill found out, he would see it as betrayal and she doubted he would ever understand.

"Johnny?" Sheriff Dan Hancock said, suddenly grasping Dede's hands. "Lord, no, Dede, don't tell me something has happened to Johnny!"

"No, Dan, it's not Johnny," she murmured. "Why I'm here today is not about an illness in my family. It's . . . it's . . ."

She found her courage slipping away as he gazed so intensely at her while waiting for her to explain. Most women never entered Sheriff Hancock's office. Most situations that required his services were handled by the men of the family.

Dede kept remembering Bill's "motto"—that it was a man's world, that women were best seen and not heard.

And she had always been willing to play along, having had nothing to say of importance to a man wearing a badge.

But now was now and she had plenty to say, and by all that was holy, she was going to get it said.

"Dan, Bill has plans that I feel are wrong," she blurted out.

She stopped short when she saw how taken

aback the sheriff was by what she had just said. She was actually tattling on a man everyone thought was her husband to another man who was his close friend. She wasn't sure she could continue.

Dan glowered at her. He crossed his arms across his barrellike chest, his badge of authority thankfully hidden behind them. He began irritably tapping the toe of one of his scuffed boots on the wooden floor, stirring up dust with each tap. His eyes were narrowed and his jaw was set.

But, no! Dede wasn't about to allow his attitude to intimidate her into silence, even knowing that once she told him everything he might go right to Bill and spill the beans. She had known even before she came to the sheriff's office that it was a chance she had to take.

"Dan, I hope that what I am about to tell you, that it was me telling you, won't go any farther than me and you," Dede said, her spine stiffening when the sheriff's eyes narrowed even more at those words.

But still, she wasn't going to allow herself to be afraid to tell him things that needed to be said. The lives of innocent people were at stake here. For now, she seemed to be the only white person who cared if the Ponca people lived or died!

"I know that I can't ask for a vow of secrecy, especially since you are one of Bill's most ardent friends," Dede continued. "But I do hope that you will consider very carefully what I am going to tell you and try to talk some sense into Bill's head about what he has planned. I doubt he will question how you knew. There are several men in on this. Any one of them could get cold feet and come to you."

"Will you just get on with it?" Dan asked, heaving a frustrated sigh. "Will you just tell me and forget who is going to tattle on who? You know I'd not want to get you in hot water with Bill. I value your friendship as much as his."

Dede then saw a slight crack in his armor as he gave her a half smile.

"You're the one bringin' me those delicious pies from your kitchen, now, ain't you?" he said, chuckling.

"I have one cooling even now," Dede said, seizing the moment to truly get him on her side. He was a bachelor—he didn't have a woman to cook special things for him.

Dede had taken pity on Dan and had often invited him to supper so that he could get a decent meal. Otherwise he ate the paltry food served in the town's few dingy restaurants where rats and cockroaches fought for space in the kitchens.

"Dan, I'll send one of Bill's cowhands into town with a big chunk of that pie as soon as I return home," Dede said softly.

"Apple?" Sheriff Hancock asked, a sudden glimmer in his eyes.

"Apples picked directly from the tree in my backyard last fall, and sliced and canned and kept especially for making pies," Dede said, smiling broadly. "The way it smelled, Dan, it is one of my most delicious."

She smiled to herself when she actually saw a slight shine of drool in the left corner of his mouth!

"Thanks, Dede," Dan said, placing a gentle hand on her arm. "Now get on with it. Tell me what's bothering you so much you'd leave your baking to come and see me."

Relieved that he now seemed friendly, Dede opened up and told him everything about Bill's plans against the Ponca Indians. She was relieved when Dan seemed genuinely shocked and just as quickly promised that he would take care of it . . . that he would stop Bill's nonsense. "And I'll never tell him how I found out about it," Dan reassured her. "I'll take care of it for you, Dede. Just you wait and see."

She gazed warmly up at him. "Thank you, Dan," she said softly. "I knew I could count on you." She turned and headed toward the door. "I'll get on home now." She smiled at him over her shoulder just before stepping on outside. "And you can expect that pie within the next half hour."

"Dede, I've already died and gone to heaven with just the thought of that first bite," Dan said, following her outside. He courteously helped her into the buggy, then waved at her as she rode away.

The minute her eyes left him he frowned and doubled his hands into tight fists at his sides. "Bitch," he whispered, then stomped to his horse, swung into the saddle, and rode at a hard gallop in the opposite direction of Dede's horse and buggy.

"What does she mean, comin' to me like that,

thinkin' I'm going to go against Bill?" he muttered as he sank his heels into the flanks of his horse. "Damn it all to hell, I want to *join* Bill and the others. I don't like the Ponca being this close to St. Genevieve any more than the next man who's got an ounce of sense inside his head."

But for certain he wouldn't tell Bill how he found out, nor would he let Dede discover that he would be one of the men riding with Bill against the Ponca. He didn't want to chance having those delicious treats from Dede's kitchen cut off!

CHAPTER FIVE

This above all: to thine own self be true,
And it must follow, as the night the day,
Thou cans't not then be false to any man.

—William Shakespeare
(1564–1616)

As Dede rode toward home, she went over everything in her mind that had been said. She could not shake an uneasy feeling about how Dan had first behaved toward her. When he had realized that she was going behind Bill's back by being there, he made her feel like the enemy.

But things did seem to turn around, she tried to convince herself. Dan did seem sincere enough in what he had said about stopping Bill and about not telling him how he found out about the plan.

"Oh, Lord, please, Dan, mean it," she whispered to herself as she drove on out of St. Genevieve toward her home.

She truly didn't want to disappoint Bill. She didn't want to look ungrateful for all that he had done for her. And Johnny. He had taken Johnny into his life as though the child was his own flesh and blood.

Dede had already taught Johnny how to ride horses years ago, but it was Bill who took the child horseback riding at least three times a week. When Bill had taken Johnny outside to show him how to shoot firearms, Dede at first had felt apprehensive. She didn't want her son to grow up believing that one had to know how to shoot to survive.

But outlaws *were* multiplying in the area, and Dede, remembering the way her husband had died, knew that it was best for her son to learn how to defend himself. She hadn't even thought about Indians and what danger they might be to him, for at the time, none lived anywhere near. But even now, with the Ponca so close, it was still white men who made her the most uneasy.

"Yes, I've done the right thing," she whispered.

She only hoped that Bill would listen when the sheriff took him aside for that talk about right and wrong ways to handle the fact that Indians now lived on land once owned solely by whites.

Yes, she was right to try and help a people that were down on their luck. Even if it meant in the long run that Bill turned his back on her and Johnny. She had survived before Bill came into her life. She could survive without him.

But it was always Johnny's education that concerned her. He needed money—for that illustrious lawyer's degree!

CHAPTER SIX

Leave all for love,
Yet, hear me, yet,
One word more thy heart behoved,
One pulse more of firm endeavor.

—Ralph Waldo Emerson
(1803–1882)

A day and night had passed. Still unsure of whether or not Dan had kept his word, and noticing no change in Bill's mood, Dede worried that Bill meant to carry out his plan at the Ponca village today. Shortly after he went out, Dede left home to follow him.

Dressed in a denim skirt and blouse, leather boots, and a Stetson hat atop her golden hair, Dede rode her black steed a safe distance behind Bill and the ranchers. She had asked Frannie to sit with Johnny again.

When Dede left the ranch in the early-morning light, Johnny and Joel were outside playing a game of marbles on the ground. It was nice that Johnny had such a good friend, but unfortunately he would lose him soon. Frannie's husband had bought land just outside of St. Louis and would be moving his family within the month.

But Johnny would make a new friend. Like his father, he was the sort of person who made friends easily. Perhaps sometimes too easily, which might someday go against him.

Dede didn't want anything to happen to disillusion her son further. He had already suffered so much when his father had been gunned down as he had. The boy had gotten over that, at least outwardly, but she had to believe he carried it inside his heart like a heavy weight.

The cries of eagles above her drew Dede's eyes upward. Against the brilliant blue sky several of the magnificent birds soared and dipped and called to one another. Never had she seen such a beautiful sight. She hoped this was some sort of omen, an omen that meant that Bill and his companions were going somewhere besides the Ponca village.

But the longer Dede followed them, the more she knew that wasn't so. They were headed directly toward the village. They had just passed the border of the small parcel of land that the United States government had handed over to the Ponca.

"Damn it, if Dan talked to Bill, Bill ignored him," Dede whispered angrily to herself. "He's going to do as he pleases, no matter that so many lives might be lost because of it."

Today the Ponca's wailing, chanting, and singing seemed less intense, but she doubted that meant anything good. It probably only meant that they were too weak to cry out to their Great Spirit any longer. Or they might have given up hope that the One Above had any control over their destiny after all.

Dede still stayed far back from Bill and the others, yet she knew that their number had multiplied along the trail, as first one rancher arrived and joined them, then another and another.

When she thought she made out the sheriff among those who arrived, she scoffed, not believing he could be so two-faced as to say one thing to her and then do another.

Dede wanted to ride up closer to see if it really was Dan, but she knew the chances of being seen were too great. She continued to lag behind, still determined to see what would happen on this beautiful summer morning.

After riding a little while longer, Dede realized that now she was much too close to the village to continue following Bill. If she truly wanted to see what transpired, she could ride to a nearby butte that overlooked everything. It was clear that Bill was going ahead with his plan. Either the sheriff had not tried to stop him, or he had failed. Or . . . the sheriff might have been in on the plan all along. If he had, she was afraid he had told Bill everything.

If that were true, she had no idea what to expect when Bill arrived home. He had never raised his voice to her. But she had never gone against him either. Would she soon see a side of him that she might have cause to fear? Or would he just quietly, in his usual kind voice, shame her for betraying him and then forgive her?

Only time would give her those answers, Dede thought to herself as she slapped her horse's reins and led him up the winding path that would take her to the top of the bluff.

Finally there, on a flat plain of rock that overlooked the vastness of the Mississippi River as well as the village down below, Dede dismounted.

After tying her reins on a low tree limb, she went to the edge of the bluff and assessed things way down below her. Her view of Bill and the ranchers was momentarily blocked by the trees, but she could see the village. Very few people were outside their lodges. Most of them were inside, and she wondered if that was because they were either dying or busy caring for the ill.

She certainly saw no strong warriors anywhere who could stop Bill and the force of white men. Those Ponca who were outside were the elderly and the young. What was sad was how subdued the children were as they sat with their dogs, instead of being involved in games, their laughter filling the morning air.

She looked slowly over the tepees that were pitched in what she thought must be their tribal circle arrangement. She was awed by their grandeur. Smoke spiraled from smoke holes and the aroma of cooking food wafted upward. At least that showed some semblance of normalcy in the village, that the women were preparing food for those still well enough to eat.

She gazed longer at one lodge in particular. It was a fine white tepee and stood out from the others in size and color. Next to it was one equal in size and almost in grandeur, except that it seemed stained brown with age. She wondered if one of these larger lodges might belong to the Ponca's chief?

A sudden movement at her far right caught her attention. She was hidden enough behind a thick bunch of brush so that the Indian warrior resting on his haunches several feet away from her had not seen her. He seemed equally absorbed in the activities below.

To be safe, she hunkered down lower behind the thick-leafed branches before looking more intently at the lone Indian. He was dressed in only a breechclout and moccasins. His long jet-black hair was fluttering in the breeze down his lean, muscled back. His skin was a beautiful copper color, and every inch of him seemed to ripple with muscle as he now stood to take a better look at things below him.

She surmised that he was from the Ponca village, perhaps a sentry who was assigned to keep watch on things below. That thought gave her a keen sense of apprehension, for if there was one sentry, wouldn't there be more? Could Bill and the others be riding into a death trap? Was that why she hadn't seen any warriors in the village? Had they somehow gotten word of Bill's plan?

Panic reached her very soul at the thought of the Ponca ambushing Bill and killing him and the others. Bill wasn't a bad man, only someone who carried vengeance in his heart over what had happened to his wife . . . a vengeance that was surely more the reason for what was happening today than the Ponca being on land that adjoined his.

Dede's first reaction was to shout at Bill to warn him, yet she knew that he wouldn't hear her. And she didn't have time to go to him. If there was to be an ambush, it would be coming about now, for surely Bill was only a few yards from entering the actual village. Her heart raced as she waited to hear the first war cries of the Ponca as they jumped out with their weapons to attack the white men.

Then her attention was drawn elsewhere as a coyote came up behind the Indian on the bluff. Her heart lurched as she waited for the wild animal to pounce on the warrior. To her surprise, the warrior turned, knelt, drew the coyote into his arms, and hugged it. It was apparent that they knew and respected one another, that they were friends, perhaps even soul mates.

The Indian put the coyote back on the ground and again gazed down at his village, then abruptly turned his eyes in her direction, as though he might sense that she was there. Dede sucked in a wild breath and waited.

He didn't see her, but she was able to see his full facial features, and what she saw made her heart skip a beat. Never before had she seen anyone so noble in appearance, or so handsome.

He turned his eyes back down to his village, and he seemed to sway, as though he might faint. Dede stood up quickly and reached out for him, then just as quickly felt foolish for her action, since he was too far away for her to help him should he actually crumple to the ground.

That he had seemed to be weak enough to faint made Dede wonder about him. Instead of being on the bluff as a sentry, was he there because he was ill? Had he left his people to keep his illness from them?

Afraid again of being seen, Dede hunkered down behind the bushes once more, then gasped when she saw Bill and the ranchers enter the village. She turned quick eyes to the Indian on the bluff and saw that he was watching in total disbelief.

A pain circled her heart to realize that Bill, a man she had so admired, could be so inhumane to a people who were already weakened by disease.

As Dede gazed down again, she stifled a sob as she watched Bill and several others hold the Ponca people at bay with their weapons drawn. Other men went into the Indian lodges and removed their weapons, while still others went to the corral and took the Ponca horses.

Thunder Heart was numb from what he was witnessing, from what the white eyes were doing! How could the whites have known that all of the strong men of the village would be out at their morning prayers. That, at this very moment, only the old, the ailing, and the women and children remained?

How could they have known that his people's acting chief would be gone for a four-day fast, so weakened that only moments ago he felt a light-headedness sweep across him?

Thunder Heart was too weak to get to his people to help them, and even if he had been strong enough, he was only one man. The others were in their private praying places, and there was no way for him to alert them of what was happening at their village. If he let out a loud cry, the whites would hear. That might panic them into shooting the innocent ones who stood at gunpoint even now.

He gasped when one of the men went inside his own lodge and removed his weapons, among them his beloved bow that he had meticulously carved. He couldn't believe it as he watched the white men stealing all of his people's horses, riding off with them as though they belonged to them and not the Ponca!

It suddenly came to Thunder Heart why this was being done to his people . . . to weaken them further at a time when they were already so weak they could hardly live one day to the next. Without weapons, his people could not defend themselves, nor could they hunt for food to sustain them through the winter months. Without horses they had no means of travel.

"No!" he cried, and as he started to run down from the bluff, his knees buckled beneath him.

Darkness enveloped him as he fainted. Four Eyes knelt beside him, yelping and howling.

Thunder Heart's fevered cry had pierced Dede's heart like a stab wound. She looked quickly over at him just in time to see him crumple to the ground, apparently lifeless. She felt torn over what to do. If Bill and the others had heard his cry, surely they would be looking up at the bluff to see who was there.

When she looked down at Bill, it was obvious that no one had heard, but nevertheless her heart sank. Bill and the others had finished their pillaging of the Indians' homes and were riding away, laden with all sorts of weapons. The Indian horses had been herded away only moments earlier.

Dede looked over at the warrior and saw that he still lay in a dead faint on the ground.

"I must go to him," she whispered frantically to herself. "I must do what I can to help."

But then she saw the coyote sitting like a guard next to its fallen comrade. If she did go to the red man's assistance, would the coyote attack her? Yet the way it seemed so devoted to the Indian made her believe it was tame enough for her to approach.

And what about the Indian? Should she help him, or leave?

Because of what he had seen the white men do, he might hold her responsible too, since her skin was white. And then there was the sickness. If she came down with the stomach ailment, wouldn't she, in turn, give it to Johnny?

She tightened her jaw with resolve. She knew what she must do. At this moment in time she could not selfishly think of herself. There was a man in need, and she could not just stand by and not offer him some assistance.

Dede determinedly ran to her black steed, grabbed the reins, and led her horse over to where Thunder Heart still lay so quietly. She tied her horse's reins, grabbed the canteen of water from her saddlebag, and crept slowly toward the red man, her eyes on the coyote as it in turn watched her approach.

She was relieved that the coyote remained beside the Indian instead of racing toward her. She knew now that it was no threat to her. Its devotion to the downed Indian was too intense to concern itself over a mere woman approaching, weaponless.

When Dede finally reached the Indian, she still hesitated before kneeling beside him. She had never been around Indians, much less alone with one. But now that she was so close, she realized that he wasn't just any Indian. She had already seen the nobleness in his features, and now, up close, it was even more pronounced. She was taken by his utter handsomeness. Never had she seen such chiseled, sculpted features, yet there was a gauntness about him, as though he might not have eaten recently . . . or perhaps as though he was ill with the stomach disease.

Although she was worried about possibly becoming ill and endangering Johnny, she thought about Bill and how he hadn't seemed to think about his own safety when he had gone among the Ponca people. And the ranchers who had entered their lodges—had they not exposed themselves to the grave disease? If they brought sickness home to their loved ones, they would then regret in their very souls what they had done today to the Ponca. The Ponca might get their revenge in the end.

Dede brushed all such thoughts aside as she again focused on this one Indian and how quietly he lay on the rocky floor of the bluff. It made her heart ache to see him this helpless. She knew that such a man would never want to seem vulnerable in the eyes of anyone, much less a white woman. But now she knelt beside him, taking advantage of his fainting spell to see him up close, to be so in awe of him!

Feeling as though she was invading his privacy, Dede started to rise, to leave, then thought better of it and removed the cork from her canteen. She trembled as she placed a hand beneath the warrior's head, and brought the canteen to his beautifully shaped lips. Her heart pounded in fear as she slowly, carefully, let the water drip from the canteen onto the man's lips.

He seemed to respond automatically to her gesture of kindness, slightly parting his lips and allowing the water to slide into his mouth. Tears of compassion filled Dede's eyes even though he was a stranger, someone who would surely hate her if he knew she was there, no matter why.

A terrible thing had occurred among his people today. It had been done by whites. She was white. Surely she would not be hated any less because she was offering a mere drink to a fallen warrior. That gesture was far less than what the whites owed the red man!

Thunder Heart was slowly awakening from his faint, the delicious taste of water on his tongue. During his fast he had turned his back not only on food but also on drink. He now realized the importance of both, for his people needed him! He gratefully swallowed the cold liquid, then slowly opened his eyes.

He found a woman kneeling beside him, her face so angelic and sweet, her blue eyes filled with such warmth, concern, and compassion, he could not help but wonder if she was real or an apparition?

Had his fasting brought him this woman as an omen for his people's future? But how could she be? She was white! Whites were the enemy, especially after today when they had taken advantage of his people's vulnerability!

Stunned that the Indian's eyes were now open and staring straight into hers, Dede gasped, fearing his reaction to her presence. She dropped the canteen and leaped to her feet. Her knees weak, she ran to her horse. Her fingers trembled as she untied the reins and then swung herself into the saddle. Knowing that the Indian's eyes were still on her, Dede was afraid to look back as she rode away.

Surely he would remember her! Would he remember her as a friend who gave him a drink? Or would he remember her as part of the white community that had taken from his people today?

"Even their horses?" she whispered harshly, sighing heavily as the thought of Bill's being so heartless came to her again. She wasn't sure how she would react in Bill's presence, for now she saw him not as the man she had always known but as someone far different.

Thunder Heart leaned on an elbow and watched the white woman ride away and knew that she was real enough. The fact that her skin was white was also real. And it was whites who had just raided his village!

He started to push himself up from the ground, then stopped when he found Four Eyes lapping up the water spilled from the canteen that lay beside him.

Yes, the woman was white, but she was a woman with a good heart. *And courage,* he thought to himself, for she had come, alone, to help a fallen red skin, which surely meant that she did not approve of what had happened down below at his village!

He patted Four Eyes, then swept up the canteen.

"She is someone I must know," he said, smiling at the coyote as it gave two quick barks.

Then Thunder Heart stumbled down the side of the bluff, his heart aching anew for all that continued to happen wrongly to his people, understanding it less and less.

Just as he entered his village, the warriors who had been gone to pray for miracles started coming in, one by one, their eyes filled with shock and sadness at the realization that something bad had happened in their absence. Everyone came together as one in the center of the village. Silently seeking some way to understand what was happening to them, a loving and peaceful people, they all looked to Thunder Heart.

Thunder Heart felt their despair deeply inside his soul, and his anger flared as if a torch's flame had gone wild inside his heart.

"The . . . white eyes . . . will . . . pay!" he shouted, angrily thrusting a fist into the air.

CHAPTER SEVEN

All are architects of Fate,
Working in these walls of Time;
Some with massive deeds and great,
Some with ornaments of rhyme.

—Henry Wadsworth Longfellow
(1807–1882)

Everyone gasped when Thunder Heart reeled as another wave of light-headedness swept through him.

He inhaled a deep breath and steadied himself just as his father's sister, his widowed *witimi,* aunt, gently took him by an elbow.

"*Wituska,* nephew, you must go on to your lodge," Silken Wing murmured as she led him toward his tepee, with Four Eyes tagging along behind. "You need nourishment."

Her gray braids were wrapped tightly in a coil atop her head, and her long fringed buckskin dress was loose, allowing her freedom of movement. Silken Wing turned her eyes from him and looked slowly over the crowd, then gazed up at Thunder Heart again. "*Wituska,* your council with our people can wait until this elderly aunt sees to your needs," she murmured.

Knowing that she was right, that he had to abandon his fast, though he had hoped to engage in it for another three days, Thunder Heart nodded. Instead, he must concentrate now on how to acquire weapons and horses, to show the white eyes that no matter what they did, the Ponca would survive.

"*Indadi*?" he asked, gazing at his father's large tepee, which sat not far from Thunder Heart's. "How is he faring? Is he stronger? Or is the stomach ailment still with him?"

"*Wituska*, the medicine of our people does not seem strong enough for your father, or for most everyone else of our village who is ill," Silken Wing said solemnly. "Do you think the white eyes might have . . ."

She didn't get the question finished before Thunder Heart interrupted her.

"Ha!" he said in a growl. "Even if the white eyes did have something that might stop the sickness of our people, do you truly believe they would share it with us? Do you not know they took our animals and weapons today to further weaken a people who are already weakened by disease?"

He stiffened his jaw. "And I would never ask for their help," he said dryly. "I would die first."

"Yes, you are right not to want to ask them for help," Silken Wing said. She waited for Four Eyes to go on ahead of them into the buffalo-skin lodge, then followed. "And even if there were those among the white people who did not have a role in what happened today, and even if they came to our village with medicine, I would be afraid to trust what they bring. They might come with smiles but give us poison."

"It is bad to distrust so much, yet we have no choice but to have such feelings for the whites," Thunder Heart said.

He sighed with relief once he reached a pallet of furs and blankets beside his lodge fire, which had burned down to embers. Four Eyes snuggled down on the pallet next to him, and Thunder Heart patted the coyote's head.

The Indian's thoughts went to the woman he had seen on the bluff. How gentle she had been as she had given him a drink of water from her canteen! After seeing her drop it when she fled back to her horse, Thunder Heart had picked the canteen up to bring it with him to his village, but during a moment of weakness during his descent from the bluff, he had dropped it and left it where it lay. His whole concentration had to be focused on making it back to his village.

Although he no longer had the woman's water vessel with him, he carried memories of her inside his heart that he doubted he would ever let go of. There was such a gentleness about her, a kindness, a genuine caring. Her eyes had touched his very soul. Her golden hair had looked as soft as cornsilk. And her face . . . it was a vision of perfect features and loveliness.

"*Wituska,* here is water for your lips," Silken Wing said. She knelt beside him and dabbed drops of water across his lips to moisten them. Then she poured water from a wooden vessel into a wooden cup. "And now drink slowly while I get you some soup from my kettle," she said softly.

Thunder Heart nodded. He sipped from the cup, his thoughts now back to where they should be. An atrocity had happened to his people today. A council must be called soon to plan a strategy . . . one that would restore things as they should be.

He started to rise, to go and call the council, but his knees were too weak. They buckled, causing him to fall back on his blankets and furs.

Carrying a kettle of soup, two wooden bowls, and a spoon, Silken Wing came back into the lodge.

"*Wituska,* soup will give you strength enough to go soon to the council house," she said as she sat down beside Thunder Heart and ladled soup into one of the bowls.

She gave this bowl to Thunder Heart, then spooned chunks of meat and some thick gravy into the other bowl and placed it before Four Eyes, who began lapping it up eagerly, his tail wagging.

"Warriors are already at the council house waiting for you so you can all discuss what happened today," Silken Wing said. "No one can understand how white people can be so cold in their hearts. Why did they do this to us today? What were their motives? Do they want the land? Or is what you said truly the way you think it happened—they took the animals and weapons to weaken us? Do they want to kill off our people because they do not want us as neighbors? Or was it done only because they wanted the weapons and horses? Do not they have enough money to buy their own? Are they perhaps even poorer than we Ponca?"

Thunder Heart ate several spoonsful of soup, his thoughts on the questions his aunt asked him, and especially on the true puzzlement and hurt in her voice. He could not understand how she could even wonder about why whites did what they did to the Ponca—the whites had never done anything good for them.

For certain, they had made fools of the Ponca again when they gave them this small plot of land that was not even near the size of the land they had been forced to leave behind in the Black Hills.

Thunder Heart thought that his aunt and his people as a whole should be used to the evil ways of whites by now. They should expect nothing other than that sort of behavior from them.

Except for the white woman on the bluff, he thought quickly to himself. What was her motive, if not kindness, for having come to him in such a caring way? There was nothing for her to gain from such generous behavior. In time he hoped to be with her, to know more about her. The fact that she was alone puzzled him. Why had she been on that bluff in the first place?

It was a bluff that overlooked his village. Yes, that was surely why she was there. Curiosity had drawn her there to see how another people lived whose skin did not match the color of hers.

People who had never been around red skins before always seemed to see them as an oddity. He was sorely tired of being gawked at by cold white eyes!

He would never forget how quickly she had run away from him once she realized that he was conscious and gazing up at her. He did not want to think that she was afraid of him just because his skin was red and hers was white.

"*Wituska,* you do not answer my questions," Silken Wing said, drawing his thoughts back to the present.

He sucked more soup from his spoon, then set the spoon and bowl aside.

"*Witimi,* Aunt Silken Wing, whites do what they do to people of different skin colors for many reasons," he said dryly. "As for what they did today? It *was* to weaken our people even more. It is a well-mapped-out scheme to . . . to . . . slowly kill off the remaining Ponca."

"To kill us off?" Silken Wing gasped, her eyes wide and frightened.

"Our people are weakened not only by disease but now also by having our horses and weapons taken from us," Thunder Heart said, his voice drawn. "No horses? No way to travel. No weapons? No way to defend ourselves or hunt for meat for our hungry people."

Speaking the sad truth made Thunder Heart

move to his feet. He still felt somewhat unsteady, but he had eaten enough to give him the strength he needed to go into council with his warriors. Each moment without him was a moment in time that was wasted.

"Are you strong enough?" Silken Wing asked as she, too, rose to her feet and slowly followed along-side Thunder Heart as he went to the buffalo-hide entrance flap and shoved it aside.

"Your soup has done its job well," Thunder Heart said, turning to Silken Wing. He smiled. "Thank you, sweet aunt."

He took her into his arms and hugged her, then left her standing outside the tepee as he and his coyote made their way through the milling crowd toward the long council lodge.

As Thunder Heart stepped inside the lodge, he found his warriors sitting around a fire in the center. No one was talking. They were silent in frustration and anger.

As Thunder Heart sat down on a blanket in their midst, his coyote curling up next to him, all eyes turned to him with a silent, devoted trust.

"What happened today must be corrected!" Thunder Heart said, his voice firm and authoritative, his weakness now only an afterthought. "Without horses and weapons our warriors are naked! We must find a way to replenish our supply of both!"

The warrior at his right side was the first to respond. "Tell us how," Dark Shadow said, his voice and eyes anxious. "For now, until your father is well again, you are our chief—our leader. What you say, we will do!"

"Thunder Heart is humbled by your total trust in him," Thunder Heart said, placing a hand on Dark Shadow's shoulder.

Then he shook his thick, black hair back so that it hung long down his muscled back. He folded his arms across his bare, powerful chest and tightened his jaw.

"I have been thinking. I do believe I have a plan that will assure getting back at the whites," he said, his eyes moving slowly from man to man. "To replenish our supply of weapons and horses, we will steal them back from the white eyes."

"How can this be done?" another warrior asked softly. "We need horses to travel from place to place to enable us to *steal* horses."

"Before there were horses for our ancestors, there were feet," Thunder Heart said, smiling as he brought a lighthearted moment into the conversation. "Do we not all have feet? Do we not all know how to use them well?"

A ripple of laughter swam along the seated warriors.

"That will be how it is done," Thunder Heart said, again serious and tight-jawed. "We will go by foot to those pastures that are the closest and steal our first horses."

"But they will be missed and the white men will immediately cast blame on the Ponca," another warrior said, drawing Thunder Heart's eyes quickly to him.

"We will leave our village each night after the sky darkens and we will steal only a few horses at a time, from different corrals so that the white people will not even notice right away what is happening. And if they do, they will not suspect it is the red man who is guilty of the crime, for they would think that if red skins came to steal back their horses they would steal them back in a much larger number."

Thunder Heart smiled cunningly. "Also, the white men are supposing that we Ponca are too weak from illness to fend for ourselves, especially since we no longer have horses for travel," he said tightly. "We are going to teach the white men a lesson, for once we have stolen back enough horses and weapons and our warriors are strong enough again, we will make those who have done this evil deed pay!"

"You did not say how weapons will be stolen from whites," Dark Shadow said, eagerly leaning forward to hear Thunder Heart's answer.

"We will watch different families of whites, and we will enter their lodges while they are gone and take firearms," Thunder Heart said. "Hopefully, as we search their property for firearms, we will find those that were stolen from us. I hope to find my loyal bow and quiver of arrows!"

Thunder Heart grew momentarily quiet as his thoughts strayed once again to the woman on the bluff. She couldn't live that far away; after all, she traveled very close to his village alone. But which house did she live in of those he had seen in the area? He wanted to see her again, to see if she was as beautiful as he recalled, or if his weakness at that time was causing him to hallucinate her loveliness.

"Thunder Heart, before we leave for our first night of searching for horses, we need meat for our families," Dark Shadow said, his voice drawn. "Yet there are no weapons for the hunt. How long must we wait to steal weapons?"

"What happened today will not stop the hunt entirely," Thunder Heart said. "You know, as well as I, that there is a certain hunt that requires no horses or firearms."

This brought smiles and nods from his warriors.

"Yes, I see you know what I am speaking of," Thunder Heart said, looking at each of them. "Clubs and dogs are all we need to hunt beaver and muskrat. But this time, my warriors, we will not all leave the village at the same time. Some must stay as sentries to watch for the white eyes."

"My chief, you stay and get your strength back while some hunt and others stand guard," Dark Shadow urged.

Knowing that he did have to get his strength back to be able to leave tonight with his warriors to search for horses, Thunder Heart nodded, but in his mind's eye he was seeing the last time that he had been on the hunt for beaver. He had trained Four Eyes as the dogs had been trained. Thunder Heart and Four Eyes had gone with a group of men and dogs and had moved along a stream, wading, looking for beaver dens.

He would never forget the time Four Eyes had located his first beaver and had eagerly dug the animal out for Thunder Heart to club to death.

Four Eyes' first hunt for raccoon had also been a successful one. Having learned quickly, Four Eyes had circled a raccoon, leaving his coyote scent, which the raccoon refused to cross. This caused it to keep doubling back. Finally the circle had become small enough that the animal was within range of Thunder Heart's arrow. One arrow drawn on the string of Thunder Heart's powerful bow had downed the raccoon.

His eyes narrowed at the thought of his bow and quiver of arrows, which had been carried away by the white men today. He would soon find his weapons—and pity the white man who crossed his path wrongly again.

The peace that he had worked hard at cultivating in his heart had been shattered today like river ice shatters with the first thaw of spring!

Now he would have vengeance—or die trying!

CHAPTER EIGHT

We crossed the pasture, and thru the wood
Where the old gray snag of the poplar stood;
Where the hammering red-heads hopped away,
And the buzzard "raised" in the clearing sky.

—James Whitcomb Riley
(1849–1916)

Dede rode onward, worried that Bill had possibly gotten home before her.

She saw no new horses grazing in the pasture as she passed. When she got near enough to the stable to see that there were none in the corral, she sucked in a breath of relief. If Bill had managed to get home before her he would have brought some of the stolen Ponca horses and placed them among his. Being the ringleader of the raid, he would not have allowed someone else to take all of the horses. He would surely want some to gaze at each day, so he could feel superior at having succeeded in this part of his scheme to weaken the Ponca.

Remembering Bill in the Ponca village, acting superior to that fine, peaceful people, made Dede's insides boil. Especially since she had been so close to one of them on the bluff and was pulled into that mystical moment when her eyes had met the Indian warrior's. It had been as though the world had momentarily stood still and it was only the two of them. She couldn't recall now what had made her scamper away from the Indian, for she had certainly not felt threatened by him.

He had been in a weakened condition, and she only hoped that he had managed to get back to his people. And if he had, she wondered what his reaction was to what had happened?

Just as she rode up to the stable and stopped to put her horse in its stall, Johnny came running toward her with Joel.

"Mama, I beat Joel in marbles *and* checkers!" he shouted, his eyes dancing. He shoved his hand inside his front breeches pocket and pulled out two fat, colorful marbles. "See these? These are my favorite of the ones I won."

Joel pulled a marble from his own pocket and showed it to Dede. "I won this one from Johnny before he beat me to win his," he said proudly. "See the colors? I like the red stripes. They remind me of peppermint stick candy at Christmas."

Dede smiled as she dismounted. "Yes, it's pretty. And it looks like you both had a good measure of winning today," she said, reaching over to run her fingers through Johnny's pitch-black hair. "It's always good to share in the winning, don't you think, Johnny?"

Johnny smiled sweetly at her. "Yes, I guess so,"

he said, then turned and smiled at Joel, who still gazed lovingly at the prize in the palm of his hand.

Then Joel turned as his mother came from the house shouting his name, telling him to come on, now that Dede was home, they should get on home themselves.

Dede waved at Frannie. "Thanks so much," she shouted. "Whenever you have need for a sitter, you know that you can count on me."

"It's always a pleasure to see our two young men playing together," Frannie said, waving back.

Joel ran to his mother's buggy and climbed inside, then eagerly waved good-bye to Dede and Johnny as the horse and buggy started down the lane.

"Mama, where've you been?" Johnny asked as he slid his marbles back inside his pocket. He ran a hand over the horse's mane. "He's hot. Did you travel far?"

"No, not too far," Dede said, herself smoothing a hand over her horse's flanks. She didn't see any need for Johnny to know where she had been, or why. Sometimes things were best left unsaid, especially to a son who could be way too daring for his own good. She was afraid if she told him where she had been, it might plant a seed in his mind to ride there someday and take a look at the Ponca himself. He was the curious sort! So far, he had gone just close enough to hear them, not see them.

She looked at the horse and again felt the heat of its flesh. Should Bill arrive home soon and happen to pet her steed, he would realize that it had been out of the stable and would certainly ask Dede where she had been.

She didn't want to be put in the position of lying *or* of telling the truth this time. The truth could get her in trouble with Bill . . . if she wasn't already.

Had the sheriff told Bill how he found out about Bill's plan? Soon she would know—when Bill arrived home!

"Johnny, would you like to go for a short ride?" she blurted out, thinking of a plan that would let her answer truthfully should Bill ask about the horse having been ridden. She could say that she and Johnny had gone horseback riding. But if she took the time to saddle Johnny's pony, she and Johnny might not be gone before Bill rode up. Her plan would have gone awry that quickly.

"Sure, Mama," Johnny said, his eyes beaming. "I'll get Charlie. My pony's been needing riding."

"Son, there's not enough time for you to saddle Charlie," Dede said, her eyes wavering as he looked up at her again, this time with a strange sort of questioning in his dark eyes. "I've neglected my chores already today. Taking time to saddle Charlie will take too long. Come on, go on my horse with me. We'll go a short way, then come back home so that I can snap the beans and get them cooking on the stove for supper."

"Well, all right," he said, the slight slouch of his shoulders revealing his disappointment. "But next time, Mama, I've got to take Charlie. He needs a lot of exercise to stay healthy."

"Yes, I know, and when we get home, you can take Charlie out in the pasture and exercise him," Dede said. She grabbed Johnny by the waist and hoisted him up into the saddle. Then she placed her foot in the stirrup and swung up behind him. "For now, let's enjoy the wind and sun together."

Johnny hung on to the pommel of the saddle as Dede swung an arm around his waist to hold him steady against her. She snapped the reins with her other hand and rode off in a gentle lope. And when they were riding free of the pasture and across land dotted with a riot of wildflowers, Dede began to enjoy this time alone with Johnny so much that she forgot why they were even there.

She giggled when his hair fluttered in the wind, tickling her chin. She laughed when he let out a loud "Whooppee" as her powerful horse broke into a gallop. She was so lost in the moment with her son, she didn't even notice that she had somehow mystically been drawn in the direction of the Ponca village.

When she realized that it was only a short distance away, recognizing the trail she had traveled to get there before, Dede's heart skipped a beat. She drew a tight rein and stopped.

Now knowing where she was, she saw just how far she had traveled from her home. She was now much closer to the Ponca village than to Bill's ranch!

"Why did you stop?" Johnny asked, as he turned

and questioned her with his dark eyes. "Are we going to go back home so soon?"

"I think we'd better," Dede said, her trembling voice revealing to her but she hoped not to Johnny feelings that were new. For at this moment she was again seeing the warrior in her mind's eye.

But in reality she was hearing the steady drone of drums, which had begun again. She was hearing the Ponca's wailing. Strange how she was having feelings for a people she did not even know—and for a warrior whose gaze had touched her very soul!

She started to yank the reins to turn her horse back in the direction of the ranch, but Johnny let out a squeal that stopped her.

"Mama, look!" he cried, wriggling away from her and quickly sliding to the ground.

She watched him fall to his knees and reach out for a turtle that had just ambled from beneath a bush.

"Mama, I want the turtle. I want to take it home with me. I want it for a pet!"

"Johnny, come on back to the horse," Dede said, nervously looking in the direction of the village. She was afraid of being this close to it. She wasn't sure what the Ponca would do to get back at the whites.

She reminded herself that the Indians' weapons had been taken from them. But had Bill and the men found them all? Or did the Ponca still have some firearms stashed away that they might use to murder white people in their sleep in retaliation for the behavior of a few misguided men?

"Mama, just give me time to get the turtle, then we can go home," Johnny pleaded, sliding his hand under the hard belly of the animal to pick it up.

Dede inhaled a nervous breath and looked down at Johnny, and just as he lifted a hand to pet the turtle, a warning shot through her consciousness. She had been too absorbed in her thoughts to realize just what sort of turtle this was.

It was a snapping turtle!

"Johnny, let it go!" she cried, then felt as though something hit her in the belly when she heard Johnny scream in anguish. The turtle bit down onto the side of his hand, instantly drawing blood that dripped from the wound.

"Oh, no!" Dede cried, scrambling down from the saddle.

She bent to a knee before her son, his desperate cries and the fright in his eyes grabbing hold of Dede as though the turtle had latched onto her instead.

"Mama, do something!" Johnny screamed, his eyes wild as he stared down at the turtle that refused to let go of his hand.

Knowing that if she yanked at the turtle it would only sink its teeth more deeply into her son's flesh, Dede dropped her hand. She looked up at the sky hopefully, but grimaced when she saw that no clouds were there, not even on the horizon. She had heard that when a snapping turtle bit a person it didn't let go until it thundered. But clearly no storms were anywhere near now, not even one clap of thunder.

"What can I do?" Dede said, desperation clutching at her insides. Johnny's cries turned to hysteria, and he had no choice but to cradle the turtle in one hand as it kept its grip on the other.

Dede was too far from the ranch, and if she even had been close, if Bill had not gotten there yet, he wouldn't be available to help. She was too far from anyone else's ranch.

But she *was* close to the Indian village. Yet she was afraid to go there, for two reasons—the sickness and the hate they surely now felt for all whites!

But she had no choice. She needed help quickly. She knew where she must take her child. It had to be the Ponca!

"Oh, sweetie, I know how badly it must hurt," Dede cried as she lifted Johnny into her arms.

Looking at the turtle still latched onto her son's tender flesh, with the blood oozing around the creature's mouth and head, she felt as though she might be sick to her stomach at any moment.

"Help me!" Johnny cried, pleading with tear-filled eyes. "Take it off! It hurts so bad!"

Johnny screamed again when the turtle seemed to bite down harder. "Help me!" he cried once more, then fainted dead away in her arms.

"Lord!" Dede cried, the color draining from her face.

She frantically placed a hand beneath the turtle to support it as Johnny's hand fell slowly away. She looked desperately at the horse, and then at Johnny. There was no way she could get in the saddle. To get to the Indian village, she had to walk. That meant that it would take more time for her to get to the village for help!

She was thankful that Johnny wasn't suffering as long as he was unconscious.

"But for how long?" Dede whispered.

Tears spilled from her eyes as she began carrying her son in the direction of the Ponca village.

Suddenly she stopped dead in her tracks, for the handsome warrior from the bluff stepped out into the open, and surveyed the scene with narrowed eyes. Dede's breath seemed to stop as she waited to see what he would do.

In her mind's eye she again saw Bill and the other ranchers rounding up the Ponca's animals and weapons. Oh, Lord in heaven, how could she expect this Indian to have sympathy for anyone whose skin was white?

CHAPTER NINE

She has a voice of gladness, and a smile
And eloquence of beauty.

—William Cullen Bryant
(1794–1878)

A child's hysterical cries coming from outside his village had alarmed Thunder Heart, and taking Dark Shadow with him, he had followed the sound.

When he saw the woman and the child and realized why the child was crying, he started to go to her and offer her help. But at the sight of the horse he stopped. He sent Dark Shadow around behind the woman and child, and just before he made himself known to them, he nodded to Dark Shadow to take the horse.

Now Thunder Heart stood eye to eye with the very woman whose kindness had stayed with him like a gentle breeze inside his heart. When he had awakened on the bluff and looked into her beautiful eyes, a part of him knew that he would never be able to forget her.

Another part of him—the part that resented whites—made him not want to care about her or the child who now lay unconscious in her arms.

But the pleading in her eyes, the tears spilling from them, made him realize that he could not turn his back on her. He owed her a debt. Today he was being given the chance to repay it. After today he would force himself to forget her.

"Please help me," Dede sobbed as she took a halting step toward Thunder Heart. "Please help Johnny."

Her plea, the softness of her voice, made Thunder Heart momentarily forget his hatred of whites. He knew he would never forget the child's cries. The pain had reached inside his heart as the woman's pleading eyes and sweet voice now reached clean into his soul. Without a word to Dede, Thunder Heart hurried to her and took Johnny from her arms.

As he laid the boy on a soft cushion of grass beneath a towering oak tree, Dede heard a sound behind her. Turning with a start, she gasped and felt her heart skip a beat when she saw another Indian and what he was doing. He was mounting her horse! With a look of defiance, he grabbed the reins, sank his heels into the horse's flanks, and rode off at a hard gallop toward his village.

Dede continued to stare in disbelief, then turned to look down at the Indian, whose very presence seemed surreal.

But he *was* real, and what had seemed at first to

be a gesture of kindness was nothing more than a way to get her attention so his accomplice could steal her beloved horse!

She started to give him a piece of her mind and demand that he get away from her son, but stopped and gasped in wonder when, as though by magic, he released the jaws of the turtle from Johnny's bleeding hand.

"How did you do that?" Dede asked, stunned. At least this part of her nightmare was over.

Thunder Heart didn't respond, for at the moment he was afraid his voice would betray him. He knew that he should feel a deep hatred for this woman because of the color of her skin, but instead he felt something that he knew was wrong. He felt an attraction to her.

Her mere presence caused his pulse to race. And as she knelt beside him to gather the child tenderly into her arms, he recalled . . . he felt again . . . the gentleness with which she had treated him on the bluff when he had blacked out.

He would never forget her kindness, or her loveliness. He even recalled her sweet smell, the same that he smelled now, the sort of scent that carried through the wind from freshly opened rose blossoms on a spring morning. Yes, she was like a wild rose, beautiful, soft, and sweet!

Dede wasn't sure how to react to the Indian's silence, but at this moment she didn't care about it. She was concerned only with Johnny. She saw with alarm that removing the turtle from her son's hand had caused the bleeding to begin anew.

She looked pleadingly up at Thunder Heart. "What am I to do?" she cried. "His hand! Look how it's bleeding!"

Thunder Heart broke his silence as he reached out for Johnny. "Give me the child," he said thickly. "I will take him to my village shaman. He has ways to stop bleeding wounds."

So glad that the Indian could speak English, and that he seemed to truly care about what happened to Johnny instead of only wanting to steal her horse, Dede eagerly nodded. "Yes, please help Johnny," she said. "Please do what you can."

She was careful not to show any doubt that she might feel about taking the boy to a medicine man, for it would show a lack of appreciation, as well as mistrust.

Her father had been a doctor. He had scoffed at the Indians' use of herbs and such things to heal their people. He believed in using the knowledge that he had acquired from medical school. To him there was no other way.

"Lightning Eyes, my people's shaman, is wise in many ways of healing," Thunder Heart said, carefully taking Johnny from Dede's arms. He looked solemnly into her eyes. "Shaman are close to the source of all things—mother nature—or the force of all things—mother earth. But there is one ailment that has not been cured by our shaman. The ailment that has attacked my people's bellies. Nothing has helped. Nothing."

His bringing up the illness made Dede tighten with fear. She even wanted to tell him to give Johnny back to her! What if she was allowing the warrior to take her son where he might contract something even worse than the bite? If he became ill with diarrhea and vomiting, could he come through it any better than the Indians?

Yes, she thought quickly to herself, hurrying on now to walk beside the Indian. She had her father's bottles of medicine, part of his legacy. Among the medicine was a potion that was used for all stomach ailments. It was something that she knew worked, for she had used it, as had Johnny.

Watching Thunder Heart now, she felt ashamed for having not thought of it earlier. She could actually offer the Ponca her father's cure! But then again, she had heard that white doctors were never allowed to minister to redskins. They were viewed as witch doctors who did more harm than good.

Johnny let out a low whimper, and Dede's concerns returned. She sidled closer to Thunder Heart and saw that her son still seemed lost in a sort of deep sleep. His cry had to mean that the pain was reaching clean past the unconscious state. He was still feeling it.

"Let's go faster," Dede said, drawing Thunder Heart's eyes to her. "He . . . he . . . seems to still be feeling the pain."

"He feels it, yet he does not," Thunder Heart

tried to reassure her. "It is only his body reacting to the pain. Inside the child's mind, where things are felt, the pain has been mercifully locked away."

"If only that were so," Dede said, tears again spilling from her eyes. "I should have never let him pick up that turtle. I—I didn't realize until too late what kind it was."

"Do not blame yourself for things you have no control over," Thunder Heart said kindly. "As chief, I have learned how to look past that which tears at my heart . . . those things that happen to my people that are not of my doing, but, instead, that are done by evil people who wish to erase red skins from the face of the earth."

Knowing that he referred to the actions of Bill and his cohorts, Dede was overwhelmed with shame. Even though she had had nothing to do with it, she felt guilty just because she was white.

She looked away from Thunder Heart and grew quiet as his village came into sight. But for the wailing, it appeared to be a normal day among the Ponca. Spirals of smoke were wafting into the air from the smoke holes of their lodges. The delicious smell of food, not the decaying stench of death, came to her in the wind.

Then her eyes went to the corral behind the village. Its emptiness was another reminder of Bill's crimes. There were no horses. There were no weapons.

Then she flinched when she *did* see a horse. Hers. It was reined in before one of the larger lodges, which she surmised belonged to this warrior. He had shown her and Johnny a kindness that she would never have expected from someone who should hate anyone whose skin was white.

She wondered how she could expect the return of her horse when so many had been taken from the Ponca. Could she even ask for it? Or should she give it up without an argument? Should she let it be her payment to them for the kindness offered to her and Johnny today?

Then it came to her in a flash what this Indian had said about himself. He was a chief! He was the most powerful man among the Ponca, who were now coming to meet him as he carried Johnny on into the village. Whatever happened to her, or Johnny, or her horse was up to him.

And up to now she hadn't felt as though she had anything to worry about. Unless the kindness he showed her was a ploy to get more from her than a horse!

"Come into my *diudipu*, my lodge," Thunder Heart said, nodding toward his tepee.

It was not surprising to Dede that his lodge was the fine white tepee that she had admired from afar. Yes, the finest would be his, for wasn't he the grandest of men? Up this close to the tepee she could see that its cover was painted, perhaps with what was this Indian's clan and personal insignia. Or perhaps the designs represented figures of all the birds and animals that he had killed. There were also realistic figures of horses, bison, and dancing men. To Dede, the tepee was beautiful and awesome.

Thunder Heart stopped and surveyed the crowd of people who were cautiously following him. He singled out his closest friend. "Dark Shadow, go for Lightning Eyes," he instructed. "Tell him that his services are needed in my lodge."

Dark Shadow nodded and broke away from the others.

Dede gazed up at Thunder Heart, her heart thundering inside her chest about what might happen these next few moments. She followed him inside his dwelling.

She saw that there was hardly any furniture in the lodge. In fact, it appeared rather bare. A fire, which she thought might be used for both cooking and warmth, was built in the center. The bed, upon which Thunder Heart put Johnny, was merely bison robes and blankets. Clothing and other gear hung from a rope strung around inside of the tepee framework. Willow rod "lazybacks," or backrests, sat beside the fire in pairs, kept rigid with chokeberry braces. The rods were decorated with geometric designs cut into the bark. The lodge was clean and smelled of sage and cooked meats.

"Soon he will be better," Thunder Heart said, drawing Dede's eyes back to him. He stepped closer to her, his gaze intense. "I am called Thunder Heart," he said, his eyes locked on hers. "Your name is?"

"Dede," she murmured. "Dede Martin."

"And the child?" Thunder Heart said. "I believe you called him by the name Johnny?"

"Yes," Dede said, moving to kneel beside Johnny. "His name is Johnny."

She bit her lip to keep from crying again as she stared at the injured hand. She was relieved, though, that the bleeding had stopped. Now it was the bruised, ugly wound that caused her concern.

Johnny's eyes slowly opened and he looked up at her, then became aware that he was in a place foreign to him. He watched as Thunder Heart slowly knelt beside Dede.

"Where . . . am . . . I?" Johnny asked, his voice low and wary. He flinched and tears spilled from his eyes as pain shot anew through his hand.

He slowly lifted his hand before his eyes, grimacing when he saw the wound.

"The turtle, Johnny," Dede murmured, smoothing locks of hair back from his brow. "It bit you. Do you remember?"

"Yes, I remember," Johnny said, fighting the pain. He looked slowly over at Thunder Heart. "Who . . . are . . . you?"

Dede was amazed at how calm Johnny was in the presence of an Indian, even as he must have realized that he was in the Indian's home. Surely his intrigue with it all helped him not be afraid. He had always had a fascination of Indians. As a small child, when he couldn't yet read, he would choose a storybook to be read to him before he went to bed, and it always had something to do with Indians.

But he had never liked the parts where the red man would be bested by whites. Even at his young age he saw the wrong in that. After Dede finished reading such a book, Johnny would tell his mother his own version of how he wished that it had ended.

Dede had always marveled at the child's vivid imagination, at how he had made the Indian the hero instead of the villain.

"My name is Thunder Heart," Thunder Heart said, then looked over his shoulder as Lightning Eyes came into the lodge. He looked at Johnny again. "Do not be afraid. My shaman is here to help you."

Thunder Heart rose to his feet and the shaman knelt beside Johnny in his place. Dede feared that her apprehension about the shaman was showing on her face. She reminded herself that she had agreed to let Thunder Heart bring Johnny to the shaman. It was best not to show that she didn't trust the Ponca's choice of how to medicate her son's wound.

When she felt a gentle hand on her shoulder she flinched, then realized it was Thunder Heart.

"Come and stand with me while Lightning Eyes helps the child," Thunder Heart murmured. "As I told you, a shaman is wise in all that he does, even when he is faced with the challenge of doctoring someone whose skin is white."

Swallowing hard, and feeling her cheeks grow hot from the magnetic pull of Thunder Heart's dark eyes and the sound of his voice, Dede almost magically reached out her hand and allowed him to twine his fingers through hers. For a moment she was transported to another world where there was no one but her and the handsome Ponca chief. She moved to her feet and stood before him, the thunderous beats of her heart threatening to consume her as she gazed into his eyes.

"Please help me . . ."

Johnny's voice, the frantic tone of it, brought Dede abruptly back to the present and the reason she was here, where everything was foreign to her and her son.

Even Thunder Heart. Although she felt something sweet and wonderful inside her heart for this man, something that she had not felt since she had been married to Ross, she knew that she must admit the foolishness of those feelings and resist them.

Yes, Thunder Heart surely saw her as an enemy. For a brief moment in time, he must be civil to her for the sake of an innocent child.

She turned away and gazed down at Johnny, then at the shaman, who placed a gentle hand on Johnny's brow.

"Little white man, do not be afraid," Lightning Eyes said softly. "What I do will help, not harm you."

Dede wanted to snatch Johnny up and hurry away with him, for she saw now that her son was afraid, and she understood why. The shaman had put on a feather bonnet over his floor-length gray hair. His flowing buckskin gown had beads sewn on it in the designs of the stars, rainbow, moon, and sun. His copper face was leathery and lined with age. The skin on his fingers was drawn tightly over bone, his fingernails long and curled.

"Give him room to do his magic," Thunder Heart said as he gently took Dede by an elbow and led her farther into the shadows, away from where Lightning Eyes knelt beside Johnny. "Look and listen. You also will feel the magic."

"White child, do you see my hat?" Lightning Eyes asked softly.

Scarcely breathing, Johnny nodded.

"It is made of pelican feathers to show my source of power," Lightning Eyes said, smiling down at Johnny. "My hat is made of the wing feathers of the same bird as my medicine bundle."

"Medicine bundle?" Johnny said, discovering that just talking and being with the shaman was making him forget his fear and the pain of his hand. "I love to read. I have read about medicine bundles. What's in yours that is special?"

"In my medicine bundle there are many things," Lightning Eyes said, opening the drawstring top and reaching a long, thin hand inside it. "I will first bring out my muskrat skin. Then I shall bring from it the root of a wild four-o'clock plant. Then I will remove some of the combplant from the bag. These will be used as an antidote for your bite."

Dede grew more apprehensive as she watched the elderly man remove all of those things from his bag. She nervously clasped her hands behind her as the shaman held the muskrat skin, nose forward, to the bite. The skin began to quiver, as though it were alive!

But she had no time to take that in, for the shaman was soon busy doing something else. He laid his muskrat skin aside and slid a piece of the wild four-o'clock plant into his mouth and chewed it for a moment.

Dede grew pale and gasped aloud with horror when Lightning Eyes leaned over Johnny and blew the chewed up root into her son's wound.

Seeing Dede's reaction, Thunder Heart reached a hand out to keep her from interfering.

Dede looked up at Thunder Heart, then relaxed when he gave her a reassuring smile. She nodded softly. She was so glad that Johnny didn't object to the way the shaman was treating his wound. She could see the seriousness in the elderly man's expression as he began to sing and chant over Johnny, but only for a moment, for soon he was gone and everything in the lodge was quiet again.

"I do feel better," Johnny said, breaking the silence, his smile an elixir for Dede as she hurriedly knelt beside him. "Lightning Eyes does hold magic in his medicine. The pain is all but gone."

"That is good. I will now wrap the wound," Thunder Heart said. He went to the back of his lodge and got a soft-looking piece of buckskin, then returned and sat down beside Johnny. "Young brave, this soft wrapping will make your bite feel even better."

Dede silently watched Thunder Heart gently wrap her son's hand. She was amazed that these people, whose very souls were being stripped bare not only by illness, but by the actions of the whites, could be so kind and gentle to her and her son.

Something within her wanted to cry out to Thunder Heart and apologize for the wrongs of her people. Yet she knew that she was only one person, only one voice, and that whatever apology she would offer would be futile in his eyes. He might even laugh at her.

"I wish there was something I could do to thank you and Lightning Eyes," Dede blurted out anyway, drawing Thunder Heart's eyes to her. "How can I ever thank you?"

"You can leave my village and not turn back," Thunder Heart said, his heart shouting inside him to tell her, no, that was not what he wanted from her at all. He wished he could tell her to stay and fill his lodge forevermore with her sunshine!

But he knew that was impossible. He had much to do, and most of it against whites!

And . . . she . . . was white.

"Yes, we must leave," Dede murmured, her eyes searching his, seeing so much there that puzzled her. He seemed to be wanting to say more to her than a good-bye.

Even she hated to leave. But she had to get home. Bill must be there by now wondering where she and Johnny were.

If he ever realized where they had truly been, she

wondered how he would react. Would he see the Ponca's goodness if she told him about how they had cared for Johnny's wound? Or would he lecture her about the foolishness of trusting Indians?

She knew now that she could trust them. Thunder Heart had even asked her to leave. Certainly she and Johnny weren't the Ponca's prisoners.

Yet, what about her horse? If she couldn't reclaim her horse to ride home, it would be very late before she got there, especially with Johnny's weakened state. And traveling alone after dark on foot was dangerous. More dangerous animals than turtles lurked about at night.

"White woman, it is best that you leave now and do not turn back," Thunder Heart repeated. "It will not be safe here among my people for you and the young brave. There are ill feelings you do not want to be faced with."

Fear that she might be wrong about the Ponca after all seized her. This chief was practically warning her, but she didn't want to be afraid of his people, especially him! Dede couldn't deny her attraction to Thunder Heart.

And she was free to love!

She wasn't truly married to Bill. It was agreed that should one or the other fall in love, they were free from each other.

It was a bitter realization that now, when she had found someone who made her insides glow, it was someone forbidden to her.

And his warning about staying longer in his village only reinforced her conviction that she must not allow herself to have special feelings for this Indian. It was something she had to put behind her, to leave in the farthest recesses of her mind, as though it had never existed.

"I will get your horse," Thunder Heart said, turning to leave. He stopped and looked back over his shoulder at Dede. "Then take your horse and leave, white woman. Leave."

She was so relieved and deeply touched that Thunder Heart was going to allow her to have her horse back. Her heart ached with wanting to find a way to help him and his people.

When he came in and lifted Johnny into his arms, then gazed deeply into Dede's eyes, she realized that no matter how hard she fought her feelings, she was lost, heart and soul, to this man forever. She was glad when he pulled himself away and went on outside to the horse.

She followed, and as he was carefully settling Johnny on the saddle, Dede noticed that the wails had resumed. She knew that inside many of the lodges were seriously ill, even dying Ponca.

She felt incredibly sad for them and she decided that no matter what Thunder Heart said, she would return with her father's medicine! She hoped the Ponca people would be allowed to use it.

Again she was aware of the constant drone of drums. She stepped up next to Thunder Heart and asked softly, "Why are the drums played so often?"

"For anyone who is not well and for anyone who

is mourning, the sound of the drums is used to help revive them and make them happy," he replied.

Dede wanted to tell him that it didn't seem as though the drums were helping anyone now, but then she thought better of outwardly questioning one of their customs.

"The songs I have heard your people sing," she murmured, "they are so sad."

"The human voice is the Ponca's main musical instrument," he explained. "Songs are part of nearly every activity. There are songs to accompany various dances and ceremonies. Medicine songs bear supernatural power and can call the spirits to heal the sick."

His eyes took on a warmth that spoke to her innermost feelings for him. "There are love songs, some of which imitate the bell-like quaver of the courting flute, and mock love songs in which young men imitate lovesick girls," he said.

He looked at Johnny. "There are also lullabies that mothers sing to quiet their children and put them to sleep . . . or to soothe them when they are ailing," he said.

Thunder Heart's words had almost hypnotized Dede. When he went quiet, it was the silence that shook her out of her reverie.

"Thank you so much for what you did for us today," she murmured, extending a hand toward him. She melted inside when he took it and held it for a moment longer than she had expected.

Her eyes met and held his for a long moment,

and it was as if a silent message passed between them, a promise that neither of them quite understood.

Shaken by this, Dede eased her hand out of his. She quickly mounted her horse and positioned Johnny comfortably on her lap. After Johnny was settled snugly against her, Dede gave Thunder Heart a smile and a nod, then rode away. She could feel his eyes on her until she was out of the village.

Then she was instantly consumed by worries about Bill. She had to make sure that he never knew where she and Johnny were today.

Making sure that Johnny didn't spill the beans to Bill about the adventure that had led them to the Ponca village, she reached a gentle hand to Johnny's cheek. "Son, it's best not to tell Bill where we were today—or anyone," she said in a tense voice. "Not even Joel. Do you understand?"

"Yes, I know," Johnny said, revealing to her his grown-up side, which had begun to surface ever since his grandfather's death. "I won't tell anyone." He smiled up at her. "But I liked being there. It's much better than reading a book about Indians. Being there, actually experiencing it, was fun."

"Fun?" Dede said, her eyes widening. "You were there because you were in pain from a terrible bite, and you saw it as *fun*?"

"You know what I mean," Johnny said, snuggling closer to her. "Mama, wasn't the medicine man kind? Wasn't Thunder Heart?"

"Yes, both were kind," she murmured, smiling at

the memory of Thunder Heart and her exchanging unspoken, wonderful things with one another.

"Did Thunder Heart mean it when he said not to go back?" Johnny asked, looking sideways up at his mother.

"I'm not sure," Dede said. "But it's wonderful that you are feeling better, Johnny, and that they saw to the bite and made your suffering less."

Suddenly it came to her like ice water being splashed on her face: the bite! How was she going to explain the bite to Bill? And the bandage! It was made of white buckskin, and Bill would know it had not come from anything Dede would have in her possession while she was out horseback riding.

She grabbed her reins tightly and drew her horse to a quick stop.

Johnny leaned away from her. "Why are you stopping?" he asked. He grew even more puzzled when she reached down and lifted the hem of her skirt to reveal her petticoat.

"Just wait a minute," she said, ripping some of the petticoat away.

Johnny seemed to understand when she unwrapped the buckskin and tossed it to the ground, then replaced it with the strip of cloth from her petticoat.

"Now things are all right," Dede said. "Let's get on home."

Part of her was feeling deceitful because of what she'd done. Bill had always been so good to her and

Johnny. But she couldn't press her luck by telling him things that she knew should be kept a secret!

She rode onward, the sun now casting long shadows on the road beside her.

CHAPTER TEN

O, lift me as a wave, a leaf, a cloud!
I fall upon the thorns of life! I bleed!
A heavy weight of hours has chain'd and bow'd
One too like thee—tameless, and swift, and proud.

—Percy Bysshe Shelley
(1792–1822)

It was just growing dark when Dede rode into the pasture. Thankfully Johnny was asleep, so the ride from Thunder Heart's village hadn't caused him more pain.

She felt so grateful to Thunder Heart and his shaman that Johnny's injury now seemed not to hurt him so much. It was as though it might already have begun to heal.

Dede thought back to how the shaman had treated the wound. It was primitive, yet there was no doubt of its effectiveness.

As the house came into view, her mind was still on Thunder Heart and his people. Although he had warned her against returning to his village—in fact, even told her not to—she knew that she must. She could still hear the wails of his people drifting toward her on the wind, paining her as though she was the one who was ill. She knew that she must return to them. She had to take her father's cure to them and hope that it might help, even though their shaman's ways had not.

"But will the shaman allow it?" she whispered to herself. "Will his people?"

And why hadn't his medicine helped? she continued to wonder. Johnny was proof that he most certainly had whatever knowledge it took to minister to wounds.

Yes, she had to go back to Thunder Heart's village. Surely his people could look past their mistrust of white cures if there was a chance it might help them. They had to know by now that nothing their shaman did was going to save those who suffered.

"Mama?"

Johnny's voice drew Dede back to the present. She must get her son inside the house to bed. But she wouldn't stay long, herself. After she bathed and fed Johnny and put him to bed, after Bill was asleep, and after it became dark enough to keep her hidden from sight when she left the house, Dede was going back to the Indian village. She must offer them help or she would forever feel guilty.

"What is it, honey?" she asked as Johnny turned his eyes up to her. "Is the bite hurting?"

"No, I'm fine," Johnny murmured. "I just wanted to tell you that I'll not tell Bill where we've been, or why. I don't want to spoil the chance we might have of going back to the Indian village. I'd like to make friends with someone my own age there."

"Johnny, I'm glad you understand about Bill, but I don't think you'd better get your hopes up of going back," Dede said. Out of the corner of her eye, she saw a movement to her left.

When she heard the sound of horse's hooves, she knew that Bill was arriving home. She stiffened as he grew closer, for she saw that he was herding along several horses that weren't his.

She knew whose they were. The Ponca's!

"Do the Ponca hate us that much because we are white, Mama, that they won't let us go into their village again?" Johnny asked, straining his neck as he watched Bill approaching on his white steed. To Johnny, that horse always looked like a ghost as it moved across the land at night.

"Yes, I'm afraid they do," Dede said. She drew a tight rein as she waited for Bill, knowing that if she didn't stop, he would question why.

"But they helped us today, Mama," Johnny said, again looking up at her.

"Because they were kind enough to look past who we were," Dede said, in her mind's eye recalling the very instant that she saw Thunder Heart standing out in the open, gazing at her and Johnny.

She would never forget that moment in his lodge when their hands had met and their fingers quickly intertwined, when he had urged her to leave Johnny's side so that the shaman could cure her son.

The wondrous thrill was something she would treasure always!

Suddenly she realized the foolishness of thinking romantically about the Ponca chief! She blamed it on the moonlight that was now so beautifully bright in the heavens as dusk turned to night.

Bill rode up and stopped beside her. "Dede, what on earth are you and Johnny doing out here on horseback this time of evening?" he demanded, then flinched when he looked down and in the moonlight saw Johnny's wrapped hand.

"Where have you been? What happened to Johnny's hand?"

Dede could feel Johnny stiffen in her arms, and she suddenly felt the wrong in bringing her son into the betrayal. Bill had been kind and generous to them both, yet she knew she could not confess everything to him, could not tell him what had happened and where they had been.

What she was about to say was not entirely a lie, just a way around the truth so that Bill would still trust them in the future. She did not want him keeping watch on her and stopping her from going to the Ponca village again.

Tonight, she planned to sneak away and go there with her father's medicine. She wished she could be open with Bill about wanting to do this, but she knew how he would react to such a plan. He might even order her to stay away!

Thus far he had never ordered her or Johnny to

do anything. Their relationship was a comfortable and amicable one.

"Me and Mama went horseback riding," Johnny blurted out, taking Dede aback that he would sense her discomfort.

Bill looked over his shoulder, and then at Johnny. "Did your pony throw you?" he asked, reaching a comforting hand to Johnny's cheek. "Is that why you are on your mother's steed with her?" He glanced down at the bandaged hand. "Did you hurt your hand badly?"

Dede stiffened again. How could she get past that truth . . . how she had chosen not to let Johnny ride his pony?

"His pony is fine," Dede said, bringing Bill's eyes back to her. "When Johnny asked me to go riding, I had already been out on my horse. It was getting late. I thought it would take too much time for Johnny to prepare his pony for the ride. I took him on mine with me, instead. When we saw a turtle, Johnny wanted it for a pet. I saw no reason not to let him have it. He picked the turtle up, but it was a snapping turtle. It bit him."

"Good Lord!" Bill gasped. "Thank God you managed to get it off. You know what they say about snapping turtles . . . that they won't let loose until it thunders."

"Yes, thank God we didn't have to wait on thunder," Dede said, laughing nervously.

There, she thought to herself, sighing with relief. The explanation was behind her. And it hadn't been all that bad. What she had said was true. There had been no need to lie!

"Frannie and Joel came over and stayed with me while mama went on her ride," Johnny said, quickly sliding his uninjured hand into his front pocket. He brought out several marbles. "See? I won these in the marble game with Joel."

Bill smiled, then tousled Johnny's hair. "Good for you, son," he said. "Good for you."

"Joel didn't entirely lose," Johnny quickly said. "He won back one of my prettiest marbles. You know, Bill, the one with the red stripes? The one you found one day down by the river?"

Dede was hearing what they were saying, but her mind was elsewhere. She looked past Bill and saw the horses behind him tied in with his own. They were fat, healthy, noble steeds. She knew they had been well cared for by the Ponca. And she knew they deserved to still be with them.

She then saw something rolled up in the blankets tied on the back of Bill's horse. She knew that the blankets held Ponca weapons that had been taken from their lodges. Her eyes moved to the Indian bow that had been too large to tie in with the other weapons. It hung loose where it was tied at the horse's side. Intricately carved, it had clearly taken some warrior many hours to make it so beautiful. Surely its owner would kill to get it back!

She looked slowly over at Bill. She had always known the good side of this man. It was hard to realize that there was a part of him that could be cruel to anyone . . . even Indians. She wondered how much more there was about him that she didn't know.

She flinched when Bill suddenly caught her staring at him, studying him as he had never seen her do before.

"Dede? What's wrong?" Bill asked, his voice wary.

He followed her gaze as she turned and looked at the horses again.

Their eyes met and held again.

"Bill, why would you do such a thing?"

"How do you even know what I did?"

"I heard you, Bill. I heard your plan."

"It had to be done is all that I have to say about it," he said, wheeling his horse away from hers. "I'll meet you at the house, Dede."

She watched him ride away, the Ponca horses following his own.

When Johnny turned his eyes to her, she knew that she had to explain. She knew that Johnny respected Bill. Would he after he knew the truth?

And she could not find it in herself to lie to her son.

So be it. Bill had made his bed. Let him lie in it.

She framed Johnny's face between her hands and told him everything, not at all surprised by the look of utter contempt in his eyes once he knew what had been done to the Ponca, and why.

"Bill couldn't have done that," he blurted out. "He's kind. He's caring."

She then told him about Bill's wife and how she had been taken from him. Dede explained the torturous search and Bill's despair when he hadn't found her.

"I guess I would hate the Indians if they did that to me," Johnny said uncertainly. His face took on an expression of wonder. "But the Ponca people are so friendly. Surely they wouldn't do anything like that, Mama. Do you think?"

She didn't want to tell him what she actually believed . . . that the Ponca would soon avenge what had happened today.

And if that's what they were preparing for, was she truly safe to go and take them the medicine? No matter. She knew that she had to take the chance or never be at peace. If she didn't lend a helping hand, like her father would have done if he were alive, she would carry shame around inside her heart for the rest of her life.

And she had to admit to herself that there was a selfish reason for wanting to go. She hoped to win Thunder Heart's trust so that he would allow her and Johnny to visit his people from time to time once the illness was over.

"Mama, you didn't answer me," Johnny prodded. "The Ponca are nice, peaceful people, aren't they? They can be trusted, can't they?"

She wanted to reply by asking him if he would just stand by and do nothing if someone took so much from him. But she didn't want to make him afraid. Neither did she want to plant a seed of fear in her own heart by saying aloud what she worried might be true.

She merely said, "Yes, they are a peace-loving people," then snapped her reins and continued onward toward the stable.

"Maybe we can find a way to take their horses back to them," Johnny said, watching Bill herd the Ponca horses into his corral.

"I think you'd best forget any notions such as that," Dede softly urged. "This is between Bill and the Ponca now. It has nothing to do with you or me."

She was more determined than ever to leave tonight, after Bill and Johnny were asleep. She didn't care any longer about the chance she was taking. She would try to help the Ponca, even though she knew that nothing she could ever do could make up for what Bill and his friends had done today.

CHAPTER ELEVEN

Hail to thee, blithe spirit!
Bird thou never wert,
That from heaven, or near it,
Pourest thy full heart.

—Percy Bysshe Shelley
(1792–1822)

Dressed in a black riding skirt and blouse so she would blend in well enough with the night, Dede rode at a gentle lope toward the Ponca village.

The closer she came to the outer perimeter, which she now knew well enough, the more her heart pounded in fear of what she had chosen to do—especially at night. All sorts of creatures roamed the land under the cover of darkness, two-legged as well as four-legged.

She even felt as though she were a part of that criminal element. She was deceiving Bill tonight by coming to the Ponca, even though she did it with a good heart, and for all the right reasons. And if Bill didn't feel such hate for Indians, she wouldn't be forced to go against him. She would have brought the medicine to the Ponca in broad daylight!

Then again, she remembered how Thunder Heart had adamantly told her not to come to his village again. Although he was a man whose very voice made her heart soar, it was the coldness with which he had told her to stay away that made her know how serious he was about it.

"But I must go," she whispered to herself, lifting her chin defiantly, causing her long blond hair to cascade farther down her back, the wind softly fluttering the wavy tips.

And surely such a man, who was so quiet and dignified in manner, would not grow angry over her efforts to do something to help his people.

When a wolf howled on a distant bluff and another gave its response, chills rode Dede's spine. She sank her heels into her horse's flanks and sent it into a faster gallop. She wanted to get this over with. Her safe, warm bed was something that she ached for at this moment.

What would the Ponca do when she arrived? What would Thunder Heart do?

And how was she going to go about awakening the Ponca? They must all be in their beds by now, although surely not peacefully sleeping. Too many were ill for everyone to just go to bed and sleep as though all was right in the world.

Yes, she concluded. Some would be awake even though the midnight hour was near. Those who were caring for the ill must rarely ever get a full night's sleep.

She hoped to change that. She hoped that her

father's bottles of stomach medicine held as much magic for the Indians as they always had for her when she had been ill with a stomachache. She would never forget how quickly her cramps had gone away after taking a dose of her father's medicine.

Surely it would be the same for the Ponca. She had to keep thinking that it would work for them as well.

She sighed gratefully when she spotted a fire a short distance away. That meant that she should be riding into the village very soon. The outdoor fires were like a beacon to her, hopefully welcoming her there.

She gazed heavenward. "Father, if you are up there watching me through your gold-framed spectacles, your blue eyes twinkling, please let this work," she whispered. "Oh, please let your medicine help these people."

She gulped hard and jerked her head to the right when she heard a rustling sound in the bushes. Then she looked quickly to her left when she thought the sound came from there. She stared into the inky blackness of the forest, and fear gripped her heart when she saw movement and the moon's glow soon revealed who was there.

Her fingers tightened on the reins and she stopped when she found herself suddenly surrounded by several Indian warriors on foot. Although they were weaponless, Dede felt no less threatened. Feeling cold inside, her pulse racing, she watched as the Indians edged in closer to her. One of them nodded at her and spoke.

"Dismount your horse, white woman. Come with us," Dark Shadow said coldly.

Dede swallowed hard, nodded, then slid from her saddle.

Holding her horse's reins, she walked toward the village with the entourage of warriors. She kept telling herself that she was right to have come tonight. It was in the best interest of the Ponca.

Now if only she could convince them of that!

CHAPTER TWELVE

The pale purple even melts around thy flight,
Like a star of heaven,
In the broad daylight.

—Percy Bysshe Shelley
(1792–1822)

Thunder Heart rode bareback on a wonderful speckled horse that he had stolen from the very first farmhouse he and his warriors had approached. He looked over his shoulder at his men, who also now rode proud, handsome steeds. The opportunity to steal more horses had been there.

But tonight they had taken only what they needed to give them the means to travel. The next several nights they would raid the white man's pastures, accumulating horses until they had as many as had been stolen from them.

They had to be cautious. If they took too many at once it would be noticed by the white people, who would more than likely come searching for their horses at the Ponca village.

But even if the white people came to search, they

would not find their animals. Thunder Heart and his warriors were riding to a valley where the stolen horses would be herded and kept and sentries would be posted on the bluffs overhead.

And the Ponca warriors now had weapons, so they could truly guard the horses. Tonight Thunder Heart and his men had watched as the whites left their unprotected farmhouses. It was easy to go inside their houses and steal weapons.

Thunder Heart smiled, clasping the rifle in his left hand while riding his steed into the makeshift corral. He wheeled his horse to a stop and slid to the ground.

As his warriors also stopped and dismounted, he smiled at them. "Tonight we were successful," he said. He ran a hand down the flank of the animal. "We now have horses and weapons. Tomorrow night we shall multiply each in number!"

"Tomorrow night I shall steal two horses and hopefully two firearms," one of his warriors said, his jaw tight.

"Tomorrow night each warrior will still take only one horse and one weapon," Thunder Heart said, reaffirming his leadership. "As I have said before, taking too many horses at once will only alert the white men about what is happening in their pastures. One missing horse will not raise their suspicions as quickly."

"We have enough firearms even now to crush those who stole from us," another warrior said, his eyes lit with fire.

"Even with firearms, we must move cautiously," Thunder Heart said evenly. "And do not let the hate you feel inside your heart misguide you into doing something you will later regret. Come now, my warriors. Let us return home on foot. We have done well tonight. We must feel proud."

After securing all of the horses, and making sure the sentries were in the appropriate places, Thunder Heart started running at a trot toward his village. His warriors ran alongside and behind him.

He glanced down at the rifle in his hand, the moonlight reflecting on the barrel. Yes, what they had stolen tonight was not much, but it was better than nothing.

And he must be cautious in how he rebuilt his arsenal and resupplied his horses. He wanted no more confrontations with whites until he and his warriors could face them on equal ground.

It tore at his heart, though, that he, a man of peace, must be thinking of war with whites. Even with each of his warriors holding a firearm, he knew the risk of never being able to best the whites. They had twice the numbers as the Ponca.

Glad to see his people's outdoor fires only a short distance away, Thunder Heart broke into a much faster pace.

Again he thought of the rifle that he carried, wishing it was his own beloved bow. Somehow he would have it again. He would keep searching the white men's houses until he found it! No white man should ever have in his possession a weapon made by the hands of a red man, especially one made by a proud chief!

His heart ached when he arrived at his village and saw so many people outside their lodges, even though it was the midnight hour when normally everyone would be asleep. But sickness didn't leave his people at night just so they could sleep. It lingered, day and night, week after week, even month after month.

If only Lightning Eyes had something to make his people well again, Thunder Heart despaired to himself. But so far nothing stopped the stomach ailment. Nothing!

Silken Wing stepped away from a family who was crying outside their lodge over the seriousness of their child's condition. She went to greet Thunder Heart, taking his hand. Four Eyes, who had stayed behind instead of accompanying his master on the search for horses and weapons, came and sniffed at Thunder Heart's heels, then sat down beside him, his eyes regarding him adoringly.

Thunder Heart saw something strange in the way his aunt looked up at him. "Aunt Silken Wing, what is it?" he asked, wondering now about the way her hand forcefully gripped his. "*Witimi,* Auntie, what has happened while I was gone?"

He looked past her at those who were ministering to the ill outside their lodges and at those who cried aloud.

He then looked with wavering eyes at his father's lodge. "Has someone else died?" he asked wearily.

"Will there be another burial at sunrise? Has . . . my father . . . ?"

"No, *wituska,* no one has died," Silken Wing said, then glanced toward the council house. "And your father has not worsened."

Thunder Heart noticed how she looked at the council house. Again she looked at him strangely.

"There is a captive being held in the council house," Silken Wing said softly. "This captive . . ."

Thunder Heart interrupted her. "A captive?" he said angrily. His rage was so quickly lit, it was hard to keep himself from shouting.

He jerked his hand out of hers. His fingers made a tight fist at his side. His blood felt as though it were boiling.

"Why, auntie?" he blurted out. "Who is the captive? And who did this? This is not the time to take captives. It can ruin my plan!"

"*Wituska,* please do not be this incensed over what was done," Silken Wing pleaded. "It seemed right at the time. Your warriors brought the woman here because they knew you told her never to return."

Thunder Heart's heart skipped a beat. His throat became dry, and he looked again at the council house. "*Witimi,* it is a woman who is being held captive? It is *that* woman?" he asked, his voice drawn.

In his mind's eye he was reliving his encounter with Dede earlier in the day, how something magical had seemed to pass between them, and how just being near her made him all warm inside. He had felt that way only one other time in his life—when he had a wife that he adored with all his heart and soul.

"It is the woman who came with the child who suffered from a turtle bite," Silken Wing answered warily. She saw his reaction at knowing who was being held captive. It was as though he looked past the color of the woman's skin and saw her only as a woman!

The white woman was not what interested Silken Wing. It was the boy, the woman's brother. So many of the Ponca's young braves had gone to the hereafter. The lives of grieving parents could be filled with laughter again if they had such a young man as the white boy in their lodges.

She smiled as an idea blossomed in her mind . . .

"Our warriors are holding the white woman captive because of your plan to steal horses and weapons," Silken Wing hurriedly added, before Thunder Heart had a chance to reply. "They felt that this was no time for whites to discover what we are doing and also that if they do come they should not be allowed to leave."

"She was told not to come, but she is different," Thunder Heart said, walking away from Silken Wing toward the council house. Four Eyes followed.

Thunder Heart looked over his shoulder at Silken Wing. "This woman can be trusted," he said matter-of-factly.

Silken Wing stiffened, frowned, then went back

to those who needed her. Thunder Heart went inside the council house, where he was needed . . . and where he had to decide what to do about Dede.

It was not a usual thing for someone, anyone, to go against his orders. And he had ordered Dede to never return to his village.

Standing in the shadows just inside the door of the council house, Thunder Heart looked toward the center of the room, where a slow fire burned in its pit and where the woman of his heart sat huddled, visibly trembling, as two of the chief's strongest warriors stood guard over her.

Knowing that she could never be a threat to his people, Thunder Heart regretted that his warriors had caused her to be so afraid. He hurried to them, drawing everyone's eyes to him. Dede's eyes were wide as they met Thunder Heart's.

"My warriors, you can leave now," Thunder Heart said, his eyes still holding hers.

He waited until his warriors were gone, then knelt before Dede. "Why did you come?" he asked, now aware that she was clutching a leather bag beside her. "Were you not told to stay away?"

He glanced over his shoulder at the darkness outside the doorway, then frowned at Dede, who was still trembling, still wide-eyed silent. "And why did you come at such a dangerous hour?" he asked thickly. "Woman, explain all of this to me. It is hard for me to understand."

Dede reached for the bag and thrust it toward Thunder Heart. "I came to bring you this," she said, her voice breaking. "Inside you will find something that might help your people's stomach ailment. It was my father's. He was a doctor and he gave this to his patients. Even I have taken it and I became well as a result."

Instantly angry, Thunder Heart shoved the bag back toward her. "You were told not to return to my village. No white man's medicine is welcome here," he said stiffly. "My shaman is all my people need."

"Your shaman's medicine has not worked," Dede responded, trying not to be intimidated by the look in his eyes. She knew, deep down, that he would not harm her.

"That is so," Thunder Heart said, sighing heavily. He stared at the bag, then again looked into Dede's eyes. "But no white man's medicine has ever been welcome among my people. Nor should it be now."

He pushed the bag back into her arms. "Take it," he said dryly. "It is yours. Keep it for your own stomach ailments."

"Please believe me when I say that this medicine is good and it does work. I don't need what I have brought to you. I . . . I have more at home," she said, trying to shove the bag back at him. She let it fall to her lap when he still refused to take it. "Thunder Heart, please give it a chance. Please give *me* a chance. When I was yanked off my horse and forced into this lodge by your warriors, I tried to explain to them that I was a friend. But they said I came falsely, bringing poison to help the white men kill off your people."

She paused, then asked, "Do you believe that? Do you truly believe that I came to you pretending to be a friend, while in my heart I was planning to poison your people?"

"No, I do not believe any of that," Thunder Heart said. He rose slowly to his feet and stepped away from her, focusing on the fire.

Then he turned toward her again. "I believe you do feel that your father's medicine might help my people," he said softly. "But our people's shaman is the only one in charge of their health."

Then he knelt before her again and grasped her shoulders. "I am touched by your goodness and your courage to come in the night to my village," he said. "I apologize for my people having wrongly imprisoned you. How is the child? Does his hand still hurt?"

"Johnny is fine. Thank you for asking," she murmured. "After we got home, he went to bed and dropped right off to sleep. I wish you would allow me to thank you for what you did for Johnny by sharing my father's medicine. I know it would help your people. I truly believe in it. I believed in my father as a physician the same way you believe in your shaman as your medicine man."

"You use the word 'believed' instead of 'believe' when you speak of your father, which means perhaps you do not believe in him that much any longer. Yet you bring his medicine to my people?" Thunder Heart asked, raising an eyebrow. "And the child . . . your brother, would he believe that his father's medicine would have been better for his wound?"

For a moment Dede was confused by what he was saying. Then it came to her that he had just called Johnny her brother! He actually thought Johnny was her brother, not her son! He thought the man she lived with was her father! She reached out toward him.

"My father . . . he . . ." she began, but a voice outside the council house calling Thunder Heart's name caused Dede to stop. Thunder Heart went and welcomed Lightning Eyes into the room.

She scarcely breathed as she watched Thunder Heart and Lightning Eyes speak quietly to one another. They both kept looking at her.

She found herself welcoming the coyote as he came and sat down beside her, snuggling close to her as though she were his steadfast friend. She began to stroke him, watching and wondering what Thunder Heart and the shaman were discussing.

Her spine stiffened and she exhaled a nervous breath when they came and stood over her. Thunder Heart offered her a hand, and she reluctantly took it, then rose to her feet at his quiet suggestion.

"White woman, I was told why you have come to my village," Lightning Eyes said, his voice tight with mistrust. "You have brought white man's medicine among my people."

"Yes, I brought a cure that works among my people," Dede said, slowly bending to pick up the bag. She held it in her arms as she spoke to the shaman, hoping that she was saying the right things to gain his trust. "Sir, when you offered your medicine to help Johnny, both Johnny and I trusted and accepted it. Can you now, in turn, trust and accept ours?"

She looked quickly at Thunder Heart and inhaled a wild breath when she found him looking at her with nothing akin to contempt. Instead, his expression held a wondrous calm, warming her through and through. He gave her a slow smile and nod.

"Too many of our people have died and will die if something is not found soon that will cure them," Lightning Eyes said, slowly reaching for the bag. "Although I am reluctant, I will try your medicine."

Dede was stunned that he was this readily agreeing to something that until only moments ago both he and Thunder Heart had fought against so adamantly.

She now knew that Thunder Heart had advised the shaman to try the white man's medicine. Surely he had convinced Lightning Eyes that if the medicine helped their people, that was all that truly mattered.

She now understood Thunder Heart's soft smile and his nod. In a silent way he was relaying to her that he was responsible for the shaman's sudden change of heart.

And she understood something else. She believed that the shaman's true reason for not wanting to use her cure was that he might be perceived a failure by his people if it worked.

She felt honored that under those conditions he still accepted her father's medicine.

"Come with me outside so that Lightning Eyes can explain to my people about the medicine," Thunder Heart said, gently taking Dede by an elbow and ushering her out into the moonlight.

He led her to the center of the village, where the flames of the great fire still leapt skyward and where his people gathered to listen.

And after the shaman's explanation, a great relief rushed through Dede, for she could sense the whole village's kindness toward her, proving that there was no animosity toward her, either for the white man's disease . . . or for the cure that might take it away.

She became choked up as she watched the medicine being given to a small child who lay outside on a pallet of furs close to the fire. As the red liquid slid between the child's lips, everyone seemed to hold their breath at once. They exhaled in a burst when they saw that the medicine did no immediate harm to the child.

Encouraged by the child's reaction to the medicine, Thunder Heart turned to Lightning Eyes. "Take this also to my father," he said, ignoring how the shaman recoiled at his command. He knew that the shaman didn't approve of the white man's medicine being used on a man who was so revered by all the Ponca.

"Go, Lightning Eyes," Thunder Heart said, his

voice more forceful. "Go, take medicine to my father." Lightning Eyes finally did as he was told.

Thunder Heart then turned to Dede. "I will escort you home," he said softly.

Dede was surprised when a young brave rode a beautiful speckled horse up to Thunder Heart, dismounted, and handed him the reins. She had thought that all of the Ponca horses had been stolen!

She started to ask Thunder Heart about it but decided that it was best not to bring up anything having to do with Bill. All she wanted to do now was get home before Bill discovered she was gone!

She nodded a silent thank you to Dark Shadow when he brought her horse to her, for he was the very one who had taken the reins from her when they arrived at the village.

Quickly she mounted her horse and rode off with Thunder Heart, his coyote following them.

Thunder Heart had seen Dede's puzzled look, and for a moment he felt that he should explain, but just as quickly decided against it.

But not because he didn't trust her. She had proved too much to him about how she cared about him and his people for him ever to believe she could do anything against them. He knew that she wouldn't tell anyone in the white community that he had somehow acquired a horse.

They rode in silence beneath the moonlight until he felt they were close enough to her home for her to go safely onward alone. He brought his steed to a shuddering halt. Dede followed his lead and stopped beside him.

Dede gasped when he suddenly reached out for her, grabbed her by the waist, and yanked her onto his lap.

Her head spun and she became weak with wonder when his lips came down upon hers in a passionate kiss. She had felt this way only one other time in her life—when Ross, her beloved husband, was still alive.

Oh, Lord, she knew now that she was in love again, but it was a forbidden love . . . one that she should force herself to forget. But the longer Thunder Heart kissed her, his hand caressing her back, the more she knew she could never live without him.

He too was stunned by the feelings aroused in him by the kiss. He felt so much for Dede, yet he knew how foolish it was to be kissing her and wanting her. He brought the kiss to an end and put her back in her saddle. With a look that completely melted her, he rode away.

He rode for a while, then stopped abruptly. He had decided that it would be best to make sure she got home and safely inside. Following far enough behind her that she would not detect his presence, he watched her ride past the corral and head for the stable.

At the corral Thunder Heart stopped in shock and stared wide-eyed at the horses in the pasture. He could not believe it! There were his very own steeds among the many horses grazing on the thick grass.

He watched as Dede came out of the stable and ran to the house.

He then stared at his horses again. Now he knew that her father was one of the men who had stolen from his people!

He wanted so badly to take his horses back now, not later, but he knew that doing so would give away his plan. His horses were too grand not to be missed by the white man! And Dede's father would soon deduce who had stolen them.

No.

He wouldn't reclaim his proud steeds. Not yet. But he would come back tomorrow night and steal something far more precious from the white man. He would steal his daughter and son!

Thunder Heart had never been one to take white captives. He had even scolded his warriors for having taken the woman as a captive tonight.

But now that had changed. Knowing that Dede's father had stolen his horses had changed everything. Frowning, he wheeled his horse around and rode off at a hard gallop. Yes, tomorrow night the white woman would be in his village again. But this time she would be there as a true captive.

His!

CHAPTER THIRTEEN

Look round her when the heavens are bare;
Waters on a starry night
Are beautiful and fair.

—William Wordsworth
(1770–1850)

A full day had passed since Dede had slipped away to the Ponca village. It was obvious that Bill had not yet discovered her escapade, and she now doubted that he ever would.

She was fresh out of her evening bath and dressed in a robe in her bedroom. Johnny, his hair still wet from his own bath and dressed in his soft flannel pajamas, sat down on Dede's bed.

She brought a box from her cedar chest and placed it on the bed beside him. But before opening the box she asked, "Sweetie, how's your hand this morning?" The bandage had been removed. All that was left of the bite was a yellow bruise and skin that was healing into a tiny, puckered scar.

"It's fine," Johnny said. "The shaman's medicine worked."

"I hope your grandfather's medicine works for the Ponca," Dede said. "If not . . ."

She didn't even want to think about the medicine not helping the Ponca, much less speak her doubts aloud. Instead, she slid the box closer to Johnny and turned his attention toward its contents.

"Johnny, I know that I've shown you these already, but I'd like for you to see them again," Dede said, opening the cardboard box. "These are your father's lawbooks."

She reached inside and gingerly picked one up, then placed it on the bed between her and Johnny. "Just look at this book, Johnny," she murmured. "See its expensive gold binding?"

She opened it so that Johnny could see the dark print on the pages. She slowly ran her fingers over the words. "You just don't know how many nights I watched your father studying these books in the glow of candlelight when we couldn't afford kerosene for our lamps," she said, her voice filled with melancholy. "It was so important to him that he become a lawyer. He wanted to follow in his father's footsteps."

"His father died young, just like my father, didn't he, Mama?" Johnny asked, reaching over to carefully touch a page of the opened book.

"Yes, very," Dede said, recalling the heartache Ross's death had caused her. She had never imagined loving anyone else, yet it had happened. Although she hadn't known Thunder Heart for very long, she knew that her love for him was real, so very true. Their kiss, their reaction to it, had proved the love they shared for one another.

But she also recalled how quickly Thunder Heart had ridden away from her after the kiss. He knew, as well as she did, the wall of prejudice that would keep them apart. If only things could be different, she despaired every time she thought of the impossibility of openly declaring their love for one another. If only she were free to, she would give Thunder Heart so much love. Perhaps, for the moments they were together, he could forget the tragedies of his people.

"Mama, where has your mind taken you?"

Johnny's voice broke through Dede's deep thoughts. She laughed awkwardly as she found him looking intently at her with his wide, dark eyes.

"I'm sorry," she said, slowly closing the book, as though that one small effort might help erase the guilt she felt for falling in love with someone besides Ross. "I was just thinking about things, Johnny."

"Things?" he asked, pinching his face into a questioning frown. He scooted to his knees and faced her. "Like what?"

"Schooling," Dede said, putting the book back with the others. Now she wished that she had never taken them from their hiding place. The memories she had held on to since her husband's burial still pained her. Now she realized that she must let go of them and allow herself to live again . . . allow herself to love again.

"Mine?" Johnny asked, sighing heavily.

"Yes, yours, silly," Dede replied, laughing as she tousled his dark, wet hair. "Since the school in St. Genevieve, is so far from our home, I have tutored both you and Joel in subjects required of children your age," she said. "But college . . . law school . . . is a different matter. Although I picked up a lot of knowledge about the law as your father studied each night, I don't know enough to tutor you on that subject, son. You must attend college to learn what is required to become an attorney."

"When Father studied, did you quiz him like you do me and Joel?" Johnny asked, with a sincere eagerness to know.

"Well, yes, I did," she said, laughing quietly. "But only after he made out the questions and gave them to me."

"Did you enjoy it, Mama?" Johnny asked, settling back down on the bed and crossing his legs beneath him. "Do you think I'd enjoy it?"

"Sweetie, I'm not sure how to answer that," she said. "I'm afraid if I say 'yes,' it might affect your decision."

Johnny took another book from the box. He opened it and slowly turned the pages. "I'd not want to disappoint Father, but I think I'd enjoy something that would have me outdoors instead of in a stuffy, crowded courtroom."

"Like what, Johnny?" Dede asked. "Do you have something in mind that you would like to do?"

He glanced quickly toward the window. "Horses!"

he blurted out, his eyes shining. "I'd like to raise horses."

"Like Bill?" Dede asked, smiling.

"Well, I don't know about that," Johnny said, his eyes narrowing. "He's become dishonest where horses are concerned. He shouldn't have ever stolen those horses from the Ponca."

Dede almost gasped when she realized the anger Johnny felt over what Bill had done.

"Yes, I think I'd like to raise horses, or something like that, that would keep me outside more than indoors," Johnny reaffirmed, his voice light and sweet again. "But I'd want Joel to be my partner, and now that he's moving, that won't be possible."

"I know you're upset that Joel is moving, but you'll find yourself a best friend again," Dede murmured.

"Like at the Ponca village?" he asked, his eyes wide.

"Well, I don't know about that," Dede said, hoping so much to be a part of the Ponca's lives, but doubting that it could ever happen.

She put the book back inside the box and returned it to the cedar chest, then pulled out another, smaller box and took it to Johnny. "Open it, son," she said. "I've never shown you these."

"Shown me what?" Johnny asked, scooting the smaller box over closer to him.

"Just look inside," Dede said, her eyes eager as he lifted the lid. He gasped and reached inside to stroke what lay beneath them.

"Gold and silver medals with velvet streamers!" He looked at Dede. "These were my father's?"

"Yes," she answered, clasping her hands on her lap. "He won many debating awards in college. I would listen to the debates. They were very intense, and hearing them helped me understand the law."

"If I go to college and become a lawyer, will I win awards too?" Johnny asked, slowly lifting one of the gold medals and resting it in the palm of his hand.

"If you are successful," Dede said, smiling at how awestruck he looked.

Johnny slowly ran his fingers over the cold metal. "I'm so proud of Papa for having won these." He gazed into her eyes. "I would love to have one of my own, yet I truly don't believe I want to be a lawyer."

Dede's eyes wavered, and she felt a strange emptiness in the pit of her stomach. She had always wanted Johnny to be a lawyer. She knew it was something Ross would have wanted. Yet she had always told herself that she would never force anything on her son. It was his life. She wanted him to live it as he chose. And if that meant that he wouldn't be an attorney, so be it. She would learn to accept his decision. She would give her husband's lawbooks to the St. Genevieve library so that someone could use them.

Dede closed the lid and put the box away.

She drew Johnny into her arms and hugged him. "No matter what you choose to do, I'll be proud of you," she murmured. "We'll work it out, son. We'll work it out."

But Johnny's confession about not wanting to be a lawyer had brought something else to light. For the first time since her father's death, Dede didn't see a real reason to stay with Bill. If Johnny didn't have aspirations to be a lawyer, or even to attend college, it was no longer important to have access to Bill's money.

For the first time since she had met Thunder Heart, she truly felt free to love him. She knew that Bill would want her to do what would make her happy. Yet she also was sure that he would not want her to find that happiness with an Indian.

She would find a way to work things out for herself, as well as for Johnny. As she had done since her husband's death, and then her father's, she would take things a day at a time.

"I'm going to bed now," Johnny said, sliding off Dede's bed. He yawned. Then he gave her a hug and walked away, his bare feet pattering along the wooden floor.

" 'Night, son," Dede called after him. "Don't let the bedbugs bite."

His giggles touched her heart. "I love you so," she whispered.

Brushing tears from the corners of her eyes, Dede went to the window and stared out at the inky blackness of the night. She flinched when she saw Bill ride away into the darkness. She knew where he might be going—to spend a night of hell-raising with his friends, drinking and gambling. Certainly he wouldn't be going to the Ponca village. He had already done his damage there.

One thing was sure. He never spent nights trying to lure her into his bed. Her relationship with Bill would always be a platonic one. He just wasn't the sort of man that she could fall in love with, or welcome to her bed. He was too much older, too much a father figure for her.

How would he react if she told him she had found someone?

Yawning, tired from her long day of washing and ironing and baking bread, Dede slid between the warm blankets of her bed. Her hair spread out on the lace-trimmed pillow like streamers of gold velvet, and she fell instantly into a soft, sweet sleep.

But suddenly her eyes were open again. She stiffened and drew her blanket up to her chin when she realized what had awakened her so abruptly. It was something in her room. A sound. She gasped when she heard footsteps stopping just beside her bed.

The moon was hidden behind clouds, giving off no light by which to see who was standing over her. The intruder's breath mingling with her own was the only sound in the room.

She didn't get the chance to ask who was there. She saw the figure of a man just before he slapped a hand over her mouth, silencing her.

"Be quiet, white woman. Make not a sound. And do not fight what I am about to do."

Dede's eyes widened with surprise, for she recognized the voice that had spoken to her! It was Thunder Heart's!

"Do not fight me. I do not want to hurt you," Thunder Heart said. He urged Dede out of the bed, one hand still over her mouth, the other at her waist. He ushered her slowly toward her bedroom door.

"Lead me now to the young brave's room," he whispered. "You and the child are coming to my village. There you will be held captive as payment for your father's role in taking the Ponca horses and firearms."

Father? Dede cried to herself. Again Thunder Heart was referring to Bill as her father.

She hadn't had the chance to correct him earlier, and she couldn't now, because he wouldn't even allow her to speak.

And if she did, would he believe her? Would he think it was a ploy of some sort to get him to change his mind?

For now, she did as he said. Although she cared deeply for him, at this moment she was afraid of him. They moved along the corridor, where candles burned low in wall sconces. With one hand he held her mouth closed, and with the other he gently pushed her ahead of him. She turned toward Johnny's room, wishing her mouth was free so that she could at least beg Thunder Heart not to include Johnny in his vengeance.

But his hand still covered her mouth. She had no choice but to do as he said.

She desperately hoped that Bill wouldn't return home while Thunder Heart was there. All hell would break loose and someone would die! The only way to prevent that was to cooperate and get out of the house as quickly as possible. She would work out a plan of escape later.

Thunder Heart ached inside over what he felt compelled to do to the woman he loved. He saw no other way but to get back at the white man where it would hurt the most.

If a man's son and daughter were taken from him it would cut deeply into his soul. Thunder Heart knew that well enough from having lost so many loved ones himself. But this white man's loved ones would not die, or be harmed. He would not know this, however. He would be led to think the worst.

For now, Thunder Heart had a different plan. He would not let the man lose hope yet. That would come in time, after Thunder Heart had what he wanted from all of the white men who had wronged the Ponca!

He worried, though, about Dede's mother. If she was somewhere in the house and awakened to see what was happening, what would he do with her? So far she was still asleep. Thunder Heart hoped she would remain so until he had fled with her children.

As Dede reached Johnny's bedroom, she hesitated before going inside to awaken him. She was so emotionally torn she felt dizzy. She wanted to understand why Thunder Heart was doing this to her and Johnny. She had thought that he knew she was a true friend—and even more than that to him! She did understand that he might want to get back at Bill, but why use her and Johnny?

The thought of being a true captive, anyone's captive, frightened her. She didn't believe that Thunder Heart would harm her or Johnny, but what about his people? If she and Johnny were brought to the village forcibly by their chief, wouldn't the Ponca feel free to do as they pleased with them?

Even when Thunder Heart finally removed his hand from her mouth so that she could go on into Johnny's room and wake him, she knew better than to ask him why he was doing this. Surely he wouldn't answer her. She doubted that he would even allow her to talk, to explain how wrong he was about so many things. And she doubted that her true relationship with Bill would matter to Thunder Heart. She lived with Bill. The fact that Bill cared for her and Johnny would be reason enough for Thunder Heart to abduct them.

She started to go into Johnny's bedroom, but Thunder Heart grabbed her hand and stopped her. "Where is your mother?" he asked, still worried that she would wake up and discover what was happening.

"Mother?" Dede asked, her voice drawn, wondering why he would be asking about her mother at such a time as this.

She turned and looked up at him with wide eyes. "Mother?" she repeated. "My . . . mother . . . is dead."

She knew that this was a good opportunity to explain her living situation to him, but it might take too much time. If Bill came home, oh, Lord . . . !

The sadness in Dede's voice when she spoke of her mother made Thunder Heart regret having asked about her. But at least now he knew that he only had Dede and the child to worry about.

He nodded toward Johnny's door. Dede hurried inside to Johnny's bed. She knew that she must wake him, yet how could she? She didn't want to frighten him. And when he was awake, what would she say?

Thunder Heart stepped up behind her. He gently touched her arm. "Awaken him," he whispered. "Now! Tell him what is expected of him."

"All right," Dede whispered back, but before she did as she was told, she turned and fully faced her captor.

The moon was no longer covered with clouds, and she could clearly see Thunder Heart. The moon's glow shone onto his sculpted features. His eyes were locked on hers. She was compelled to reach up and gently touch his face.

"I want to understand what you are doing, what you are forcing me to do," she said. "Please help me to."

"In time," Thunder Heart whispered back, taking her hand and sliding a slow, caressing kiss across its palm. "Just know that neither you nor the boy will be harmed."

"I do know that," Dede said, restraining herself

from falling into his arms to prove how much she did trust him, how much she loved him!

She forced herself to turn away from him, then knelt beside the bed. Her fingers trembled as she reached out for Johnny. "Johnny," she whispered. "Sweetie, wake up. We've someplace to go."

Johnny stirred in his sleep but didn't wake.

Dede swallowed hard, then turned to Thunder Heart. "Must I?" she asked, her eyes pleading.

"You must," he responded, gently placing a hand on her shoulder. "Now. Time is passing too quickly. The white man might return home. You would not want me to come face-to-face with him tonight. Someone would surely die."

Panic seized Dede at this confirmation of her earlier conclusion. She stood up and shook her son's shoulder firmly. "Johnny, you've got to wake up," she said, her voice no longer a gentle whisper. There was a sound of authority there that Johnny only heard when he had done something mischievous.

He awakened with a start and bolted to a sitting position, then grew wide-eyed when he saw Thunder Heart standing behind Dede.

"Why are you here?" he asked, wiping sleep from his eyes.

"I have come to take you and the woman to my home," Thunder Heart said, trying to keep his voice steady, though, in truth, the child's innocence tugged at his conscience.

"Really?" Johnny asked, instantly excited. He

looked at Dede. "Is that true? He's come for us? We can really go with him?"

"Yes, we're going with him," she replied, rolling back his blanket. "Hurry, Johnny. We must leave now. Not later."

She turned to Thunder Heart. "Can we have a moment of privacy while I help him get dressed?" she asked softly.

When Dede saw the look of distrust in Thunder Heart's eyes, she put a hand on his arm and led him outside to the corridor. "I promise not to do anything foolish," she said. "I most certainly wouldn't do anything that could put Johnny in danger."

She glanced down at her gown, then pleaded at him with her eyes. "I would also like to dress more appropriately," she said. "I'll help Johnny and then I'll go to my room and hurry into my clothes."

Thunder Heart's eyes narrowed, then he nodded. "Make haste," he said, then turned his back to her as she rushed back into Johnny's room.

"Does Bill approve of what we're doing?" Johnny asked, leaping from the bed.

"Bill doesn't know yet," Dede said, her voice guarded.

"He'll not like it," Johnny giggled.

"No, I doubt that he will," Dede said, nervously looking over her shoulder at the door, where Thunder Heart waited.

She rushed Johnny into his clothes, then led him out to the corridor. She smiled clumsily at Thunder

Heart when he gave her a look that made her insides melt.

"Now I would like to go and get dressed," she said quickly. "I'll only be a minute. I'll truly hurry, Thunder Heart. Truly I will."

He studied her eyes and saw nothing in them that indicated she was lying or planning to deceive him. Something told him that she understood why he was doing this, even though she had questioned him as though she didn't. He knew that she was a woman of compassion and that she surely understood the wrong her father had done the Ponca. She would also understand his need for vengeance!

In time he would make it up to both her and Johnny. He hoped that she would welcome this.

"Go. Change clothes," he said. "I shall be waiting here with the young brave."

"Thank you," Dede said, then ran down the corridor to her room.

As she rushed to her chifforobe to choose clothes, her heart pounded hard. What was happening tonight had been set in motion the moment she and Thunder Heart had first seen one another.

It seemed as if destiny had brought them together and that destiny still worked in their favor, even if he was taking her against her will. Yet being taken captive by him was somewhat romantic, especially knowing that he meant her no harm. Perhaps this was the only way they could have ever gotten together again.

For now she was not going to fight it. She would

wait and see how far he went with his act of vengeance. She was sure that he would never harm her or Johnny.

She dressed more quickly than ever in her life and soon emerged in riding skirt, a white, long-sleeved blouse, and leather boots.

Perhaps even more than Thunder Heart, Dede understood the need to get out of this house before Bill returned. If Thunder Heart knew the extent of Bill's hatred toward all Indians, he would realize that Bill would shoot him the moment he saw him and ask questions later.

Dede ran her fingers through her hair, since she had not taken the time to brush it, then pushed Johnny's hair back from his face with a quick sweep of her hands.

She turned toward Thunder Heart. "We're ready to go," she said, clutching Johnny's hand.

"Take me where there is paper and pen," Thunder Heart said flatly.

Dede questioned him with her eyes, but led him to Bill's study. She was glad that Johnny didn't seem afraid. Every time she looked at him she saw excitement in his eyes. She hoped that wouldn't change.

"Light a lamp," Thunder Heart instructed.

Dede nodded and lifted the chimney from a kerosene lamp on Bill's wide oak desk. She struck a match and held it to the kerosene-soaked wick, and once it was aflame, she turned the wick higher so it gave off more light. What she saw made her go cold inside. Thunder Heart was standing over Bill's weapons, and in his right hand was a powerful bow.

"This was stolen from my lodge," he said coldly, turning fierce eyes toward Dede. "I spent many hours making it, especially carving the pictures into the wood."

He nodded toward a quiver of arrows. "Those, too, are mine, made by my own hands," he growled.

"Take them with you," Dede blurted. "They are yours. Take them."

She was confused when he leaned the bow back against the wall where he had found it. He came to her, nodding toward the desk.

"Take up a pen," he said. "You will write a note. In this note say that you have taken the child to visit an ill relative."

"Why would I say that?" Dede asked, searching his eyes for answers.

"This note is a way to keep the white man and his friends for a while from knowing where you and the child are, and with whom," Thunder Heart said. He picked up the pen and forced it between Dede's fingers. "There is a time when the men who stole from my people will know who bested them tonight, who took what is precious to this one white man, in particular. That time will be only when Thunder Heart chooses it."

"Are you certain this is the best way?" Dede asked, shocked that she was actually helping Thunder Heart in his plan to take hostages.

"It is the best way. For now the white man who

owns this house, and who has my horses in his corral, must think that you are somewhere besides with the Ponca. Time is what I need. The amount of time it will take for him to check on your whereabouts will be time enough for me to get enough horses and firearms to fight him," Thunder Heart said. He folded his muscled arms across his powerful chest. "Think of an aunt who you might go to if she were ailing and requested your presence."

"If that's your plan I don't understand why you are taking me and Johnny now," Dede said. "Why not wait and take us when you can brag about having done so?"

"Because this is how I wish to do it," Thunder Heart said tightly. "Now is better than later to have you."

He nodded toward the paper. "Write," he said.

Dede knew better than to question him further. He was a man who made decisions and stuck with them. She must go along with this plan.

"Who can I say we went to visit?" she asked aloud, frantically trying to think of a name. She was relieved that Johnny was too absorbed in studying Thunder Heart's bow to pay attention to their conversation. She concentrated even harder, then her eyes brightened when a name finally came to her.

"There *is* an aunt," she exclaimed. "My Aunt Mae. She lives in St. Louis. She is elderly and no one expected her to live this long. It would look normal for me to go to her if I received a telegram requesting my presence at her bedside. And it would look normal if I took Johnny as well, for he adores Aunt Mae."

"Then write the note and say that you will be at this Aunt Mae's house," Thunder Heart said, smiling as Johnny came up beside him, clutching the bow in his right hand.

"It's very pretty," the boy said, sliding his free hand over the carved figures. "I'd like to learn how to make a bow and carve it." He gazed wide-eyed at Thunder Heart. "Will you teach me how to do this one day? Would you even teach me how to shoot a bow and arrow?"

"Child, I will do all of those things," Thunder Heart said. He placed a gentle hand on Johnny's shoulder. "It is good to see your interest in my people's ways."

Beaming, Johnny said, "I want to learn everything."

As Dede was writing her note, she listened to Thunder Heart and Johnny talking. She hoped that Johnny would not call her "Mama" in Thunder Heart's presence. She hoped to be able to explain the truth soon. It didn't seem right for him to continue thinking that Bill was her father and Johnny was her brother.

But for now that wasn't important. There would be time later to tell him.

Now she must get them out of the house before Bill arrived!

She would tell Thunder Heart as soon as she could, because she didn't want to give him a reason to look at her as a deceitful person. And although she was his captive at this moment, she still could not help but love him with all of her heart.

She no longer feared his people's reaction, now that she realized Thunder Heart cared too much for her and Johnny to allow anyone to harm them.

"There, it's done," Dede said, laying the pen aside. She leaned down and blew on the wet ink, then stood up and smiled at Thunder Heart. "He'll have no reason to doubt what I wrote in the note."

Thunder Heart gazed into her eyes, then looked down at what she had written on the piece of paper. He knew that she could have written anything she wished and he wouldn't be the wiser, for he did not have the ability to read or write. If she wanted to deceive him by writing the truth, he knew that she could have done so.

But something deep inside told him that she wouldn't do such a thing. He knew that she sympathized with his people's plight. After all, she was willingly turning against her own father. That proved everything to Thunder Heart about her feelings for him.

"It is time now to go," he said, putting a hand gently around Dede's waist. He nodded at Johnny. "Return the bow where you found it."

Dede looked quickly up at him. "But it's yours," she blurted out. "You are only right to take it."

"Taking it would show the white man I was here," Thunder Heart said, still eyeing his bow hungrily. "I regret leaving it and my arrows, but if the white man found them gone, it might give up the true plan . . . that you are not with your aunt but with a Ponca chief."

Feeling true sympathy for Thunder Heart, Dede resolutely walked over to the glass weapons case, reached inside and took out a rifle. Then she put it into Thunder Heart's hands.

"This is now yours," she said, seeing his eyes wide with questioning. "I shall just add a line or two to the note and say that I have taken the rifle for my protection."

As Dede wrote this down, Thunder Heart stared at her in disbelief. He was stunned by her generosity even though, in truth she should hate him for taking her as his prisoner.

She smiled to herself, put the pen aside, and went to Thunder Heart, who was still studying her so closely.

Yes, perhaps she was crazy for giving this Indian a deadly weapon while he was stealing her away in the night as his captive. Yes, perhaps she was crazy to be so cooperative with him about writing the note! But she just couldn't find it in her heart to truly be afraid of him. She understood why he was doing this, and she didn't blame him.

Bill and his friends had left the Ponca defenseless. And deep down inside, although she felt such gratitude toward Bill for taking her and Johnny in when they had lost everything, she could not help but hate what Bill had done to the Ponca.

She kept telling herself over and over again that

she had no control over what was happening. None of this, except her stealing the rifle for Thunder Heart, was of her own doing.

In time Bill would know. He would know everything, especially her love for a man whom she should consider an enemy. But she knew most of all that she could never, ever hate Thunder Heart.

She did worry about Johnny and what he might be thinking about her willing assistance to Thunder Heart tonight. Johnny knew that she was not a person who made it a habit to lie, yet he had seen her writing all of those lies to Bill.

But Johnny also understood the plight of the Ponca and Bill's role in it. She knew that was why he didn't openly question her. He must know that her deceit was done for the right reasons.

She and Johnny rushed out of the house with Thunder Heart. Bill would think that she had gone to St. Louis, and he would expect her to travel in her buggy with Johnny, so that was how they set out for the Indian village.

She wondered, though, how Thunder Heart was going to keep her and Johnny hidden from white men, should any come to check on things. She wondered where the horse and buggy would be hidden.

And she was still afraid of the stomach disease, afraid that Johnny would continually be exposed to it at the village. Should he become ill, her understanding and love for Thunder Heart would turn quickly to hate.

She snapped her reins, and her black steed trotted briskly beneath the moon, the buggy wheels making ominous sounds as they rolled along the road that led away from Bill's lovely ranch house.

Dede wondered if tonight was the true beginning of the rest of her life—or the beginning of its eventual end!

It all depended on two things—how the Ponca as a whole received her and Johnny, and how Bill reacted when he discovered that she wasn't at Aunt Mae's after all!

CHAPTER FOURTEEN

How sweet the moonlight sleeps upon this bank;
Here we sit, and let the sound of music
Creep in our ears; soft stillness, and the night,
Become the touches of sweet harmony.

—William Shakespeare
(1564–1616)

Knowing that they were now near the Ponca village, Dede looked over at Thunder Heart, who rode bareback on his speckled steed beside her horse and buggy. Although she understood much of what had happened tonight, many things were left unanswered.

She glanced down at Thunder Heart's horse. Where had he gotten it? And why hadn't Thunder Heart stolen some of the horses that filled Bill's pasture to take back to his people? It only would have been fair, since many of them actually belonged to the Ponca. He must have recognized his own people's horses, yet he had left them behind.

And although she had persuaded him to take one of Bill's weapons, he could have had the whole slew of them.

But perhaps Thunder Heart was right. Bill would have figured out who had taken them.

Sighing heavily, Dede let her thoughts stray elsewhere as she again studied Thunder Heart's magnificent profile. He sat so tall and dignified, on a horse that was a magnificent animal itself.

Oh, but if only things could be different, Dede thought sadly to herself. If only there was no "unwritten law" that forbade whites and redskins to fall in love. Of course, it had happened in the past, but not without consequences.

Now that Dede had finally found a man who sent such a sensual thrill through her, it was unfair that so many obstacles prevented her from revealing the intensity of her love to him.

She had no idea just how far Bill and his accomplices would go. If they discovered that taking the Ponca's horses and weapons was not enough to defeat them, what else would they do? Dede had read of Indian massacres out west. Could it happen here in this gentle land of Missouri, where rivers ran sweet and clear, where eagles soared so beautifully in the sky?

Oh, Lord, she hoped not. Should Bill's hate for the Indians and greed for land that he had been forced to give up cause anything to happen to Thunder Heart, she herself might go gunning for Bill. Dede's admiration for the man was fast changing to resentment.

Even Johnny had shown his distaste for what Bill had done to the Ponca, and he was only a child.

Johnny would never forget the kindness of the Ponca, the way Thunder Heart had effortlessly removed the turtle, and then the way the shaman had magically made his wound heal. Now only a trace mark remained to show where the bite had been.

Dede's thoughts came to an abrupt halt when Thunder Heart turned and gazed at her. She felt a warmth spinning through her blood as she recalled another time when he had looked just as intensely at her. It was right before he plucked her off her horse and gave her that passionate kiss. Even now she felt the bliss of that kiss, of that embrace. It would have been so magical had he come tonight and swept her away because he loved her, not because he viewed her as a way to get back at an evil white man.

Thunder Heart saw how Dede was looking at him, and he could not help but want her with all of his soul. He could see the need in her eyes—the passion that he had seemed to awaken with a kiss. A kiss that he even now tasted on his lips, so sweet and meaningful.

If only he could have gone to her tonight with different intentions. He would rather have brought Dede's father a bride price and left it at his door. Then Dede could have come willingly with him to be his bride.

But knowing how this woman's father hated the Ponca with a passion much different from the passion between a man and a woman, Thunder Heart knew that he would never pay a bride price to the man. When he took Dede as his wife—and he would, when the time was right—he would pay no one for her. She would be his woman. And he would be the kind of husband who sheltered, protected, loved, and provided for her, always.

Knowing that now, when so much was at stake, was not the time to dwell on the subject of marriage, Thunder Heart tore his gaze from hers. He looked ahead at the shadows of the bluffs that rose high over the place he had readied for Dede and the child. She would soon know that he had planned this abduction well.

"Thunder Heart," Dede said, drawing his eyes back to her. "Thunder Heart, I'm concerned about Johnny's welfare—his health. If he is taken among your people and forced to stay there, he might come down with the stomach ailment. If he does, do you have enough of my father's medicine left for him? Had I thought quickly enough back home, I could have . . ."

"Woman, you are worrying unnecessarily," Thunder Heart interrupted her. "Neither of you will be near those who are ill. I have made you a camp away from the main camp."

Just as he revealed this to her, Dede realized that they had taken a turn away from his village. She had been so lost in thought earlier that she had not noticed.

"Where are you taking us?" she asked softly, now looking all around her for something familiar about the lay of the land.

"You will soon see," was all that Thunder Heart would say.

They traveled onward in silence. Johnny had scooted close to Dede and stretched out on the seat beside her. He had fallen asleep, his head resting on her lap and her hand on his cheek.

Now she saw horses grazing in a low, deep valley. On one side loomed bluffs that shadowed everything beneath them. She was aware of a heady scent, of leaves and fresh water, of acrid rushes in the nearby shallows, and of spicy evergreens. She could hear a loon crying somewhere in the distance. An owl hooted from a tree limb close by.

It was a place of tranquility, yet one thing was out of place here. Horses! Where had the horses come from? They must have been stolen back from the whites! She smiled at that thought.

"This is where you and the child will stay," Thunder Heart said, motioning toward a makeshift lean-to. He rode up to it, stopping a few feet away. "I will build you a substantial lodge later, one that will keep you out of the rain and the wind, a place where you will be comfortable until this thing between my people and the whites comes to a conclusion."

Dismounting beneath a cluster of cottonwood trees, he tied his horse's reins to a low limb, then took Dede's reins. "After I get a fire burning for you and Johnny, I will take your horse and buggy and hide them where no white man can find them," he said.

Dede was only half hearing him. She looked past the lean-to at the grazing horses. She saw some Ponca warriors on horses, obviously standing guard.

"You see the horses," Thunder Heart said, reaching a hand up to help Dede from the buggy.

"Yes, I see them, and I . . . I . . . think I understand where they came from," Dede said softly.

When he smiled, she knew that she had guessed right, and she felt a sense of relief that he and his warriors had gotten back at least a portion of what had been taken from them. If she could, she would ride with them and help them reclaim the rest of what belonged to them.

Thunder Heart waited to help her down from the buggy. She glanced down at Johnny, still sleeping soundly, as if he were in his comfortable bed, without a care in the world.

Then she looked at Thunder Heart again. "Johnny is asleep," she murmured. "If I move, I'll awaken him."

Thunder Heart nodded, then walked around to the right side of the buggy and gently lifted Johnny into his arms. In his sleep, Johnny trustingly slid an arm around his neck. Thunder Heart bent low and brushed a soft kiss across Johnny's brow. Dede saw this and was moved.

Then Thunder Heart carried Johnny into the lean-to and put him down on a pallet of blankets, taking time to cover him. Dede hurried in from the buggy and sat down beside Johnny.

She watched Thunder Heart make a campfire, fascinated by how he was doing it. He was making a fire by friction. First, he picked up a piece of soft stone that had a small depression on one side. Then he placed some rotten ashwood in the depression and just outside it. He took the stem of a soapwood plant and twirled it in the depression until enough heat was generated to make the rotten wood smolder. He blew on the smoldering punk until he had a spark large enough to ignite his dry grass tinder.

When the fire was lapping at the logs in the fire pit and the burning oak filled the night air with its pleasant aroma, Thunder Heart turned to Dede. "I must leave you alone for tonight," he said. "I have things to do. But I will return tomorrow. I will bring food, water, and more blankets."

"We're going to be left alone?" Dede asked, suddenly apprehensive, not wanting to think about what roamed the land at night.

Thunder Heart nodded toward his warriors. "They are here to protect you," he said. "And to keep watch to make sure you do not try to escape."

"Escape?" Dede said, for it truly had not even occurred to her to take advantage of his absence tonight.

Then it came to her just how odd it was that she hadn't thought of escaping. She actually felt as though she was part of this plot against Bill and his friends, as though she had been a part of it from the beginning. She most certainly didn't feel like a captive.

But now that he had put it to her in such a way, she realized that she should be scared.

"I did not think you were considering escaping," Thunder Heart said. "You are here because I forced you to come with me, yet in your heart you are here because you want to be. Is that not right, beautiful white woman?"

A blush rose hot and rushed to her cheeks. She turned her eyes away from him, for she didn't want to admit to him how she felt at this moment. Perhaps she would later, under different conditions. But now other things must take precedence over her feelings for a red man.

She could not help but be somewhat afraid at being away from her warm, comfortable, safe environment. She knew that if Thunder Heart were to stay, it would alleviate her fear. But as it was, he was leaving and she and Johnny would be at the mercy of warriors they did not know.

"Morning will come soon," Thunder Heart reassured her, then walked away.

After he took her horse and buggy to their hiding place, he came back and swung onto his horse, bareback. He looked down at Dede for a long moment, then flipped his long hair back and rode off at a hard gallop.

Dede grabbed one of the folded blankets. Trembling slightly, she looked guardedly at the sentries, then slid the blanket around her shoulders.

"Mama, where are we?" Johnny asked as he woke up. He leaned on an elbow and peered around him. His gaze stopped on the campfire and then he looked past it, realizing they weren't in the Ponca village.

"Where is Thunder Heart?" he asked, scrambling to a sitting position. "Where has he brought us?"

"It's a place safe from those who are ill at his village," Dede murmured. She slid a blanket around Johnny's shoulders, then nodded toward the blankets stretched out beneath him. "Sweetie, go on back to sleep. We're safe enough here. And morning can't be that far away."

"I am sleepy," Johnny said, yawning and rubbing at his eyes as he slowly fell back down on the blankets again. "Mama, lay down with me. Snuggle?"

"Yes, I'll snuggle," Dede said. She stretched out beside him and pulled a blanket over them both. She stroked his hair as he rolled over closer to her. "Sleep tight, Johnny. Don't let the bedbugs bite."

"Don't let them bite you either," Johnny said, giggling.

They both fell silent. Dede felt Johnny stiffen against her at the same moment that she heard a noise.

He propped himself up on an elbow as she sat up and looked around, trying to identify what was sniffing around in the dark close to their lean-to.

"It's Thunder Heart's pet coyote!" Johnny cried, as Four Eyes came slinking up to the entrance of the makeshift dwelling. "Four Eyes. I remember Thunder Heart calling the coyote by the name Four Eyes."

He reached a hand out for the coyote. "Come to me, Four Eyes," he called. "I'm a friend."

Four Eyes went straight to Johnny and licked his hand, then his face.

Proud of his new friend, Johnny smiled at Dede. "See, Mama?" he said, stroking the coyote's stiff grayish-white fur. "See how friendly he is?"

Dede smiled and petted the coyote herself. She felt a bond with the animal, for it was Thunder Heart's.

Her thoughts lingered on the proud, handsome Ponca chief. She did not resent him for what he had done tonight. In fact, she worried about him. Should Bill ever figure out where she was, he would be out for blood.

She shivered when she thought of whose.

Thunder Heart's!

CHAPTER FIFTEEN

We hope, we aspire, we resolve, we trust,
When the morning calls us to life and light.

—Josiah Gilbert Holland
(1819–1881)

A meadowlark was letting out its crisp song in the dawn's early light when Bill arrived home. He had not meant to stay so long in St. Genevieve, but the cards had been good to him last night. He laughed to himself at how his poker game had improved with his age.

He halfheartedly slung his reins around the hitching rail. He was too tired to take his horse to the stable and brush it down. He would go to bed and sleep for a while, then take care of the horse and the other chores awaiting him.

Actually, he wasn't even sure that he could make it to his bed. The hours in the smoky gambling parlor, drinking way too much whiskey and playing way too many hands of poker, had taken their toll.

He lumbered up the front steps and half fell into

the front door. He tried to be more quiet. He didn't want to awaken Dede, yet he did want to take a peek at her and Johnny just to see that they had been all right without him.

Why, hell, he hadn't even been with them for the evening meal. Did they think he had let them down?

"Naw, they know better'n that," he whispered, tripping his way down the long corridor.

When he saw Dede's wide-open bedroom door, he frowned. She generally slept with it closed, and it was too early for her to be up working around the house or in the kitchen.

He went on to her room and looked inside, taken aback when he saw that her bed had been slept in, but she wasn't there.

"Did she awaken and find me gone and become alarmed?" he wondered. He headed down the corridor and stopped to look in on Johnny, truly alarmed when he found that he wasn't in his bed either.

"Dede!" Bill shouted as he walked on toward the kitchen. "Johnny! Where are you?"

There was no response, only a strange, muted silence. Bill picked up his pace until he came to the kitchen. When he stepped inside, he saw no coffee boiling on the stove, nor any sort of preparations for breakfast at all.

He stumbled to his study. Perhaps Johnny and Dede were waiting for him there, even though they hadn't answered his calls. In the study he found the kerosene lamp burning on his desk, its fuel almost gone.

He went to blow out the flame, then saw a note lying on the desk.

"What on earth is this?" he whispered, picking it up and reading it.

"Aunt Mae?" he said, raising an eyebrow. "Dede must've received the telegram right after I left last night. And she was probably too concerned about her aunt to bother searching for me in St. Genevieve."

He knew she hated saloons and gambling halls and loathed even the thought of brothels being a part of the town.

"But just leaving so fast isn't like her," he said, nervously wiping his brow. "I've got to go to St. Louis. I've got to be sure she and Johnny got there all right."

He felt suddenly light-headed and knew that the lack of sleep and the amount of whiskey in his gut prevented him from taking off for St. Louis right now. First he would sleep off the foolishness of the long night.

Then, after he was rested, he would set out for Dede's aunt's house. He knew Dede was responsible enough to have gotten herself and Johnny there without mishap. They could do without him for a little while longer.

"Damn it, I sure messed up last night," he thought as he left the study and went toward his bedroom. "Just you wait and see, Dede, I'll sure as hell make it up to you."

CHAPTER SIXTEEN

Oh, to love so, be so loved, yet so mistaken!
—Robert Browning
(1812–1889)

Dede had been awakened at the break of dawn by the sun splashing streamers of gold into her eyes. She had crawled out of the lean-to and seen that the sentry was asleep, so she had taken advantage of the moment to awaken Johnny and go with him to a nearby stream for a quick bath.

Though she had considered stealing a horse and leaving while the Ponca warrior slept, she knew that she wouldn't get far, for there was another sentry nearby who would surely catch her.

She thought it was strange that she didn't make more of an effort to flee. If anyone besides Thunder Heart had abducted her, she knew she wouldn't be taking her captivity so lightly. She would be worrying about all sorts of ungodly things that she did not want to think about.

But she knew Thunder Heart could be trusted. In fact, she hungered to be kissed by him again. That alone made her want to be near him, whether captive or free.

"I'm hungry," Johnny said, crawling over to sit beside her and clutching a blanket around his shoulders. "What can we eat?" He looked quickly around him. "Four Eyes is gone. I wish he had stayed."

"Sweetie, I'm sure Four Eyes returned to Thunder Heart, and as for food, I am sure Thunder Heart will bring us nourishment soon," she said, settling down beside him on a blanket.

She slid an arm around his waist and drew him close. "Are you all right with what's happened?" she asked softly. "You seemed to be last night. But you are used to waking up in your own bed, used to coming into the kitchen and having a hot bowl of oatmeal waiting for you."

"With lots of sugar," Johnny said, smiling up at her. "And with raisins."

"Yes, with lots of sugar and raisins," Dede laughed. She cuddled him closer. "But, Johnny, how do you feel? Aren't you just a little bit afraid?"

"When I woke up in the middle of the night and was not in my bed, yes, I was afraid, but only for a little while," Johnny said. He looked at her with his dark, innocent eyes. "But then I saw you beside me and I knew that I was safe."

His words touched her so deeply, showed his trust in her to be so strong, that Dede had to fight off the urge to cry. She drew him up on her lap and for a moment he was a little boy again. She slowly rocked her body back and forth as his cheek rested trustingly on her bosom.

Then the sound of a horse's hooves came to them like small bursts of thunder in the quiet morning air. Johnny crawled quickly out of Dede's lap and stood up, watching for the approaching rider. He smiled broadly when he realized the rider was Thunder Heart. She rose to her feet and placed a hand on Johnny's shoulder as they waited for Thunder Heart to rein in his horse a few yards away.

Four Eyes soon appeared. His tail wagging, he leapt up and put his front paws on Johnny. Johnny laughed and petted him, then sat down and pulled the coyote onto his lap to hug him.

Dede's heart thudded in her chest as Thunder Heart's eyes met and held hers. She knew now why she had slept less soundly than usual last night. It was not because of her captivity. It was because she had been eager to see Thunder Heart again.

With no white people around, she felt free to care for him, to love someone whom most whites called savage. In truth, the white people were the savages, taking and taking from the red man, leaving him with scarcely an ounce of pride.

"I have brought food and more blankets for your comfort," Thunder Heart said, wrenching his eyes away from her. Passion stirred within him that had lain dormant since the death of his wife. It was good, he thought to himself, smiling. This passion . . . the ability to feel it again!

Dede found it hard to speak. She was tongue-tied not only by Thunder Heart's presence but also by the compassion he showed her and Johnny.

The way he had looked at her said things that neither of them felt at ease to speak in front of Johnny. She wanted this man with all of her heart and being. Feeling the way she did, how could she ever resent him for having stolen her and Johnny away in the middle of the night?

It was for a purpose, a purpose that even she, a captive, believed in. She felt that Bill should pay for his sins against the Ponca. To have stolen from them when they were so weakened by disease was the worst crime of all.

"Let me help you," Johnny said, shrugging the blanket off his shoulders and easing the coyote off his lap.

He hurried to Thunder Heart and smiled. Thunder Heart handed him a parfleche bag, and Johnny's nose twitched at the good aroma wafting out of the bag. He recognized the delicious smell of freshly baked bread. He also smelled baked meat.

"I will bring more blankets and water," Thunder Heart said, smiling as Johnny practically skipped over to Dede.

Thunder Heart could tell that the child still held no resentment, even though he had been taken from his home and brought to an unfamiliar place. In fact, the excitement that Thunder Heart had seen in the child's eyes last night seemed doubly evident today. Yes, the young brave seemed to be enjoying this little adventure.

"Look at the bag," Johnny said, holding it out for Dede. "Smell the food?"

Dede laughed softly. "Yes, I smell it. It's making my stomach growl," she said, a blush rushing to her cheeks as she looked at Thunder Heart.

But he was too busy bringing over blankets and a water pouch to notice. He knelt beside her. "These are also for you," he said, his eyes locking on hers again as she took the blankets from his arm.

"Thank you," she murmured, laying the blankets aside and taking the water pouch that Thunder Heart handed to her.

"While you and the child eat I shall build you a more substantial lodge," he said, stepping away. "I have already eaten. My *witimi,* aunt, prepares my morning meals. She prepared this food for you."

Dede didn't get a chance to respond. He had already left to cut long, green limbs from the nearby cottonwood trees.

As she and Johnny ate venison and bread, and took deep gulps of water from the pliable buckskin pouch, she watched the small lodge take shape.

"I am building you and Johnny a *diudipu,* a wigwam," Thunder Heart told them. He stripped the long green poles of leaves and stuck them into the ground, then bent them over and tied them at the top. "It will keep out the wind and the rain. It will keep in the heat on cool nights."

Dede continued watching him as he tied poles and vines horizontally to make the framework. And when this was all done, he went to his horse and untied a large folded hide, which he spread over the poles, leaving a space at the top center for the smoke hole. After staking the covering to the ground on all sides, he carried rocks inside and made a fire pit.

"I'll help you. I'll carry wood inside for the fire," Johnny said, his stomach now comfortably full. He ran around beneath the trees and gathered up several good-sized twigs, then took them inside the wigwam.

Once Thunder Heart had cut more substantial wood for the fire, and flames were licking at the logs, he stood back with Johnny and Dede and surveyed the wigwam.

"Do you like the lodge?" he asked, and smiled.

"Yes, I do. It will be fun to stay in it," Johnny said, stepping just inside. His eyes slowly roamed the interior, seeing how everything had come together to make a place for him and his mother to stay while they were Thunder Heart's captives.

Dede stepped inside with Thunder Heart. "Yes, I think it's very nice," she said, noticing how her approval made his eyes light up.

"Soon I will bring mats for the floor," he said, sliding another log into the flames.

"How long will we stay here?" Johnny asked, gazing intently into Thunder Heart's eyes.

Thunder Heart didn't respond. He reached over

and patted Johnny on the shoulder, then sat down beside Dede on a blanket spread before the fire.

"It's much bigger than I thought it would be," Dede said. "It's even large enough to stand up in."

"I would not make you a lodge that made you walk with a bent back," Thunder Heart said, following her gaze, admiring what he had built for the woman he loved.

He was well practiced at building such lodges. Although his people preferred tepees, they had learned the art of constructing a quick *diudipu* for the times they were away from their homes, hunting, or staying at the sugar bushes.

"I want to thank you for your kindness, yet it sounds strange to be thanking you, since Johnny and I are not here of our own choosing," Dede said, avoiding the word "captive."

She didn't even want to think of herself in that way. In a sense this was an adventure, something she would have never imagined in her wildest dreams.

"I will never treat you harshly as some people treat their captives," Thunder Heart replied. "I will always make things comfortable for you and the child."

"We appreciate that so much," Dede said. It was wrong of Thunder Heart to take them, yet right. She hoped never to have cause to be sorry for cooperating with him.

"The medicine that you brought to my people is helping most of them," Thunder Heart said. "But my *indadi*, my father, is still gravely ill. I am losing hope. His body seems unable to fight off disease as it could before he was weakened by long travel and the sadness brought on by the death of his beloved wife."

"It was so wrong that you were forced out of your homeland," Dede said, lowering her eyes. She was truly ashamed, for those who did this to the Ponca were her own people.

"My people could have adapted to the change had they not been weakened by disease," Thunder Heart said, his voice drawn. "Even now they are trying to accept it."

"How can they?" Johnny asked, hugging Four Eyes to his chest.

"My people, at night, tell their children myths to keep their heritage alive in their hearts, even while the white man is trying to rob them of it. In this way, the children learn the art of adapting to all situations, good and bad."

"Can you tell me one of your myths?" Johnny asked eagerly. "I truly want to hear."

"I have time for one tale and then I must return to my people," Thunder Heart said, watching the flames lapping around the logs. "I will tell you about *Indadige*. The children listen with an anxious heart when this myth is told to them."

"Oh, please do tell me," Johnny cried, scooting closer to Thunder Heart.

"*Indadige* was a monster in human shape that came one day to Ponca hunters in the forest. It attacked a group of hunters who were roasting a wild turkey," Thunder Heart said, smiling at Johnny's attentiveness to the story. "It was tall, with long hair. It hooted like an owl. It had bunches of grass tied to its upper arms and just below the knees, and it carried a club. Its eyes were close together and continually watering."

He turned slowly to look at Dede, then smiled at Johnny again. "When we lived in our homeland, where the creature was known to roam, parents kept their children indoors as soon as the sun set behind the distant mountains," Thunder Heart said, chuckling when he saw Johnny visibly shiver.

"You don't think it came with your people to Missouri, do you?" Johnny asked, his voice wary. "Do you think it is causing the stomachaches?"

Thunder Heart laughed throatily. "No, it did not follow us to this new land," he said, reaching up to tousle Johnny's hair. His smile faded as he lowered his hand. "And, no, it did not cause my people's illness. That was brought to them by whites."

Dede had become so immersed in the tale and in Johnny's attention to it that she hadn't paid any mind to an elderly woman approaching the wigwam.

But her insides tightened when the woman came and sat just outside the entryway, her gaze singling out Johnny, as though he was her sole purpose for being there. But that made no sense, Dede argued to herself. Surely it was her imagination. Yet it was definitely strange how the woman just sat there, staring—and staring only at Johnny.

Dede gently touched Thunder Heart's arm. "Who is that woman?" she asked. "Why is she sitting there? Why is she . . . staring at Johnny in such a way?"

Thunder heart looked past Dede toward his aunt, then turned back to her, guardedly. He offered no explanation about his aunt and why she was looking at Johnny as she was, yet he did know why. It was something that he doubted Dede would want to hear.

He wasn't sure, even, if he would allow it, although his people would say it was a normal thing to happen. If it harmed the white woman, he doubted he would let his aunt go through with it.

"Thunder Heart, surely you know the woman. Who is it? Why is she here?" Dede insisted, her cheeks flaming with anger the longer the woman sat there and stared at Johnny. She was feeling more and more ill at ease because of the woman's presence, and because of Thunder Heart's refusal to explain.

When Thunder Heart still ignored her and slowly rose to his feet, his gaze now also on the child, Dede knew that something was terribly wrong. The way the woman was staring at Johnny was threatening. It was as though she was studying him for a purpose.

But what?

She flinched when the old woman stood up and left as mysteriously as she had arrived.

"Thunder Heart, what's going on?" Dede demanded as she pushed herself up from the ground and put her hands on her hips. "Why have you gone quiet? Why aren't you answering my questions?"

Knowing that there was no explanation that Dede would accept, and not altogether approving of what was soon to happen, Thunder Heart still did not respond. Instead, he went to his horse and swung himself into the saddle.

Four Eyes came to him and barked. Thunder Heart leaned low and caught the coyote as he leapt into his arms.

"Please . . ." was all that Dede got out before Thunder Heart wheeled his horse around and rode away.

"What was that all about?" Johnny asked, coming to Dede's side, taking her hand.

Dede's heart was beating fast. Her dread now overwhelmed anything good that she had thought before. When it grew dark, she would find a way to flee!

The instant her son's safety came into question, Dede could no longer sit idly by. Her heart ached to think that Thunder Heart wasn't being honest with her. The old woman's actions were too peculiar for Dede not to believe that something was going to happen to Johnny.

"But what could it be?" she thought to herself.

She knelt beside Johnny and pulled him desperately into her arms.

"Mama, you're frightening me," Johnny said, sensing her mood.

"Don't be afraid," she soothed. "Son, I would protect you with my life."

"Are you suddenly afraid of Thunder Heart?" Johnny asked, leaning away from her so that he could see her face.

The question cut like a knife into Dede's heart. She looked away, afraid to answer. She did not want to tell her son the truth—that she could not help but feel betrayed by the Ponca chief.

CHAPTER SEVENTEEN

Trust, that's purer than pearl—
Brightest truth, purest truth in the universe—
All were for me—
In the kiss of one girl.

—Robert Browning
(1812–1889)

The day had seemed very long to Dede, but now it was finally dark and she and Johnny had eaten.

"Mama, why are you putting out the fire?" Johnny asked. Dede was pouring water onto the fire inside the wigwam. "It gets chilly at night. The fire would feel good."

"We're not going to be here tonight, so a fire is not necessary," Dede replied flatly. She gave Johnny a sidewise glance. "Roll up two blankets, Johnny. We'll take them with us."

"Where are we going?" he asked, moving to his knees as Dede poured more water onto the sizzling flames. "We're supposed to stay here."

"Johnny, just do as you are told while I put this fire out," Dede said, hating that she sounded annoyed. "I never leave a fire untended. I will not leave this one to burn down the wigwam."

But only because the resulting fire would draw undue attention to her escape, she thought heatedly to herself. Otherwise, she would have enjoyed burning the lodge that Thunder Heart had so carefully built for her and Johnny! That would show him a thing or two about her. She would not allow anyone to take advantage of her and her son. Not even the man who set her heart racing. She would forget him as quickly as she had become enamored of him!

Dede stopped and sucked in a shaky breath as she slowly looked around, remembering the care with which Thunder Heart had constructed the wigwam for her and Johnny. It was something a man would not do for just any captive. Were she truly a hostage, held by someone who hated her, she would not have been given such a warm, comfortable shelter. But she could not forget the change in Thunder Heart. She and Johnny had to try their best to escape.

"You're mad at Thunder Heart," Johnny said, reaching out for Dede's arm. "What did he do, Mama? What did he say?"

Dede took both of his hands in hers. "It's what he didn't say that frightens me."

She would not go into the details of why she felt this desperate need to flee from the man she would always love. She didn't want to frighten Johnny by telling him how the old woman's presence had unnerved her so much that she would risk their safety to make sure the woman didn't see her son again.

Yes, she had to get Johnny away from here. And she had to do it tonight!

"What do you mean?" Johnny asked. "Don't you trust Thunder Heart anymore?"

"Should we have trusted him at all after he came and stole us away in the middle of the night?" Dede blurted out. She dropped Johnny's hands and dumped ashes onto the smoldering embers.

"Damn him, I should just let this wigwam burn," Dede muttered.

"Mama, you're talking to yourself," Johnny said, gently tapping her on the shoulder. "And . . . you are saying a bad word that you never say. That means you are really mad. I wish I knew why."

Her face hot, blushing over being caught talking to herself and saying a curse word, Dede gave Johnny an awkward smile.

"Yes, I guess I was," she murmured. She wanted to say that that was what loving a man who had tricked her did to a woman. "I guess I'd better watch myself, huh, Johnny?"

Johnny gave her a half smile. "I've got the blankets rolled up," he said, pointing to them.

"And I've finally got the fire extinguished," Dede said. She turned and faced him. "Now, Johnny, as soon as the sentry goes to sleep, we're going to run out of the wigwam. We're going to get my horse and go home."

"Why didn't we do that last night when the sentry went to sleep?" Johnny asked. The outdoor fire cast its golden glow through the entryway.

"Well, now that is a very good question, isn't it?" Dede said, sighing. She knew why she hadn't left last night. Then she had felt as though she might be helping Thunder Heart. But now she felt foolish, and she could not help but feel used.

"Come on," she said. "Let's go sit beside the outdoor fire. We'll watch the sentry. It might take a while, but I know he'll eventually go to sleep."

"If we can stay awake ourselves," Johnny said. He wiped sleep from his eyes with a fist, then yawned.

He looked past the sentry, who was sitting on the ground beneath a tree. "There are other sentries, you know," he said.

"Yes, I know. We'll just have to make a wide circle around them so they won't see us," Dede said, having already mapped out everything in her mind. "That's why we're not taking the buggy. It would draw attention to our departure."

"I guess I'll never learn more Ponca customs now," Johnny said, keen disappointment in his voice. "I loved to listen to Thunder Heart tell about the Ponca myths. I'm sure there are many more he could tell us."

"Well, he can just tell someone else," Dede said, stubbornly tightening her jaw.

"What if he comes for us and finds us gone?" Johnny asked.

"We'll worry about that when, and if, it happens," Dede replied. "Once he finds us gone he might think it's good riddance."

"I don't think so," he said, scooting closer to Dede. "I'm sleepy, Mama. I don't think I can stay awake."

"Take a nap and I'll wake you when it's time to go," she said. She slid an arm around his shoulders and drew him even closer.

"Night, night. Don't let the bedbugs bite," Johnny said, giggling.

Dede was glad that Johnny could still have his sweet sense of humor in light of the danger that lay ahead. She knew it wasn't safe for them to take off in the dark, weaponless. But her protective instincts deep inside her told her that Johnny was in danger if they stayed. Yes, they had to leave. Tonight!

She looked over at the sentry. Her heart skipped a beat when she saw that he was sound asleep. The time had come!

If they didn't leave now, the opportunity might never come again.

"Johnny, wake up," Dede whispered. She gently shook him by the shoulder. "Come on, sweetie. It's time to go."

Johnny stirred and yawned, then looked up at Dede with questioning eyes. "Do we have to?" he asked. "Can't we wait until morning?"

"You know that we can't escape when it's daylight," Dede said, grabbing one of the blankets. She shoved the other one into Johnny's arms. "Come on, son. Time's a wastin'."

"Oh, all right," Johnny said, yawning again as he got to his feet, the blanket bulky in his arms.

"Just consider this another exciting adventure, and you'll be all right," Dede said. She bent and brushed a kiss across his brow. Then they ran into the darkness, Johnny close at her side.

Panting, Dede spied her horse grazing with the others. She ran on, ducked low beneath the rope corral, then waited for Johnny to follow. When she turned toward the horses again, her heart stopped dead still and her knees grew instantly weak. She saw the outline of a man standing in the shadows only a few feet away, directly in front of her.

"Because of what happened today I thought you might consider escaping tonight," Thunder Heart said as he stepped out into the moonlight. "I waited. You came. But now you must return to the wigwam."

"No, we won't go," Dede said. She lifted her chin defiantly, yet she knew that no matter what, she would be taken back to the wigwam.

And this time he might even tie her up to make sure she didn't try to escape again.

Thunder Heart came to her and gently touched her cheek. "I know why you felt the need to leave," he said huskily. "And I apologize for that. I will make your fear for Johnny's welfare go away."

"Then you know there was something wrong in how that woman watched Johnny as though . . . as though she was contemplating taking him," Dede blurted out.

"Yes, I know, and I understood her reasoning. In the past, when there were other available children, I even felt that what she wanted to do was all right," Thunder Heart said. "Until I saw your reaction."

He dropped his hand away. He stooped before Johnny and framed the child's face between his hands. "Johnny, go back to the wigwam," he said softly.

"But the fire is out," Johnny said, looking over his shoulder.

"I will come soon and rebuild the fire," Thunder Heart said. He looked at the blanket in Dede's arms.

He took it and gently gave it to Johnny. "These will warm you enough," he said. "Go to the lodge. Sleep. Things are all right in your world again. I will let nothing change that."

Listening to Thunder Heart's reassurances, Dede became confused. She must have been right that the woman wanted Johnny. But now everything seemed alright. Thunder Heart wouldn't let anything happen to her or Johnny. She wanted to be thankful, but the fact that he had sided with the old woman, even for a while, made her not trust him as much as before.

"We will watch you until you are safely inside the lodge," Thunder Heart said, waving at Johnny as he ran away.

When Johnny was in the wigwam, Thunder Heart turned to Dede. He placed gentle hands on her waist and drew her into his embrace. "Let us say no more about what you feared," he said thickly.

"Then I will say no more about your attempt to flee. I promise that no one will ever take the child from you."

Thunder Heart's kiss, and the magic it brought into her heart, made Dede forget everything except her love and passion for this man.

As his kiss deepened and his hands moved higher, cupping her breasts through her cotton blouse, she felt dizzy with a rapture unknown to her before.

Thunder Heart swept Dede into his arms and carried her away from the horses to a place of singing water. A stream meandered beneath high cliffs and through umbrella-like cottonwoods that hung over the moon-reflected water.

Everything that had troubled Dede only moments before was swept away and replaced by ecstasy as Thunder Heart laid her down on the thick, cool grass. Close by, wild roses released their sweet aroma into the night.

"Are you here with me now because you wish to be?" Thunder Heart asked huskily. "You do not feel forced?"

"I do want this," Dede replied, so glad now that her plan of escape had failed.

"You want Thunder Heart?"

"Oh, yes, I want Thunder Heart."

"I want you," Thunder Heart said, running his fingers down the front of her blouse, unbuttoning it. "My woman, there are no cares in the world at this moment. There is only us. There is only the passion we share."

"I have never wanted a man as passionately as I want you," Dede said.

She threw her head back, gasping, when he leaned low and swept her blouse open, his lips covering one of her nipples.

She writhed and wove her fingers through his long, thick hair as his tongue lapped at one nipple and then the other. She gasped in a wild burst of pleasure when she realized that one of his hands had slid up her skirt and was now stroking the center of her womanhood.

"Yes, yes," she whispered. She felt herself floating away on wings of pleasure when his mouth covered hers recklessly, his caressing fingers lifting her higher . . . higher . . . higher.

With a moan of ecstasy she kissed him back and clung to him.

She felt his knee spreading her legs wide apart, then gasped anew as he pressed himself down onto her throbbing center. His breeches were still on, yet she could feel his thick, long shaft straining against the buckskin fabric.

She knew that once he released his manhood and gained access to her wet and ready place, she would be transported to another world.

She had never felt as brazen, but she had never wanted a man so badly as now. She pulled her mouth free from his. "Please," she whispered, her hands on his face, her fingers eagerly caressing his handsome features. "I want you. Please want me as much."

"I have never wanted any woman as much as I want and need you," Thunder Heart said, his breath coming in short, painful rasps. "I want you for my wife, white woman, not only for the pleasure I take from your body."

"But how can it be?" Dede asked, her voice revealing her heartache. "You know it is forbid . . ."

He gently slid a hand across her mouth to stifle the word he abhorred. "Never say that word to me," he said firmly. "Anything we wish to do together because of our love is right. No one can ever take it away from us. No one."

Dede wouldn't allow herself to think of Bill and how he would react when he discovered where she was, and with whom. She let herself be lost in the wondrous moment as Thunder Heart stood up and slowly undressed in the moonlight.

As each portion of his muscled, copper body was revealed Dede's desire was aroused even more. When finally he dropped his buckskin breeches to the ground and she saw how well endowed he was, she felt heat rush to her cheeks. Then when he wrapped himself within a hand, a sensual shock rippled through her.

"Come to me," Thunder Heart said, his voice drawn and husky. He reached his hand out for Dede. "Come and feel my heat. Know that it is yours."

Dede rose slowly to her feet.

She stood before him and her fingers trembled as she reached down and placed her hand on his throbbing member.

"Move your hand on me," Thunder Heart said, his eyes glassy with passion.

Dede gazed into his eyes. His warm flesh made her insides melt in rapture.

She pleasured him for another moment, then questioned him with her eyes when he gently pushed her away.

"Undress," Thunder Heart said.

Her eyes locked on his, her heart pounding, Dede removed her blouse and shoved her skirt down over her hips.

When she was finally nude, she watched how his eyes feasted on her flesh. He reached out both hands and filled them with her breasts, his thumbs tweaking her nipples.

She, in turn, again grasped his manhood. While one hand moved on him, she ran the other over his powerful chest.

He drew her into his embrace. As he kissed her, he slowly pulled her down with him to the bed of soft grass.

Stretched out beneath him, Dede twined her arms around his neck. She moaned in ecstasy as he positioned himself inside her and began rhythmically thrusting.

A spinning sensation flooded Dede's body. She closed her eyes and let the ecstasy move over her in its bone-weakening intensity.

She wrapped her legs around him, only half aware of making whimpering sounds. She thrust herself closer to his heat, then gasped when he reached between her legs to stroke her sensual place, all the while continuing his constant, deep thrusting within her.

Thunder Heart felt quick, hot bolts of electricity flashing through him with each thrust. He was almost delirious with sensation. His whole universe seemed to be spinning.

He bent low and sucked on her nipple, his hand still stroking her, her woman's center throbbing against the tips of his fingers.

Yes, he could tell that she was near, as was he. He wanted to prolong the pleasure, but it had been too long since he had let himself give in to the temptations of the flesh.

And since he had lost his wife, there had been no woman with whom he wished to share such moments.

Not until now.

Not until Dede.

He would not let anything take away what they had found.

He felt foolish now for even having considered allowing his aunt to give Johnny to a Ponca family to be raised as their own, even though such arrangements were customary among his people.

No. He would do nothing to harm his relationship with the woman he loved. She was a woman of character, of strong morals, of honesty!

Ah, how proud he was to have found her and to have found a way to make her love him in return.

He swept his arms around her and kissed her with a deep, hot passion as his body and hers quaked together in the final throes of ecstasy, their climaxes sought and found at the same moment of bliss.

Afterward they clung to one another. Dede did not want to let him go. Never so happy, Thunder Heart smiled.

"Do you see the stars tonight?" he asked as he rolled away from her and stretched out on his back.

"Yes. I don't think I've ever seen as many, or seen them as bright," Dede said, staring up at them as she snuggled closer to Thunder Heart.

This moment was so right . . . so perfect.

She hated for morning to come, for with it would come reality.

"My people pay a lot of attention to the stars," Thunder Heart said, motioning toward the sky with a slow sweep of his hand. "My people use the position of the sun and stars as a rough measurement of time."

"The Milky Way is the most fascinating to me," Dede mused, staring at the thick cluster of stars overhead. "Isn't it beautiful how the stars shine and glimmer almost as one?"

"My people have names for many of the constellations," Thunder Heart said. "The Milky Way is called *waka-ozage* in my Ponca tongue, or 'the holy path.' Its movement is used for reckoning time."

"The north star," Dede said, smiling over at him. "How do you say that in your language?"

"It is called *mika-ska-azi*, or 'the star that doesn't move,'" he answered. "That star is used by our hunters and travelers to find their way."

He gazed up at the full moon. "My people pay much attention to the moon, too," he told her. "In its last quarter the moon is called *mi-t-e*, or 'dead moon.' My people look for signs of storm at that time."

"I see the full moon as the 'lovers' moon,'" Dede said. "Tonight we are the lovers."

He swept her beneath him again, and his mouth came to hers in a trembling, passion-hot kiss.

His hands moved over her, awakening her to a desire so overwhelming that she seemed to melt inside.

"I love you so much," she whispered against his lips as he filled her and once again took her to the stars, and beyond.

CHAPTER EIGHTEEN

Keen as are the arrows of that silver sphere,
Whose intense lamp narrows
In the white dawn clear,
Until we hardly see,
We feel that it is there.

—Percy Bysshe Shelley
(1792–1822)

Feeling deliciously wonderful, Dede rose from her bed of blankets, the memory of last night so vivid she felt as though Thunder Heart was still with her, touching her, lifting her high on clouds of rapture.

When he had left after their lovemaking to steal back more of his horses, Dede had sat outside beneath the moon for some time, reveling in the knowledge that Thunder Heart loved her as much as she loved him!

Oh, how wonderful it would be to be his wife, to have him as Johnny's father!

And that he wanted her to marry him was everything to her . . . everything!

Feeling a chill in the wigwam, Dede realized that the fire had died down to low embers. She moved to her knees beside the fire pit and scooted several logs into the hot coals.

Trembling, she pulled a blanket around her shoulders, then turned and gazed at Johnny, still sleeping so peacefully amidst his blankets.

She wanted so much for him.

She wanted everything to be perfect.

She wanted him to have everything in life that he wished for.

She had accepted that he didn't want to be a lawyer and thanked the Lord that it was so, because when Bill found out about Thunder Heart and Dede's feelings for him, he would never understand. And when Bill turned his back on Dede, he would turn his back on Johnny too.

Yes, the one thing that diminished the wonder of falling in love again was Bill.

But Bill actually wasn't the only problem. Everyone who thought they were man and wife would learn that they had never been married at all.

She hoped that people would believe her explanations, or she could end up looking like a harlot. If everyone thought that, unmarried, she had shared a bed with Bill, her reputation could be scarred forever.

But there was something that concerned her even more. She just now realized that she hadn't talked to Thunder Heart about Bill and Johnny. He still thought that Bill was her father and Johnny was her brother. When she had started to tell him, she had been interrupted, and then it had slipped completely from her mind.

Well, she would tell him now. The next time he was with her. She only hoped that he wouldn't mind having an instant son! Until now he would have been thinking of Johnny as a nephew instead.

Wanting to get her day started, Dede decided to make breakfast from the supplies that Thunder Heart had brought. There were plenty of unperishable foods in the parfleche bags.

Before he had left last night, he had told her that someone would bring fresh meat and vegetables today for her to make a stew over the lodge fire.

She smiled at the thought of learning to survive without her fancy kitchen and cookware. She and Johnny were even growing used to wooden plates and utensils.

To Johnny it was fun. To her it was a challenge.

She needed to go to the nearby stream and freshen up before preparing breakfast. She took one more look at Johnny to make sure he was still sleeping soundly. When she heard his even breathing and saw the contented look on his face, she leaned low, kissed his forehead, then went quietly to the entry and pushed the buckskin flap aside.

She stopped short when she saw something lying on the ground just outside. Her heart warmed and she smiled, reaching out for the buckskin dress, which was neatly folded for her to find when she awakened today. Beside the dress were beautifully beaded moccasins, as well as a necklace made of matching beads.

"Oh, Thunder Heart, I do love them so," she whispered as she swept them up and clasped them to her bosom. "I will wear them with such pride."

She glanced down at herself. She had worn the same skirt and blouse since she had been taken from her home, not only during the day, but also to sleep in.

She had not even had the chance to wash them yet, as she hadn't wanted to part with them long enough to wait for them to dry. With nothing else but blankets to wear, she would have felt too vulnerable if any of Thunder Heart's people had made a sudden appearance.

Now that she had this buckskin dress she could change and wash her clothes.

She hoped that Thunder Heart would also think of Johnny's need for clean clothes. She smiled as she envisioned her son in fringed buckskins and moccasins. With his long black hair and his smooth summer tan, he could even pass for an Indian.

She started to go on to the stream where she would use the blanket around her shoulders for a towel. But she stopped short and felt the color drain from her face when she saw the elderly woman from yesterday walking toward her.

Not wanting to jump to conclusions, especially since Thunder Heart had assured her that Johnny was safe, she thought about his promise to have meat and fresh vegetables delivered to her today.

Maybe that was why the woman was coming, or perhaps even to apologize for her rude behavior yesterday!

The first hope was dashed when Dede realized the woman carried nothing with her. That only left an apology. She had to believe that was why she was approaching, was now only a few feet away. But the woman wore no smile on her face, and Dede could not help but think the worst. She was there because of Johnny.

But . . . why . . . ? Dede despaired.

"Oh, Lord, why is she doing this?" Dede whispered, clutching the dress and moccasins to her chest. She looked quickly over her shoulder and gasped when she saw Johnny coming out of the wigwam, his fists rubbing his eyes, his hair twisted and unkempt.

She dropped the lovely gifts from Thunder Heart to the ground, turned quickly, and placed trembling hands on Johnny's shoulders. "Get back inside," she said sternly. "And don't come out until I tell you to."

The expression in his eyes tore at Dede's heart. Rarely had she spoken so coldly to her son. But this was a rare circumstance.

She felt threatened by the woman. She wanted Johnny to be safe.

She was glad when the entrance flap dropped down and Johnny was no longer where the woman could see him. Dede stood stiffly as the woman stopped only a few feet away from her. She inched back toward the entrance flap and placed her hands behind her, clutching the flap closed with determined fingers.

"I have come for the boy," the woman said in perfect English.

Stunned speechless, her whole world seeming to crumble around her, Dede gaped in disbelief. She dropped her hands to her sides, her fingers doubled into tight fists. Dede rushed out of hearing range of the wigwam, and the woman followed her.

"Why do you think you have the right to come and take Johnny with you?" Dede asked, her voice filled with rage. "Who are you?"

"My name is Silken Wing," the woman replied. "I am aunt to Thunder Heart."

"You . . . are Thunder Heart's aunt?" Dede gasped, not knowing whether to feel better or worse. Thunder Heart had promised that no one would take Johnny from her. And why on earth would the elderly lady think that she could?

"Yes, I am Thunder Heart's aunt," Silken Wing repeated. "My reason for coming for the child is that many sons his age have died in my village because of the stomach ailment."

"I'm sorry about that, but what could that have to do with Johnny?" Dede asked warily.

"It is a Ponca custom that when a son of one family dies, the family looks for a boy their son's own age to adopt, to take the place of the one who died," Silken Wing explained. "I have watched Johnny. He is strong. And I know that your mother is dead.

Thunder Heart shared that with me. That means that Johnny has no mother. It is important that a child, especially a boy, have both father and mother to guide him into adulthood. I know of a family who will take Johnny in as their son. You are only his sister."

Dede's insides went cold. She felt the blood draining from her face. And then she felt Johnny's hand clutch hers and realized that he had come out of the wigwam and had heard everything.

Dede could feel desperation in the way Johnny held her hand.

She fiercely twined her fingers around his, her heart thudding so wildly that she felt light-headed.

But she couldn't allow herself to faint. She had to stay strong for Johnny. She was his protector. His mother!

Stunned by Silken Wing's words, Dede was finding it hard to breathe, much less speak. She bent down and wrapped her arms protectively around Johnny. "You can't have Johnny!" she cried. "He's *my* son!"

She heard a sharp intake of breath behind her, and she knew who had gasped in disbelief.

Caught up in the moment, she hadn't heard Thunder Heart arrive. He must have left his horse with the others and come from the corral on foot. And he must have heard her exclamation. He had heard her confess to something she had not yet told him!

Oh, Lord, she had been planning to tell him.

Today!

But not in this way . . . surely the worst way possible for him to learn the truth.

As she spun around to face him, she felt everything they had shared slipping away from her.

"Your *wizibe*, your son?" Thunder Heart asked, his spine stiff as he looked from Dede to Johnny incredulously. His eyes held Johnny's for a moment and then he glared at Dede. "You have just said that this child is your son."

Eyes wide, her breathing shallow, Dede slowly nodded. "Yes, Johnny is mine," she said, her voice breaking. "Please let me explain."

"The man that I thought was your father is instead your *husband*?" he asked tightly.

He stepped closer to Dede. He looked down at her with angry eyes. "You who I thought was honorable and pure are instead a lying, deceitful woman," he said furiously. "You made love with me. I made love with a married woman? Do you not know how dishonorable an act that is for a man? For . . . a woman?"

He looked past her and motioned his aunt. "Aunt Silken Wing, take the child," he said angrily. "I was going to tell you today not to come for the boy, to search elsewhere. But now, knowing how deceitful this woman is, I give you permission to take the child. She does not deserve such a fine son as he!"

Dede was shocked by what was happening, not only because Johnny was going to be taken from her but because the man she adored thought so little of her now. She didn't know what to do. She felt as though the earth had just opened up and swallowed her whole.

It was the worst day of her life, even worse than the day she had buried her husband. Today she was losing not only the man she loved but also her son.

But she wasn't deceitful! She would have never purposely kept this from Thunder Heart!

"You must let me explain," she exclaimed. "If your love for me was true, you will listen."

"I . . . will . . . listen," Thunder Heart said, his jaw set. He so badly wanted to believe that there was a good reason for Dede to keep the truth from him. He had no choice but to listen and to weigh her words. Yes, he must give her a chance, for no matter what she might be guilty of, he still loved her.

Relieved to be given an opportunity to set things right, Dede hurriedly explained. "You see, Thunder Heart, I didn't purposely not tell you," she said after she had told him the truth. "The first time I tried, I was interrupted. Then I forgot that you didn't know."

When he didn't say anything, but continued to look at her in a way she could not interpret, she began to lose hope that things could ever be the same between them again.

"Please tell me that you understand," she begged, reaching out for him. Her heart sank when he clasped his hands together behind him, denying her touch.

Dede grabbed Johnny and held him tightly. His

eyes were wide as he still stared at the woman waiting to take him away.

"You mustn't allow this to happen," Dede insisted, fighting back the tears that threatened to spill from her eyes.

She knew the importance of looking courageous and brave in the light of what had happened. She wanted to feel the courage. She also wanted to continue fighting for Thunder Heart's love.

"Please believe me, Thunder Heart," Dede pleaded, and again she told him about her relationship with Bill, about Johnny's father having died, and about her own father's death.

"Everything I have ever done I have done for my son," Dede said, her voice breaking. "Living with Bill, pretending to be married so that it would not look shameful for us to share the same house—all that was for Johnny. I didn't expect to meet someone I could truly love again. Not until I met you, Thunder Heart. Not . . . until you."

"You share the man's house," Thunder Heart said huskily. "Did you ever share his bed?"

The color drained from Dede's face. "Heavens, no," she blurted out. "But that was why I had to pretend to be Bill's wife, so that people wouldn't misunderstand."

She lowered her eyes, then raised them slowly to look straight at Thunder Heart. "Last night was so beautiful," she said. "I shall never forget . . . last night."

Thunder Heart's eyes wavered as his feelings

toward her softened. He looked at Dede, then at Johnny. "Young brave, you will stay with your mother," he said.

He went to his aunt and led her away, toward his village.

A sob lodged in Dede's throat as she watched Thunder Heart walking away. She truly believed that when he had more time to think about what had happened, he would return to her with love in his heart.

For now, it was wonderful to be with Johnny.

"Mama, you asked Thunder Heart to understand many things, but even I don't," Johnny said. "What is this about Bill? You aren't his wife?"

"Oh, Johnny, I shouldn't have waited so long to explain things to you, either," Dede cried, grabbing him and holding him tight. "I will now. Yes, I will tell you everything."

CHAPTER NINETEEN

This I beheld, or dreamed in a dream;—
There spread a cloud of dust along a plain.

—Edward R. Sill
(1842–1887)

Fueled by confusion, Thunder Heart raided ranches with vigor that night under the cover of darkness. When he returned to the hidden corral in the valley, several horses had been added. He mentally counted them and smiled, realizing that almost all of the horses that belonged to the Ponca had been stolen back.

Worn out, his heart aching from loving Dede so much, yet needing time to think things through, he went to his lodge.

When he arrived there he found his aunt waiting beside the fire. She looked up as he entered, her eyes red from crying.

He knew by the way she spoke his father's name that his father was dead.

He hurried outside and looked heavenward. "Mighty One above, what have I done to deserve so much heartache?" he cried angrily. "Will it ever end?"

CHAPTER TWENTY

There are souls like stars, that dwell apart,
In a fellowless firmament.

—Sam Walter Foss
(1858–1911)

After a restless night, when her emotions battled within her constantly, Dede finally got up. The break of dawn came across the land in muted colors of pinks and blues.

She brushed her fingers through her hair to straighten it, then slid logs into the slow-burning embers of the fire. Torn over what to do, she simply sat and stared into the fire, its flames slowly caressing the logs in satin streamers.

"Why didn't he come last night?" she whispered, tears running down her face. She had explained everything to Thunder Heart. Wasn't that enough?

Or had he not believed her? Did he now see her as a lying, deceitful person, undeserving of his love?

She looked at Johnny, who was still asleep. It seemed like a miracle that he was even there. She still couldn't believe that Thunder Heart's aunt thought Dede would hand Johnny over so easily.

Even if Johnny had been only her brother, Silken Wing must have known their bond was intense . . . too strong for her to relinquish him to total strangers.

Dede had to keep reminding herself that what Silken Wing had wanted was not devious. It was a Ponca custom. Silken Wing had seen in Johnny a way to bring comfort to a couple whose son had died.

"But my son is mine," she whispered, a sob lodging in her throat. "He is my happiness."

Dede flinched when she heard the whinny of a horse just outside. Her pulse raced at the thought that it might be Thunder Heart coming to tell her that all was forgiven. If he came this morning and said he understood, oh, then surely things between them would be right once more.

The horse whinnied again, and Dede got quickly to her feet. She realized that she hadn't actually heard the horse approaching. That must mean that the horse belonged to the sentry, and that he had secured it closer to her lodge than usual.

But she had to see. She could not give up on the chance that Thunder Heart was outside, perhaps talking to the sentry, waiting to come to talk to her after he saw her moving about.

She watched the smoke of the fire spiraling upward and then disappearing through the smoke hole. The fire alone would have told Thunder Heart that she was awake. If he had been waiting for that, he should have been in the wigwam by now.

Hurrying to the entrance flap, Dede swept it aside, then stopped and stared in disbelief. She found her horse standing there, only a few feet from the wigwam, grazing on thick, green grass. It was saddled, and its reins were tied to a low-hanging cottonwood limb.

She looked past the horse at the sentry. His eyes were on her, but as she slowly reached for the horse's reins, he made no sign of getting ready to stop her.

"This has to be a test," she whispered to herself.

But nothing mattered except that her horse had been returned to her and, with it her freedom. She hurried inside, awakened Johnny, and carried him to her steed.

"Mama, where are we going?" Johnny asked, getting comfortable in the saddle as Dede slipped up behind him.

"I'm not quite sure yet," she answered. She gave the sentry a guarded look, and when he still did nothing to stop her, Dede knew that she was free to ride away from her place of captivity. Sinking her moccasined heels into the flanks of the horse and holding Johnny securely against her, she found herself riding in the direction of the Ponca village—instead of riding toward freedom.

But, in truth, that freedom no longer appealed to her. She wanted a life with Thunder Heart. As long as it was a life that included Johnny.

At least today she was being given the chance to try again to make things right with Thunder Heart. That must have been the purpose of her being given her horse back.

But she couldn't understand why Thunder Heart had decided to let her go, to let her and Johnny return home. Wouldn't he risk that she would tell Bill everything? That Bill might bring many men to the Ponca village, and this time take more than horses and weapons? That this time they might take lives?

None of it made any sense.

But she would play along. If it was a trick of some sort, she would soon find out. She wouldn't be allowed to get far. Or she might be allowed to get just inside the perimeter of the village, to think things were going to be all right, and then be stopped and taken back to the wigwam in some sick sort of trick.

No. She didn't think that Thunder Heart was that kind of a man. She couldn't believe that he could ever do anything to harm her. Even though he may have lost faith in her, surely he couldn't fall out of love with her so quickly. It was that love, and the beautiful private moments they'd shared, that gave Dede hope.

Regardless of how she would be received at the village, Dede could only ride onward. She had to do everything possible to make things right between her and Thunder Heart.

Soon she would know. She so badly wanted to believe in a future with him. She wanted to be his wife! She gazed heavenward and prayed that was how it would be. Chills suddenly ran down her spine as she came closer to the village and heard the wails that until now had ceased. The air seemed to vibrate again with the sad cries of mourning.

Dede shivered to think that perhaps someone powerful had died, for the people's cries today were twice as intense as before.

"Who?" she whispered, then swallowed hard. She wondered what it might be like when someone mourned a chief. Wouldn't the cries and chants be as loud and as sorrowful as they were now?

But it can't be Thunder Heart, she thought desperately. *He's young. And he wasn't ill yesterday.*

Then it came to her. It might be his father! Wasn't he the true chief? Wouldn't his death elicit such mourning? And Thunder Heart had told her that his father was no better after taking the medicine.

Yes, surely Seven Drums had died.

Her heart went out to Thunder Heart. If it was true he would be torn apart with grief.

She wanted to hold him, to help him through his hurt. She understood too well the devastation one feels at the loss of a loved one. She had lost too many. Her beloved mother, her husband, and the most recent loss . . . her father.

She knew that Thunder Heart had suffered many great losses as well. Yes, if he had lost a dear one today, she would do what she could to go to him. She hoped he would allow it . . . that he would want her there.

She saw the outskirts of the village through a

break in the trees. She looked inward to find the courage to ride among Thunder Heart's people. She felt weak in the knees at the thought of being denied entry.

She silently prayed that he had decided to give her and Johnny their freedom for all the right reasons and that she could resume her life as she chose. If he had truly forgiven her, he was her choice for the future, now and forevermore.

"Lord, please let it happen that way," she prayed. She held her chin high and her back straight as she rode into the village. Soon two warriors stepped into her path. Then another came up quickly on her right and took her reins. She suddenly felt as though she and Johnny had ridden into a trap. The Ponca's wails had stopped. Everyone was staring at her and her son.

But what puzzled Dede was that no one looked at her with resentment or hate. There seemed to be compassion in their faces. She followed their eyes as they looked past her.

When she saw Thunder Heart standing just outside of a tepee, his face covered with the black ash of mourning, she knew that Seven Drums had died.

She was torn over what to do. The one warrior was still holding her reins. The people were again looking at her and Johnny, waiting for her next move. For the moment everything seemed frozen in time.

Finally Thunder Heart came to her. Her eyes locked with his, her pulse racing.

"Come to my lodge with me so that we can have private time together," he said, offering Dede a hand. "Your son will be safe with my aunt Silken Wing."

Dede swallowed hard. Then Silken Wing came toward her and Johnny, a look of apology in her eyes, and Dede felt better. The elderly woman must feel sorry for having frightened Dede so much when she had tried to take Johnny away from her.

"He will only be with my aunt until your time with me is over," Thunder Heart reassured. "My father has died. Come. Help me accept my loss."

"You no longer resent me?" Dede asked softly.

"I need you" was all that he would say.

Dede slid off the horse and into Thunder Heart's arms.

She gave Johnny a quick look as he walked away with Silken Wing. He seemed unafraid, especially now that a young brave his own age was walking with him and talking to him. Johnny had wanted to make a Ponca friend. Perhaps this would be the boy.

She went on to Thunder Heart's lodge with him. He urged her to sit beside the fire, then he sat facing her.

"My *indadi*, my father, lost the battle with the stomach disease," he said, his voice thick with remorse. "No *maka*, no medicine, was strong enough to heal my father, neither yours or my shaman's."

"I'm so sorry," Dede murmured. She reached a soft, comforting hand to his cheek, relishing the warm feel of his skin. She looked past the black ash and into his eyes.

"What can I do to help you?" she asked.

"Why did you come to my village when you saw that I had returned your horse to you?" Thunder Heart asked. "Did you come today to make things right with Thunder Heart?"

"When I saw the horse I was confused," Dede admitted. "I wasn't sure why it was brought to me." She lowered her eyes momentarily, then looked quickly up again. "Why was it?"

"I brought the horse to give you your freedom," Thunder Heart said, taking her hand away from his face and gently holding it. "Then I waited to see what you would do with this freedom. Return to the man who is not your husband? Or come to me, the man who loves you."

"It . . . was . . . a test?" Dede asked, her voice wary. "Did I pass?"

"Yes, in a sense it was a test, and yes, you passed," Thunder Heart answered. "By not returning to your ranch, you proved that you do truly care for me, that you trusted me enough to come into my village, even though, until this morning, you had been held captive."

He lowered his eyes, then looked into hers again. "I apologize for having allowed my anger to cloud my judgment," he said. "But I would like to ask your permission for Johnny to stay with my aunt for a while."

Dede slowly slid her hands free from his and

clasped them tightly in her lap. "What do you mean?" she asked, aware of the distrust in her voice.

"I need you, my woman," Thunder Heart said, his eyes imploring her, his heart aching at the thought of his father lying in repose, awaiting burial.

He reached over and unlocked her fingers, then took her hands and held them.

"My woman, I have many days of travel ahead of me," Thunder Heart said quietly. "I would wish for you to accompany me on my journey of the heart. But I would not want to ask this of your son. He would be better off staying in my village. Aunt Silken Wing has agreed to keep him until you return. She understands under what conditions. She knows that when you return from the journey, Johnny will be returned to you, his true mother."

His words spun crazily inside her head. But what mattered was that she was forgiven and that Johnny would never be taken from her, and that Thunder Heart needed her . . . wanted her.

"Where are you going?" she asked softly.

"I must return my father to the Ponca's true burial place at *Ma-azi*, in South Dakota, near Wind Cave," Thunder Heart said, tears shining in the corners of his eyes.

"South Dakota?" Dede gasped. "You are planning to travel to South Dakota, the place you were forced to leave?"

"It must be done," Thunder Heart said, his jaw tightening. "My father was a proud Ponca chief. He deserves to be buried among his ancestors, among all the proud chiefs that came before him . . . including my beloved grandfather and great-grandfather."

"But if the white authorities find out, they will stop you," Dede said, her thoughts suddenly on Bill and how he might take advantage of these circumstances. If the Ponca left the reservation and began a journey back to their homeland, where their presence was restricted, she knew that Bill and those who sided against the Indians would cause trouble. Thunder Heart might even be thrown into prison for violating the treaty laws.

"No matter what obstacles I must face to get there, I will take my father to his homeland for burial," Thunder Heart said, his eyes lit with a determined, angry fire. "Do you not see? Doing so will be the last respectful, loving deed this son can ever do for his father."

"And you want me to accompany you?" Dede asked, knowing that if burying his father in South Dakota was so important to him, she must do everything within her power to help him.

Yet there was Johnny!

If she left him behind, wouldn't that give Silken Wing time to place him with a family who would convince him to stay with them out of his intense fascination with Indian life?

And what if Bill realized where Johnny was and came for him in Dede's absence? And if he discovered Dede's plan to marry Thunder Heart, might he take Johnny far away to keep him from being a part of the Indians' lives?

So much troubled her, yet she knew that she must help Thunder Heart during his time of sadness. She did fear the whites coming and stopping him. But if she was with him, perhaps she could find a way to make the whites understand his need to give his father a proper burial among his ancestors.

"Yes, I will go with you," she said, thankful that Thunder Heart had been patient while she wrestled with all of this in her mind. "But I think Johnny should go with us."

"Because of problems from whites that we might confront on the trip north, Johnny would be safer among my people, where there are many warriors to guard against intruders," Thunder Heart said. "Only a few warriors will ride with us."

"But won't that give the whites an advantage should they try to stop you?" Dede asked warily.

"I cannot think the worst," Thunder Heart replied. "It would not be wise to think about fighting the whites, as my father's body might be violated during a fight. No. I must hope for good, not bad, while I do what is right for my father. His spirit awaits a proper burial among the Ponca ancestors."

"I understand," Dede said.

He held his arms out for her, and she went to him.

His arms enveloped her, sending a gentle peace throughout her. She only hoped that being there for him would give him some peace during his time of anguish.

"The Ponca believe that after a person dies, his spirit continues to exist," Thunder Heart said softly. "Each person has a *wandze*, or spirit, which does not perish at death. I know that many whites believe that there is one day to be a resurrection of all bodies from the ground. But in my world there is a continued existence of the ghost, or spirit."

He gently held her away from him, his eyes locking with hers. "It is believed that if you are good, you will go to the good ghosts," he said. "If you are bad, you will go to the bad ghosts. My father will go to be among the good, where many of those I have lost before will be awaiting to celebrate his presence among them."

Dede knew that as he talked about those who had died, he was thinking of his wife and unborn child, and his mother and grandparents. She hoped that when all of this was behind them, she could fill the places in his heart that had belonged to those he had loved and lost.

Her thoughts went back to Bill. She knew that he deserved to know that she and Johnny were all right. By now he might realize that the note had been a lie.

She had to wonder whether his search for her would take a back seat to going after Thunder Heart, once he received word that the Ponca were returning to their homeland? There was no doubt that he would find out. Whoever spied Thunder Heart and his entourage first would alert the authorities, who would then report to Bill that she had been seen among the Ponca travelers.

She owed Bill a lot for having taken her and Johnny in, yet now she owed Thunder Heart even more. He needed her more than Bill ever had. And she would be there for him forever!

"Tomorrow I must be initiated into true chieftainship, for up till now, I was only acting chief," Thunder Heart said, interrupting Dede's thoughts. "Nothing about this is fair, for my father should still be alive and still be chief!"

He rose to his feet and stared into the flames of the fire. "Whites have taken so much from me," he said, his voice breaking. He looked slowly down at Dede, then reached out a hand to her. "You are white and I should hate you, yet it is certain that you have my heart, my woman."

Dede flung herself into his arms. "You have had mine since the very moment we met," she said, clinging to him. "I'm here for you now, and I shall always be."

"And nothing or no one will separate us again," Thunder Heart said, holding her tenderly in his arms.

"No, nothing or no one," Dede whispered, pushing away all thoughts of Bill, the white government, and anyone else who might try to stand in Thunder Heart's way.

At this moment she was doing what she could to help the man she loved. She felt so blessed to have the opportunity to be with him. Last night, when it seemed as if her whole world had been torn apart, she didn't see how being with him would be possible ever again. But here she was, with his arms so wonderful around her.

CHAPTER TWENTY-ONE

The ill-timed truth we might have kept—
Who knows how sharp it pierced and stung?

—Edward R. Sill
(1841–1887)

Totally confused, so frustrated that he didn't know which way to turn, Bill rode away from St. Louis. He had not been able to find Aunt Mae so he could check on Dede and Johnny. When he had arrived at the boarding house where Aunt Mae used to reside, he discovered that relatives had moved her and had not left a forwarding address.

It was totally out of character for Dede not to have mentioned in her note that her aunt no longer had the same address.

Perhaps that had been innocent enough, he tried to persuade himself. Maybe Dede wouldn't have expected Bill to go looking for her. She would have assumed that he would stay home and await her return.

But she must have known, he thought gloomily

as he rode beneath a row of tall elms on the narrow dirt road, that leaving as she had—in the middle of the night, without first telling him—would have disturbed him enough that he would want to check on her. No lady should be traveling without a gentleman escort these days, especially not one with a small child.

"No," he whispered to himself. The breeze was warm on his face as he sank his heels into the flanks of his horse, hurrying him along. "Something just doesn't seem right here."

He yanked on the reins and stopped suddenly, then wheeled his horse around and sent it back at a hard gallop toward St. Louis.

With his jaw set and his heart pounding, Bill made a decision. He was going to check all over town. Damn it, he was going to find Dede. He was going to make sure that she and Johnny got home safely. And when they did, he was going to give Dede a lecture that she would never forget.

Taking the rifle with her for protection was a smart thing to do, but she should have known that it wouldn't be enough should a bunch of outlaws happen along and find her and the child, so vulnerable and alone.

Bill would never forget how his wife had gone out for a ride alone and had never returned to his arms again. It was as though she had been swept clean off the earth. And Dede knew how that had happened. She knew the dangers of traveling alone!

Bill rode harder until he came to the outskirts of

St. Louis again. He went down Chippewa Avenue and recognized an inn that was run by friends. They would know the city well. They would know how to find Aunt Mae. And when he found her, surely he would also find his Dede! Although he and Dede weren't man and wife, he felt no less protective of her. She was so sweet, so caring. She was like a daughter to him.

At Junction Inn, where his friends George and Sara McKee greeted travelers with open arms, wonderful food, and comfortable beds, Bill wheeled his horse to a stop and dismounted.

As he flipped the horse's reins around a hitching rail, his gaze moved to the quaint two-story brick inn. Comfortable-looking wicker rockers sat along the spacious front porch, and windows revealed lacy curtains behind sparkling panes of glass.

When a familiar face looked out one of the windows, Bill smiled and gave Sara McKee a nod.

George, all two hundred pounds of him, came rushing out of the door, his arms extended. He wore a black fustian suit, his thick gray hair outlining a cheerful face with laughing eyes.

"Bill!" he cried as he wobbled down the front steps. "I'll be damned, if it isn't Bill Martin."

Bill stepped forward to meet him and was almost swallowed whole in a hefty hug.

"It's good to see you, too, George," Bill said, laughing.

Then petite Sara came out, wearing a pale blue velveteen dress. She had sparkling green eyes and her face was framed by bright red hair. She yanked George away from Bill, then embraced him herself. "Why on earth didn't you bring your wife and child?" she asked, her voice as soft and demure as she.

Bill stepped away from her. "That's why I'm here," he said, his smile fading as he looked almost clumsily from George to Sara. "Seems I've misplaced them."

"What?" Sara gasped. She placed a hand to her throat. "What do you mean?"

"Come inside and have a cup of coffee as you tell us," George said. He took Bill by an elbow and ushered him inside, where smells of spices and lemon pudding filled the air, and where overstuffed chairs in the spacious parlor tempted one to sit down.

Everywhere Bill looked he saw Sara's handiwork. Crocheted pieces, dainty little things sitting on tables, and bouquets of summer flowers were all around.

"Sit," George said, motioning toward a chair close to an open window, where lacy curtains fluttered in the gentle breeze.

Bill nodded and sat down. George sat on one side of him, Sara on the other, and a maid brought out a tray of sweets and piping hot, wonderful-smelling coffee in a silver pot.

"Now tell us everything," Sara said, lifting the pot and pouring three cups of coffee. She sat back and sipped her coffee as Bill told them how he had found the note and then how he had discovered that Aunt Mae had been taken somewhere else.

"We know of three new places that might take in elderly boarders," Sara said, setting her cup aside. "One is up past the city proper. Two more are out by Ulysses S. Grant's huge farm. We can take you to each one, if you want."

"Please. I would appreciate it so much," Bill replied. He took two sips of coffee, then set the cup down beside Sara's on the table. "And I need to do it now if you can spare the time. If I don't find Dede at those places, I must hurry back to our ranch and see if she has returned. I hope I'm worrying over nothing."

"Anyone would worry about a missing wife and child," Sara said, rising to grab a cloak from a peg on the wall.

After slapping a gun and holster around his thick waist, George ushered Bill and Sara out of the inn. "I'm sure you'll find out that everything is all right," he said encouragingly.

They boarded a horse and carriage and rode in a tense silence. When Bill discovered that no one had heard of a Mae Hoots at the first place, and when he got the same answer at the second, he became concerned that something was truly wrong.

And when they arrived at the third place, which was more like a hospital than a boarding house, and he finally found Aunt Mae, his hopes were shattered the moment he saw her. She sat in a rocking chair in a gloomy room filled with many elderly women just like her. She slowly rocked back and forth, a blanket wrapped around her from her shoulders down past her feet, with only her ashen face and gray hair visible. Her eyes told him that she no longer could recognize anyone, not even her loved ones.

"She doesn't know me," Bill said, kneeling down and gazing into Aunt Mae's blank gray eyes. He swallowed hard. "Aunt Mae? Please hear me. Tell me about Dede. Was she here? When did she leave?"

"Bill, I doubt she even knew that Dede was here," George said, laying a heavy hand on Bill's shoulder.

Bill gave George a desperate look. "Then how would she have known to send Dede a telegram?" he asked, rising slowly to his feet. "Some of Dede's other relatives must have contacted her," he reasoned, kneading his brow in frustration. "I don't know any of them. Dede has never been that close to them, not enough to introduce me."

He paced back and forth for a moment, then stamped over to the desk where a nurse sat reading a book and drinking a cup of coffee.

"Miss, I need some information," Bill said, growing impatient as she continued to read and ignore him. "I need to know if a Dorothy Martin and her son, Johnny, were here to see Mae Hoots."

The nurse looked up at him and frowned. "No one by that name has been here," she spat out. "Now can't you see I'm tryin' to read?"

"Miss, who would be the one to send a telegram from this place?" Bill asked, not to be dissuaded.

"Sir, I ain't no fortune teller," she answered, her sour, pinched expression causing Bill's temper to flare.

"Who in hell is in charge of this damn place?" he asked heatedly. "Surely it's someone besides you—you don't seem to know anything."

"You don't need to use curse words or insult me," the nurse said, slamming her book closed. She rose quickly to her feet, her long white dress whisking around her ankles as she walked in a huff toward the door. "Come with me. I'll take you to Donald Bloomington, the owner. He'll tell you what you need to know."

"Thank you," Bill said, relieved to finally have her cooperation. He smiled over his shoulder at Sara and George, who walked behind him, but tensed up when he was led into a small office. A lean, bald man sat behind a desk, working on a journal.

Bill stepped up to the desk. "Sir, I need to know if you are in charge of sending telegrams for your patients here," he asked, nervously clasping his hands behind him.

The man looked up. He smiled. "Yes, I'm the one who sends out all correspondence," he answered. "Who do you need to know about?"

"Mae Hoots is one of your patients," Bill said. "Did she, by chance, send a wire a day or so ago to a Dorothy Martin, who lives just outside of St.

Genevieve?" He quickly added, "Or she might have addressed the wire to Dede . . . Dede Martin."

"Sir, Mae Hoots isn't capable of telling me her name, much less remembering anyone else's," Bloomington said. He sighed heavily.

"Then who wired Dede?" Bill asked, his voice puzzled. "Who in the hell sent her a wire?"

"All that I can say is that I didn't, nor did anyone on my staff. I can tell by your expression that it wasn't what you wanted to hear."

"Something like that," Bill said, nervously raking his fingers through his hair. "Thank you, anyhow."

"Anytime," Bloomington said, then resumed placing figures in his journal.

Bill returned to George and Sara. "I don't know what's going on here, but I know one thing. I've got to get home and see if Dede is there," he said, his voice breaking. "If anything has happened to Johnny and Dede, I've only myself to blame."

"Why is that, Bill?" Sara asked, her eyes innocently wide.

"When I was gallivanting around gambling and drinking something could have happened to my Dede and Johnny," he said, tears sparkling in the corners of his eyes. He went outside and boarded the carriage with his friends, confused over what to think. Dede must have written a false note, he decided, but why would she have done that?

Unless she was forced to . . . he thought to himself, a cold fear settling in at the pit of his stomach.

"The Ponca Indians . . ." he blurted out, drawing

George and Sara's attention. The carriage wheels rumbled over St. Louis's cobblestone streets.

"What did you say about Indians?" George asked, raising an eyebrow.

"It'd better not be," was all that Bill replied, his eyes filled with searing hate.

CHAPTER TWENTY-TWO

The Soul that rises
With us, our life's Star,
And cometh from afar.

—William Wordsworth
(1770–1850)

There was a solemn quiet at the Ponca village. Dede sat with Johnny before the lodge fire in Thunder Heart's tepee, awaiting his return. He would come to her as the true chief of his Ponca clan. Even now he was at the council house participating in the brief rites that would make him officially the chief.

"I wish we could be there," Johnny said, drawing Dede out of her deep thoughts.

She watched Johnny as he stroked Four Eyes' silver-gray fur. Even the coyote had been barred from the proceedings, which included only Thunder Heart, a few of his most favored warriors, and all of the elders of the Grizzly Bear Clan.

"Women and children aren't allowed at such an important meeting," she explained. "Just be happy for Thunder Heart, Johnny, that he will now be the true leader of such a proud people as the Ponca . . . their beloved chief."

"I am, but it's so sad that his father had to die, and all because of the disease brought into the village by a white man," Johnny said. He turned and faced her. "Mama, I've been thinking about something. I want to go with you to the Black Hills. I've heard so much about Wind Cave. I want to see it. Surely it's a place of great mystery."

"Just as the meeting today at the council house is no place for a child, neither is the journey to the Ponca burial grounds," Dede said.

She reached out and ran her fingers through his hair, which now was growing past his shoulders. He could surely pass for an Indian with such long hair, his deep tan, and dark eyes, especially now that he would be living among them.

"You'll be gone for a long time," Johnny said, sighing. "I'll miss you."

"As I'll miss you." She did not want to admit how uneasy she was about leaving Johnny in the care of a stranger. "But Silken Wing has promised to take care of you. You have wanted to learn the customs of her people. This is a good time to take advantage of the lessons that she and others will gladly teach you."

"I like her already, Mama," Johnny said, turning to face the fire again and lifting Four Eyes onto his lap. He hugged the coyote, then smiled at Dede. "And I've made a friend. His name is Young Blood. He said that he'll teach me how to use a bow and arrow." He smiled mischievously. "His bow and quiver of arrows were well hidden when Bill took the Ponca's weapons."

Dede's eyes wavered. "Son, be careful with weapons. Promise me?"

"I won't use them until I have learned how to," Johnny reassured her. Then he frowned. "Mama, what about Bill? When are we going to let him know that we're all right?"

His question disturbed Dede deep down in her heart, for she knew that it was wrong to keep Bill wondering and worrying about them. He had been good to them both. And she had never lied to him about anything, until recently. The biggest lie of all was that she and Johnny were in St. Louis visiting Aunt Mae. The truth was that Dede had not seen or heard from her Aunt Mae for some time now.

"Mama, you didn't answer me," Johnny said, reaching over, quietly shaking Dede's arm. "What about Bill?"

"Yes, what about Bill," Dede said, swallowing hard. In her mind's eye she recalled the stolen Ponca horses in Bill's corral. She was also remembering what she had heard outside the door of Bill's study. She would never forget him going into the Ponca village and stealing from them.

So did Bill truly deserve their consideration? Had he considered the wrong that he was doing to an innocent people when he had stolen their horses and weapons?

"What am I to do if Bill comes to the village looking for us while you are gone?" Johnny asked.

Dede sighed heavily. "I hate putting you in the middle, making you a part of this," she answered. "But, Johnny, what Bill did to the Ponca is so wrong. I'm trying hard to understand why he did it . . . because of his wife. I just wish he could let go of the past and live life as it is now."

"But he can't," Johnny said. "And what he has done to the Ponca can't be undone. I bet if he knew we were here, he would stop at nothing to get us."

"Yes, I know, and when that time comes, we will deal with it," Dede assured him. "But now? I must concentrate on the upcoming journey with Thunder Heart. Are you certain you feel all right about staying behind at the Ponca village?"

"Even though I would rather go with you, I'm fine about staying behind," Johnny said softly. "And I think it's wonderful that you are going to marry Thunder Heart. He'll be my father. Imagine having an Indian chief for a father!"

"Yes, that will be wonderful," Dede said, sighing with relief because he seemed so happy about this new twist in his life. "I truly love Thunder Heart. All I ever felt for Bill was the way one feels about a father, or perhaps a big brother."

She lowered her eyes, then looked at Johnny again. "That's why I hate having had to lie to Bill," she said solemnly. "It isn't the nicest way to repay someone who took you in and gave you a home."

"What he did to the Ponca wasn't nice, either," Johnny reminded her.

She reached for his hands again. "Son, while I am gone, don't wander far from the Ponca village," she urged. "You know that Bill might go to St. Louis and discover that we aren't there. When he gets back, he'll surely search for us. We can't allow him to find you among the Ponca, especially with me so far away. I wouldn't want him to take you home with him, not under these circumstances. Do you understand, Johnny? Do you see why you mustn't allow Bill to know where you are?"

"Yes, and I'll be careful," Johnny said. He lifted the coyote from his lap, then moved into Dede's arms. He wrapped his arms around her neck and hugged her. "I just wish it was over . . . the long trip . . . the time we must spend apart."

"Yes, I wish things were different, too," Dede said, returning his hug.

"Tell me what Thunder Heart told you about how he is becoming a chief," Johnny said, crossing his legs beneath him.

Dede was deeply touched by her son, who seemed twice his age in the way he accepted things so easily and the way he had taken to the Indians so quickly. She was glad that he was more intelligent than the white children who mocked Indians and called them savages. His heart was filled with caring, not with prejudice.

"As Thunder Heart told me earlier today, chiefs are installed in a solemn ceremony," Dede explained. "He told me that when his people were one large group, when they had not been forced to separate and go in two different directions, there was a head chief of the whole tribe who presided over the initiation rites. But there is no head chief anymore. There is only one chief per clan. And Thunder Heart is the one who will now lead his clan."

"I only saw a few warriors enter the council house for the ceremony," Johnny said, drawing his knees up before him and hugging them. "Then I saw many elderly men go in."

"Yes, only a few warriors and elders are required to be present for the ceremony to be completed," Dede said, smiling as her glance took in the way her son was dressed. He looked so handsome in his fringed buckskin outfit and his beaded moccasins.

She knew by the way he strutted around in the buckskins that he was proud to wear them. She was glad, because she doubted that he would wear denim clothes again. While living among Indians, one dressed as they did, as she now even dressed.

"After they enter the council house they are to walk around in a clockwise direction and then take their seats," she continued, Johnny still listening attentively to what she was saying. "Then a sacred pipe is to be passed around, starting at the door. Each man is supposed to take three puffs and then pass the pipe to the man on his left. Prayers are to be interspersed with the smoking of the pipe."

She paused and looked at the closed entrance flap, envisioning Thunder Heart so noble and handsome as he took part in the ceremony. She knew that he would be torn . . . sad over the loss of his father, yet proud to serve his people in the capacity of chief.

She wished she could be there, seeing it all, but she was glad enough to be in his village at all, to be the woman who would soon become his wife.

"Mama, you're daydreaming again," Johnny said, interrupting her thoughts.

"Yes, I guess I was," she said, laughing awkwardly.

"Tell me more, Mama," Johnny urged her eagerly.

"Yes, more," she agreed. "When the pipe gets clear around to the door it will be passed back the way it came, but it will never be passed over the doorway."

She smiled and gently touched Johnny's cheek. "No man is a chief until he has smoked the sacred pipe," she said. "Once that is done tonight, and after a few words are said by each attending warrior, Thunder Heart will be proclaimed to be chief."

"Then he should be chief by now," Johnny said. He turned his head quickly to the entrance flap and smiled as Thunder Heart entered, his bare, bronze shoulders proudly squared.

Johnny leapt to his feet and ran to him, grabbing his hand. "You are now chief?" he asked, his eyes beaming. "For real? You are the true chief?"

"Yes, it is done," Thunder Heart said to Johnny, but he was looking at Dede, who gazed up at him in wonder.

He knelt before Johnny. "My Aunt Silken Wing has prepared a place for you in her lodge for sleeping," he said. "Young brave, it is best that you go there now. It is late. All children your age are asleep."

Johnny looked over his shoulder at Dede. "Must I?" he asked, with a rare whine in his voice.

Dede knelt beside Thunder Heart and took Johnny's hands in hers. "Yes, you must," she told him. "You and I have had our special time together tonight. And it must stay in our hearts until I return. We plan to leave tomorrow morning while you're still asleep, before the sun rises. That will give us more time for our first day of travel."

Johnny swept his arms around Dede's neck. "I shall miss you so," he said, a sob catching in his throat. "If anything should happen to . . ."

"Nothing will happen to your *inaha,* your mother," Thunder Heart said, interrupting him. "I vow to keep her safe from all harm."

Johnny leaned away from Dede and looked at Thunder Heart with a deep seriousness. "Sometimes white men might make you break your vows," he said, again speaking with the intelligence of a person twice his age. "I've seen it, Thunder Heart. You've seen it. It can happen and no one can stop it."

"I vow to you, still, that no harm will come to your *inaha,*" Thunder Heart said, his voice more stern, more determined.

"Run on now, Johnny," Dede said, tousling his

hair. "But, first, give me that one long, last hug . . . one that will sustain me until we are together again."

When he flung his arms around her neck even more tightly than before, she could feel his desperation and his fear. At that moment she almost decided not to go. But she knew how important it was to Thunder Heart that she accompany him. She couldn't let him down. Too many people had already done that.

"I love you, Mama," Johnny said, then tore himself away from her and gazed up at Thunder Heart. Suddenly he flung himself into the chief's arms. "As I also love you, Thunder Heart. I look forward to having you as my father."

With that he ran out of the lodge, leaving Dede and Thunder Heart to stare in silence at one another.

"Yes," Dede said, breaking the silence. "Yes, he loves you. He already looks to you as a father."

Thunder Heart reached out for her. His lips came to hers, quivering and sweet, but she was aware of something else. A saltiness on his lips.

Which meant that he had been crying.

Quietly, softly, she drew away from him. A sob caught in her throat when she saw his sorrowful eyes.

"Oh, darling, I'm so sorry about everything," she cried. She moved into his arms again and clung to him. "It has to be so hard . . . knowing what lies ahead of you. The long journey with your father."

He eased away from her and went to sit on blankets before the fire. He gazed into the flames and said somberly, "I am now the true chief of my people. Chiefs are expected to be circumspect in their behavior and to hold themselves above the passions of ordinary people."

He turned slowly to look at Dede as she sat down beside him, her gaze never leaving him. "Tonight my passions run rampant throughout me," he said tightly. "The passion of loss, and the passion of pride at being my people's leader."

He turned to her and held his arms out. "My biggest passion is for you, my woman," he said. "Come to me. Let me hold you next to my heart. Never have I needed anyone as badly as I need you tonight."

She moved into his arms and held him. For just a moment he forgot that he was a powerful leader who was not supposed to show emotion. His whole body shook with sobs as he allowed himself to feel everything that had been overwhelming him.

"Let it all out," Dede whispered to him, stroking the long column of his muscled back. She was so touched that he, a great chief, could allow himself to show his vulnerability to her, a woman. But, she reminded herself, she wasn't just any woman. She was going to be his wife!

"To have lost my *indadi* in such a way, for his body to have to make the long journey to get to his proper burial place, is the hardest of all my recent hurts," Thunder Heart said hoarsely.

Then he leaned away from Dede and framed her

face between his hands. "But you, my woman, take so much of the hurt away," he said, swallowing hard. "Thank you for giving of yourself to this man who most whites see as savage."

"I love you so much," Dede said, hating his use of the word "savage," yet knowing that nothing she could say or do could erase the ugly word from his mind. "I will always be here for you. Always."

"Tonight, in our bed of blankets, I wish to just lie quietly with you," he said, his voice breaking. "Lovemaking comes after my heart aches less than it does tonight. Is that something you can agree to?"

"Darling Thunder Heart, I want what you want, when you want it," Dede said. She gently took his hand and led him down to the blankets. "Come and lie beside me. We shall say no more. We will just hold one another."

Thunder Heart stretched out beside Dede and held her tightly. "Thank you, my woman, for being you," he said. He stared into the flames of the fire and, in his mind's eye, relived special moments with his father. He needed to do this before he could lock them away in the book of memories that was stored in the depths of his heart.

Dede could sense that he was reliving his past. It was in his eyes. It was in the way he sometimes flinched, then would relax and smile.

She snuggled closer and rode the waves of memories with him, but she was reliving her own past, including those she had said her own good-byes to these past several years. It was good to have someone to cling to while remembering.

But she hoped that once the journey to the Black Hills was over and they were man and wife, they would no longer have any reason to look back in time, to relive the past.

She wanted to begin making fresh memories, of just him and Johnny, inside her heart!

CHAPTER TWENTY-THREE

Tell them, dear, that if eyes were made for seeing,
Then Beauty is its own excuse for being.

—Ralph Waldo Emerson
(1803–1882)

It had been a long day of travel through Missouri for Thunder Heart and his entourage. The journey was a slow one, for the travois transporting the body impeded their progress.

Four Eyes traveled with them, crude moccasins on his paws to make the journey easier for him when he walked. Other times he was carried in a sling at the side of Thunder Heart's horse.

Tonight the moon was a sliver of gray in the sky. The stars were like millions of teardrops glistening against the night sky. A fire burned softly, the late-evening meal of baked rabbit only a memory now. Dede and Thunder Heart sat away from the others on a slight rise of land that overlooked the campsite. Four Eyes slept beside them.

The rustling of cottonwood leaves overhead reminded Dede of times long past when she had sat on her mother's lap on the front porch of her parents' Missouri home. She had nestled close to her mother one night as she rocked slowly back and forth in a wicker chair. Her mother had called the evening Indian summer, she remembered. The leaves had been brilliantly colored, and the day's temperature had soared into the high eighties. Too hot to sleep, and awaiting the return of her physician husband, who had been called from the supper table to deliver a baby, Dede's mother had taken her outside and held her on her lap while she sang lullabies.

Tonight, the songs of those who sat vigil over the wrapped body of Seven Drums wafted softly through the air. Unlike the wailing and singing Dede had heard from her kitchen window, tonight there seemed to be a sort of quiet peace in the voices. Although their beloved chief was dead, the Ponca were finally winning the battle with the stomach ailment.

"You are thinking deeply about something," Thunder Heart said, reaching over to draw Dede closer to his side.

She straightened the blanket beneath her, the warm air like a caress on her face. She smiled at him. "The pleasantness of the temperature tonight took me away to a time long ago," she said. "I was on my mother's lap on the front porch of our home. She was singing to me."

She inhaled deeply and closed her eyes. "It's as

though she were here now, her breath sweet and warm on my face as she brushed soft kisses across my brow," she said, sighing.

"My *inaha*, my mother, sang to me often, too," Thunder Heart said, envisioning himself as a little boy. He had idolized his mother. She had been a vision of loveliness. And her voice had been so soft and comforting, like a sweet caress.

Tonight, as his mother's husband lay amidst his blankets awaiting burial, surely she was there in spirit with him.

Thunder Heart wished that he could join them, at least for a moment, to experience their love and devotion again.

"It's wonderful to have good memories," Dede said, seeing by the look in Thunder Heart's eyes that he, too, had been transported back in time for a moment. She could even see him as a child on his mother's lap, his dark eyes looking adoringly at his mother.

When she and Thunder Heart had a son, oh, how she hoped that he would be the exact image of his father. She would adore holding their son on her lap, his eyes smiling at her, his tiny hands touching her cheeks.

Thunder Heart's laughter brought Dede out of her thoughts, feeling awkward for having been caught twice in one night daydreaming.

"And what was on your mind this time, my woman?" he asked, his eyes twinkling.

She smiled almost bashfully at him. "The son that

we will have one day," she said softly. "I want him to look just like you."

"And we will have a daughter, also, who will be a picture of you," Thunder Heart said huskily.

He turned to Dede and placed his hands on her cheeks and drew her lips toward his. "I want you, my woman," he said. "I need you. I need you now."

His lips trembled as he kissed her.

Dede reeled with passion as he slid his hands downward and cupped her breasts through the buckskin fabric of her dress.

It had seemed forever since they had made love. But now it seemed as though it was only moments ago when he had transported her to a place of joyous bliss.

She was glad that he felt free now to make love. She had not expected him to until after his father's burial. If so, the wait would have seemed endless.

And they might not even make it to the Black Hills. She hadn't mentioned this concern to Thunder Heart, that she didn't think that he and his people would be allowed to travel on to Wind Cave country. All day long she was aware of people coming from their country homes to stand on their porches and stare at the slow procession of Indians and the *abawai*, the travois. It was made of two tepee poles tied together so that they crossed at the horse's withers, and on it was a blanket-wrapped body.

Dede was concerned for more than one reason. She knew that Thunder Heart and his warriors were breaking the law by leaving the land assigned to them by the United States government.

They were going against the government by returning to their homeland!

And now Bill and the other ranchers who had taken the Ponca's horses would learn that the Indians had stolen them back. Then there was the fact that everyone had seen her, a white woman, with the procession of Ponca Indians. She was afraid that word would spread and that Bill would soon know the truth of where she was. She just couldn't help but worry about Johnny too. If Bill discovered she was with Thunder Heart but that Johnny wasn't, he would definitely conclude that Johnny was with the Ponca at their village.

Dede couldn't shake off her fear that Bill would take Johnny away from the Ponca. Out of humiliation at her having joined the Ponca against him, who could say what he might do with Johnny.

She had decided that she had to turn around and return to the Ponca village and make sure Johnny was safe. She just hadn't told Thunder Heart. She had planned to tell him tonight while they sat alone away from the others, but she didn't know how to break the news to him.

She only hoped that he understood and did not think her return home meant she was abandoning him and their love for one another.

Before the night was over she would know his reaction, for she had to tell him. She had to leave at daybreak tomorrow and hurry back to Johnny.

As slow as the journey had been, they had not covered that much distance so far. Riding alone, with nothing impeding her travel, she could make it back to the Ponca village in less than half the time it had taken to travel this far.

She had another reason for wanting to turn back before Thunder Heart's people themselves were stopped and made to return. She was afraid they might be arrested. If so, after they were returned to St. Genevieve, she could be there to argue their case. She had learned many things about the law while helping her husband study for his exams and observing his court cases. If the Ponca were taken to court for having defied the United States government, she would fight to the end for them!

She only wished that she had thought ahead and realized that there would be many people along the trail to witness the Ponca defying the white man's law.

She would have stayed behind and prepared for a fight, ensuring that Thunder Heart's journey to his homeland wouldn't be sidetracked for long. She didn't want him to feel the humiliation of being stopped, perhaps even arrested.

But she doubted that even if she had thought ahead to these possibilities, Thunder Heart would have heeded her warning. He was determined to return his father to his proper burial place. It was something that he felt deeply must be done.

She hoped that it wasn't too late for her to help.

"Your heart is not in the kiss," Thunder Heart whispered against Dede's lips.

"I'm sorry," she whispered back, feeling guilty for allowing him to realize that her mind was elsewhere when he needed her so badly tonight. She swallowed hard. "Truly I'm sorry."

"I shall try again," Thunder Heart said huskily, then brought his mouth to hers again in an all-consuming kiss. He swept his arms around her. His body pressed against hers as he gently helped her down to the blankets.

He had purposely led her this far from the campsite so that they could make love. In the shadows of the cottonwoods, only the stars and the moon would witness their sweet, precious lovemaking.

And he needed Dede tonight more than ever before. In her he would find some semblance of peace.

Today, as he had traveled with his father's body wrapped in blankets behind him, it had been hard to think past his sorrow.

Tonight, while alone with Dede, he felt as though a weight had been lifted from his shoulders.

Still kissing her, he reached down and slid a hand up the inside of her dress. Slowly he felt his way up the silken length of her leg. He felt her quick intake of breath against his lips as he slid his hand inside her undergarments and found her moist and ready for him.

He heard her gasps as he stroked her bud of pleasure with flicks of his fingers. And when he thrust a lone finger up inside her, he heard her moan and felt her body gyrate against his.

Desire raged through Dede as Thunder Heart stroked and thrust with his fingers. She was becoming delirious, her senses yearning for the promise of ecstasy that he was offering her.

Her hand trembled as she reached between them and felt him hard and ready, his manhood pressed tightly against his fringed breeches. As she stroked the full length of him, she could hear rumbles of pleasure surfacing from deep within him.

He moved away from her and stood up and began disrobing. Her eyes feasted on each portion of his copper body that shone back at her in the moonlight as he tossed his clothes aside, piece by piece. And when he was standing fully nude over her, and she saw his magnificence, she felt as though she were in a trance. She moved to her knees before him and cupped his manhood in her hand, and she swept her tongue out and touched him. He tasted sweet of river water.

As he wove his fingers through her long hair and brought her face even closer to his heat, she began to pleasure him in the way most men hungered for. She had learned it from her beloved husband, this particular way of giving her love. At first, she had thought it was wicked and strange.

But in time she had accepted it as a part of their lovemaking, especially when he had reciprocated by showing her how he could awaken such passion in her own body with his tongue and lips.

"My woman . . ." Thunder Heart whispered huskily, his head thrown back, his eyes closed as the pleasure built within him.

When he felt too close to the brink of total ecstasy, he urged her head away and brought her to her feet before him.

As she stood there, gazing with a heated passion into his eyes, he slowly undressed her.

When she was silkenly nude, he wrapped his arms around her and again led her, with his body, down to the blanket.

She was only half aware of making whimpering sounds as he worshipped her body with his mouth and tongue, leaving none of her secret places untouched.

Thrilling inside, she parted her legs as he knelt over her. She reached up and twined her arms around his neck as he entered her and began his steady, rhythmic strokes. She, in turn, thrust her pelvis toward him and moved her body sinuously against his. Her breath caught and held as he lowered his mouth over one of her breasts, his tongue flicking the nipple.

Her breath became ragged as he kissed her again, his mouth urgent and eager, his body moving powerfully against her, his thrusts growing more maddening. The pleasure was so intense and beautiful, she felt as though he was touching the very core of her universe.

Thunder Heart felt the heat spreading through him. He stiffened his legs, paused, and then thrust into her again, his heart pounding, his lips quivering against hers, the pleasure suddenly overtaking him. He clung to her and buried his mouth against the slender column of her throat as spasms gripped him in total ecstasy.

Feeling her own pleasure overtaking her, Dede clung to him and threw her head back, her moans awakening Four Eyes.

When he began howling, and another coyote answered in kind from a distant hill, Dede and Thunder Heart came out of their reverie. They rolled apart, laughing, thankful that they had reached the ultimate pleasure before being interrupted by Four Eyes.

"We awakened the animal in him," Dede said. She turned on her stomach and rested her chin in her hands as she watched Four Eyes lifting his eyes to the moon, yelping his own love song. And then he ran off in the direction of the other coyote.

Alarmed by him suddenly taking off like that, Dede sat up quickly and grabbed for her dress. "We'd better go after him," she said, then stopped when Thunder Heart took her dress and put it back down on the ground beside him.

"He will go make love and then return to us," he said. "Tonight is for lovers."

"Yes, and I do so love you," Dede said. He placed his hands on her waist and turned her over so that she was stretched out beside him on her back. "I do love you so very much."

Thunder Heart leaned up on an elbow and questioned her with his eyes. "I sense that you said that more out of apology than passion," he said, their eyes meeting and holding. "Why is that, my woman?"

"I didn't mean it to sound like that," Dede said. She looked suddenly away from him, for she knew that the moment of truth had arrived. She had to tell him her plan. It wasn't fair to keep it to herself any longer. She knew that he would need time to digest what she said before she actually left him at daybreak.

"But I do have something to tell you," she said, again gazing into his eyes, her own wavering.

"What is it that makes you suddenly so serious when you should be only thinking of our time alone together?" Thunder Heart asked, sitting up. He sensed that something was wrong. He saw it in Dede's eyes. He heard it in her voice. And in the way she sat up and grabbed her dress, as though she was determined not to make love with him again tonight.

Dede saw his reaction to her having picked up her dress again. She just as quickly laid it aside, for she didn't want tonight to end. She only hoped that he would want to make love again after what she said to him.

And not only tonight, but every night.

She blurted out how she felt about everyone along the trail having seen them today traveling away from their assigned land, and her with them.

She told him about her fear of what Bill might do

to Johnny—that if Bill, in his anger toward her, took Johnny far away, she might never see him again.

She also told him how concerned she was about the government possibly stopping their march north.

She explained that she would prepare herself for defending them, that she had a knowledge of the law because of her lawyer husband.

When she was through, Thunder Heart seemed stunned by all of the assumptions that she had come to.

"None of that will happen," he said tightly. "When the white men see that my mission is one of the heart, that I only wish to see my father buried among his ancestors, they will not interfere."

He then drew her over and held her close. "And your son will not be stolen away by the man who cared so much for him," he tried to reassure her.

"You don't know the extent of Bill's hatred for all men with red skins," Dede said. "That I have taken your side against him, might be the last straw for Bill. He might do anything to get back at me."

"You feel that strongly, do you?" Thunder Heart asked, leaning away from her and gently gripping her shoulders. "You truly believe that all of this will come to pass?"

Dede nodded. "Yes, all of it," she said, swallowing hard. "It is best that you prepare for the worst, as should I. I promise you, Thunder Heart, that I will do what I can to prevent anything bad from happening to you and your people. I do know the law and I plan to use that knowledge to protect you."

Thunder Heart dropped his hands, stood up, and gazed into the far distance. "Nothing comes easy for my people," he said wearily. He turned and gazed down at Dede. "Nor for you, since you are now a part of my people's lives."

He reached out a hand for Dede. She took it, stood up, and moved into his arms, their naked bodies fusing as though they were one.

"Then you do understand my need to leave in the morning?" she asked.

"Yes, and I shall send a warrior with you to protect you."

Dede looked quickly up at him. "No," she said. "You will need those who are here with you."

Thunder Heart placed a hand beneath Dede's chin and lifted it to look into her eyes. "I fear for your safety," he said thickly.

"I will be all right," she said, then flung herself into his arms again. "But while I am away from you, I shall fear for you."

"What will be will be," was all that he could say. At this moment he felt the dread of defeat all over again, as though it were reborn inside his heart like a knife, digging and twisting.

CHAPTER TWENTY-FOUR

Over our manhood bend the skies;
Against our fallen and traitor lives
The great winds utter prophecies.

—James Russell Lowell
(1819–1891)

The stillness of the house as he entered it made Bill's worst fears about Dede a reality. When he had taken his horse to the stable to its stall and given it a bucket of oats to feast on after its long, hard ride to and from St. Louis, Bill had noticed that Dede's horse and her personal buggy were not there. Fear had gripped his heart. Everything that he had been dreading during the trip home from St. Louis was confirmed.

She . . . was . . . still gone.

And now, as he searched frantically from room to room, hoping that she was there, somewhere, he finally realized that not only was she gone, but she had been since she had written the note.

"Why?" he whispered, raking his fingers through his hair. He left the parlor and headed back to his study. "Where? And . . . with whom?"

He didn't want to think the Ponca were responsible, for that would be the worst possible scenario. He had lost one wife because of some Indian's need for vengeance against white men. *Oh,* he prayed to himself, *don't let it have happened again.*

In flashes he recalled how proud he had felt when he rode into the Ponca village, finally having found a way to settle an old score with redskins, even though he knew this tribe was not responsible for his wife's death. Any redskin suffering because of him was enough to make him feel as though he had, in a small way, avenged what had been taken from him so long ago.

In his mind's eye, he recalled how he had enjoyed seeing the Ponca's eyes as they watched not only their horses, but also their weapons, being taken from them. To Bill it had been the same feeling of victory that he had felt when he had ridden into the Indian villages in the Black Hills with his cavalry friends. They had left death and devastation behind them as he searched in vain for his beloved Julia.

But if having done this to the Ponca had brought Dede and Johnny any pain, perhaps even caused their deaths, Bill would regret his decision for the rest of his life.

He hung his head, the fight seemingly wrung out of him. He went into his office. The morning sun was streaming through a window. When Bill saw where it rested—on the bow and the quiver of arrows that he had taken from Thunder Heart's lodge—it was like a message sent to him from above.

"The bow . . . the arrows," he said, stopping in his tracks as he stared at them. Both were still there, untouched, which made his conclusions about what might have happened to Dede and Johnny seem all wrong. If one of the Ponca had come into his home and had seen the bow and the arrows and concluded they had been stolen from a redskin's lodge, wouldn't the Indian, *any* Indian, have taken them? He knew that to an Indian they were precious weapons.

And as he examined the intricate designs carved into the bow, he realized the hours it must have taken to make it and the love that would have been put into the task. He just couldn't believe that an Indian could leave it behind if he had come into this home to take a woman and child hostage.

"No, it has to be something . . . someone . . . else," he said, sighing heavily. He sat down behind his desk, his shoulders slumped. He picked up the note again and read it. Dede's handwriting did not show signs that she was afraid when she wrote it. It was smoothly written, the same as everything else he had seen her write. Surely if she had been forced to write the note it would show!

"I just don't know," he said, gently putting the piece of paper back on the desk, still staring at it. "Where are you, Dede? Where have you taken Johnny, and why? Wasn't I good enough to you? What did I do to make that change?"

He winced as though someone had splashed cold water on his face when he recalled exactly what could have changed her mind about him. She never approved of his taking the horses and weapons from the Ponca, removing their means to hunt and protect themselves.

Yes, being the Christian woman that she was, Dede would abhor such an act against a weakened people, even those whose skin was red. She had studied her Bible and followed its teachings well, especially the Scriptures about the wrong of prejudice. She saw everyone as equal, no matter the color of their skin, or . . .

His thoughts were brought to a halt when he heard the thundering of many horses' hooves approaching his house. He rushed to the window.

Drawing back the sheer curtain, he saw Sheriff Hancock and what seemed to be a posse.

"Who are they going after?" he wondered, then hurried out of his study down the long corridor to his front door. Just as he stepped outside on the porch, Dan and the men came to a wheeling stop.

"What's going on?" Bill asked, leaning heavily on the porch rail.

"Haven't you heard?" Dan asked, pushing his Stetson back from his brow with a forefinger.

"Heard what?" Bill asked. "I've been gone. I went to St. Louis."

"What took you to St. Louis, Bill?" Dan asked, toying with his horse's reins.

"It's a long story," Bill replied with a sigh. He

looked past Dan at the men and saw that they were listening raptly to everything that was being said. Except for Dan, what Bill had to say about Dede and Johnny, for the moment, was to be a private affair.

"Dan, I'll tell you about it in a minute," he muttered as their eyes met and held. "I'd like for you to come into my office. I'd like to talk to you alone."

Bill once again looked at the men who were waiting on their horses. "What's the posse for, Dan?" he asked, before turning to go into the house.

"To go after some Injuns, that's what," Dan said, frowning.

"Which Indians?" Bill asked. "What are you talking about?"

"The damn Ponca, that's who," Dan said. He slid out of his saddle and sauntered up the front steps to the porch. "They're headed for the Black Hills, Bill. We're gonna stop them."

"Do you mean the Ponca have all packed up and left?" Bill asked, his eyes widening. "They are going against the United States government by returning to their homeland?"

"No, not all of them. Only a few," Dan replied, resting his hands on his holstered pistols.

"But why?" Bill asked. "Why would only a few go back? If they are going up against the government, I'd think they would stand together as a unit. Lord, they'll need as many warriors as they can get to fight off the law."

Bill took an unsteady step away from Dan. "Damn, Dan, how are they traveling?" he asked, his voice drawn. "They don't have any horses. They don't even have any weapons to defend themselves."

"They've got both," Dan growled out. "Seems they've been busy at night stealin' back what was taken from them. But they were clever sons of guns. They only took a few horses each night so no one would realize what they were up to."

"Damn!" Bill exclaimed. "You said they also have weapons. How in the hell did they manage that?"

"Who can say?" Dan answered with a shrug. "All's I know is they have horses and weapons and they are going against the law by traveling back to their homeland."

"I still don't understand why there are only a few going," Bill said, frowning. "Why not the whole bunch of them?"

"Because it only takes a few to take a dead man back to be buried with his ancestors," Dan replied.

"What's that you say?" Bill said, again raising an eyebrow.

"From what I have been able to understand about what's happening, the old chief died, and his son, who is now chief, and a few others are taking the old chief back to their ancestral burial grounds in the Black Hills," Dan said, folding his arms across his chest. "And that ain't all, Bill. There's a white woman traveling with the Injuns. Several people have seen her."

"A white woman?" A sinking feeling grabbed Bill

at the pit of his stomach. "Lord, no! Don't tell me it's so."

"Why would you care if a woman is with them, or not?" Dan asked, idly scratching his brow. Then he dropped his hands to his sides and leaned toward Bill. "Oh, I know. It's because of what happened to your wife. Injuns. They abducted her." He assumed a wide-eyed expression of surprise. "Do you think this woman with the Ponca is being forced to travel with them?"

"Did anyone describe the woman?" Bill asked warily.

"Yes. They say she's pretty, petite, and has long blond hair," Dan said. Then he gasped. "Damn it all to hell, Bill, I've just described Dede."

"Seems so," Bill said, shaking his head back and forth in disbelief.

Dan looked past Bill, toward the front door. "Where is Dede, Bill?" he asked. "It's not like her not to come out and greet visitors." He laughed. "Of course, I'm sure she ain't all that glad to see so many gents arriving at one time, especially what's obviously a posse."

Bill looked over at the men, weighed down with all sorts of weapons. "So you're going after the Indians, huh?"

"Sure as hell am," Dan said, snickering. "Can't let the government down, now, can I, by lettin' the savages get away with something like this?" He frowned. "You never said where Dede is," he said.

"Surely she'd at least stick her head out of the door with a brief 'howdy.' "

"She isn't here," Bill said, his voice breaking. "She's gone, Dan."

Bill put a hand on Dan's shoulder. "Was there any mention of a white boy with that white woman?" he asked tightly.

Dan paled. "Lord, Bill, do you know what you're implying?" he asked.

"Yes, that the white woman with the Indians is Dede," Bill answered, his voice catching. He motioned toward the door. "Come inside. I want to show you something."

They went to the study and Bill showed Dan the note. They exchanged worried stares.

"Do you think the Ponca are stupid enough to pull a stunt like abducting Dede and Johnny and taking them to the Black Hills?" Dan asked.

"I don't know what to think," Bill said, sighing as he went to the window and stared out of it. "And then there's Johnny. If that woman riding with the Indians is Dede, where on earth is Johnny?"

"Let's go to the Ponca village and question the Indians," Dan said, stepping up next to Bill. "We should do that first, and then go after the sons of bitches. If Dede is being forced to go with them, who's to say what their plans for her are?"

Bill took another deep breath as he looked at the bow and arrow. "Damn it all to hell, if an Indian came for Dede, why didn't he take the bow and the quiver of arrows with him?"

"The only way to get answers is to go to the Ponca village," Dan said, turning toward the door. He waved a hand toward Bill. "Get your rifle. Let's go."

Bill grasped Dan's arm. "No, we can't do that," he said, his voice tight.

"Don't you want to know if Johnny is there and if Dede is with the others?" Dan asked, raising an eyebrow.

"Damn it, you know I do," Bill said, dropping his hand. "But we can't just ride into the village demanding answers, not if we don't want one of the warriors to sneak away and warn the others that we are on our way to get them. We don't want to tip our hand about what we're doing. If Johnny is being held at the Ponca village, nothing will happen to him. The women wouldn't let harm come to a child even if he's white. It's Dede I'm concerned about, first and foremost. We've got to save her. Then we'll find Johnny."

"I'm sure you're right," Dan agreed.

Bill looked at the fancily carved bow, then shook his head. He opened his gun cabinet. For a moment he stared at the empty space where his prize rifle had been hanging. Dede had written in her note that she had taken it for protection. Now he believed that wasn't so. He believed that whoever came and took Dede away also took his rifle!

"Whoever is responsible for all of this, I'd like to be the one who puts the noose around his neck," he spat out. "I'd even like to be the one who slaps the horse's rump so the savage is left hanging and choking to death."

"Yeah, I second that motion," Dan said, chuckling.

They left the house together.

Bill ran to the stable and saddled his horse again, then rode away with the rest of the posse, a cloud of dust bursting from beneath their horses' hooves.

"I've been waiting what seems a lifetime to hang me an Indian for what happened to my darling Julia," he whispered to himself.

Smiling, he envisioned a Ponca warrior hanging lifelessly from a rope, a breeze swinging his body slowly back and forth as Dede watched, as proud as Bill that the savage was dead. The savage would pay for having taken Dede and Johnny. And he would pay for what one of his kind had done to Julia. Finally Bill's vengeance would be achieved. Then he could truly begin to live again. The bitterness inside his heart would be wiped away at the very moment the savage took his last breath.

"It shouldn't take us long to catch up with the Indians who are taking the old man to his burial place," Dan said, interrupting Bill's thoughts. "The stupid savages are carrying the dead body on a travois. Because of that, they can cover only a small parcel of land each day."

"Even if we do catch up with the Indians, are you within your rights to arrest them and take them back to St. Genevieve to your jail?" Bill asked. He reached down and rubbed his horse's mane as a silent apology for making him travel again so soon.

"I've taken care of everything legally," the sheriff said, smiling smugly. "I sent a telegram to the Secretary of the Interior about the savages leaving their government-assigned land and heading toward the Black Hills with a dead body."

"And?" Bill asked, listening raptly.

"And the Secretary of the Interior wired me back, ordering me to go and arrest the runaways and take them to St. Genevieve," Dan said. "I'm to place them in jail. Representatives from Washington will come and take care of the rest."

"The hanging, don't you mean?" Bill asked, anxious to hear Dan agree with him.

"That's for the higher-ups to decide," Dan shrugged.

"Well, I've had some luck a time or two persuading who you call 'higher-ups,'" Bill said, laughing. "Yeah, St. Genevieve will have itself a hanging or two for its citizens to watch."

Dan nodded. "Can't happen soon enough for me," he laughed. "Nope. Can't happen soon enough for me. I've never wanted redskins so close to my town. This is one surefire way of taking care of at least a few of them."

"What's to become of the old chief's body?" Bill asked warily.

"Cain't you just see the shock in the savages' eyes to know that one of their kind will be buried like natural people?" Dan said, his eyes twinkling.

"Surely you won't put him in our town's cemetery!" Bill gasped.

"Why not?" Dan asked. Then he laughed. "Oh, I see. You're afraid of a spirit or two of that old man's ancestors comin' to spook you."

"Hell, no," Bill said nervously. He swallowed hard. "Sure as hell, no."

But deep inside, Bill was somewhat afraid of the Indians' hocus-pocus, that they might have ways to come back and haunt those who wronged them. He squirmed uneasily in his saddle, then pushed such thoughts out of his mind. Nothing would stand in the way of what he had to do today. Especially not worrying about ghosts and goblins!

CHAPTER TWENTY-FIVE

I wandered lonely as a cloud
That floats on high o'er vales and hills.

—William Wordsworth
(1770–1850)

Dede rode long and hard, stopping only for herself and her horse to drink great gulps of water from the rivers and streams. Finally she was back at the Ponca village, Johnny beside her.

"Johnny, I was so afraid that Bill might figure out where we were and come and take you away," she murmured. Having her son safely in her arms was like pure heaven within her very soul.

"I'm all right, Mama," Johnny said. Then he slipped away from her and gazed up at her with a frown. "And I'm so glad that you came back because . . . because . . ."

When Dede saw how he was struggling with what he had to tell her, apparently something that really bothered him, she felt tight inside. She knew that Johnny wasn't the sort to worry about things.

He was always carefree and laughing. He saw only the good, which sometimes worried her. But he knew, from having experienced heartache, that not everything in life was pleasant and good. So for him to worry about something made her almost afraid to hear what it was.

"What is it, Johnny?" Dede asked, aware that the Ponca had come out of their lodges and were now circled behind him, their eyes questioning.

And she understood. The last time they had seen her she had left with the funeral procession for their homeland. They had to believe that something was wrong, or she wouldn't have returned, especially alone.

But she placed their concern second to what Johnny still struggled to tell her. She gazed down at him intently, waiting.

"Mama, I wanted my pony, Charlie," Johnny began, seeing the alarm enter Dede's eyes. She must already know what he was going to say about the horse, and maybe even what else he had to tell her. It didn't make sense that she would leave Thunder Heart and come all the way back to the Ponca village unless she knew that something had happened.

Johnny understood her dedication to the Ponca chief. And he was glad that his mother loved such a man as Thunder Heart. But to have left him? Yes, his mother must know that something was wrong.

"You didn't go to the ranch and get Charlie, did you?" Dede asked, almost afraid to hear the answer.

"Yes, I did, Mama," Johnny said, lowering his

eyes. Then he shot them up again and looked anxiously at Dede. "Young Blood and I went and got Charlie, Mama, but only after I knew it was safe. I had already seen Bill ride away with the posse. That was how I knew it was all right for me to get my pony and bring him here."

Dede wasn't aware of how her fingers tightened on Johnny's shoulders, but everything within her had grown cold after hearing what Johnny had said about Bill and who he was with.

"You saw Bill leave with a posse?" she gasped, aware now of Young Blood stepping up beside Johnny.

"Yes, Mama, and after I got Charlie, Young Blood and I followed the posse," Johnny said carefully.

"Oh, Lord, you didn't!" Dede exclaimed. "Even knowing the danger of being caught, you followed them?"

He nodded.

"Where did they go? Which direction?"

"They are headed the same way as Thunder Heart," Johnny answered.

"But that doesn't necessarily mean they are following him," Dede said, not wanting it to be true. She didn't want to envision the posse catching up with Thunder Heart, though they certainly would, in only a short time, since the procession was moving so slowly with the travois.

"Johnny, I came from that direction," Dede said. "I didn't see them."

Yet, now that she thought about it . . . she had

taken a shortcut. She wouldn't have seen them had they been on the same trail that Thunder Heart was on!

"I'm sure they are after Thunder Heart and those who ride with him," Johnny said, eagerly nodding. "You see, Mama, Young Blood and I followed until the posse stopped to rest. We left our ponies staked behind thick bushes and then sneaked up and listened to what the men were saying. They said something about the government giving permission to arrest Thunder Heart. That's their intention, Mama. They are going to go and get Thunder Heart and the others and put them in jail. They are going to take Seven Drum's body to St. Genevieve."

Dede's head was swimming as she took in all of this information. She so wished it was only the product of her son's very vivid imagination. But she knew that what he had told her was true. All of it. Her son couldn't . . . wouldn't . . . conjure up such a tale.

And hadn't she expected as much from the white people who hated everything the red man stood for?

Well, she had a thing or two to show them! She did know the law. She would see to it that if Thunder Heart was taken to jail, he would be there for only a short while.

"Come on, Johnny," Dede said, grabbing his hand. "We've got to get to the ranch. I've something to do."

"What, Mama?" Johnny said, holding back. "What are you going to do?"

She stopped and gazed down at him. "I'm going to put your father's lawbooks, and my knowledge of the law, to good use," she said, her voice tense. "And you're going with me. I'm not going to let you out of my sight again."

"Can Young Blood come with us?" Johnny blurted out. "He's my best friend, Mama, more than Joel ever was."

Dede glanced over at Young Blood. He was such a fine young man—so polite, and it was obvious what he thought of Johnny. He looked to him as a "blood brother," and that made Dede proud.

"Yes, he can go with us, but only if his mother approves," Dede answered, searching the crowd for Young Blood's mother. When she found her and the woman smiled and nodded at Dede, Dede returned the greeting. Then she turned to face the group.

"I want you all to know that I am going to do everything within my power to help your people," she said, as though her beloved Ross were there, with a guiding hand on her shoulder.

She singled out Silken Wing from the crowd and smiled reassuringly at her. "Your chief Seven Drums will be buried near Wind Cave," she said. "I promise you that."

"Mama, I forgot to tell you that several of the Ponca warriors left in an attempt to catch up with Thunder Heart and warn him," Johnny said. "They left only moments before you arrived."

"No!" Dede gasped, paling. "There's nothing they can do. They'll be shot or arrested along with Thunder Heart."

She ran toward her horse. "I've not a minute to waste," she cried. "I've got to set things right. Oh, Lord, if only I can!"

Johnny and Young Blood mounted their ponies and rode with Dede to the ranch.

Once there, as Dede ran into her bedroom to grab the box of her husband's lawbooks, Johnny took Young Blood to his room and showed him things that were precious to him, things he had been forced to leave behind.

"Marbles?" Young Blood asked, his eyes wide as Johnny shook his collection out of the leather pouch onto his bed.

"When we have time, I'll show you how to play the game of marbles," Johnny said, pride in his eyes as Young Blood picked up one of his shiniest, most colorful marbles.

"It is very pretty," Young Blood said, stroking the round glass ball.

"It's yours," Johnny said, smiling broadly as Young Blood looked up, wonder in his eyes.

"Mine to keep?" he asked, in awe of so much that he had seen in this white person's house. He had never seen anything as grand, yet it felt sinful to envy what he knew belonged to a white man who hated his blood kin.

"Yes, yours," Johnny answered.

He watched Young Blood pick up other marbles

and hold them against the light to marvel at the different colors and designs. Then he glanced toward his door, wondering if his mother was finding what she needed in his father's lawbooks to help the Ponca people.

Dede sat on her bed. Her fingers trembled as she rushed through one book after another, reading passages that might help her with her upcoming argument. She hoped it would be enough to free Thunder Heart and those who traveled with him.

"I must hurry," she whispered to herself, memorizing things that she knew would be of value and setting aside the most important books, which she would take with her. Surely she would be able to say the right things and protect those who were innocently traveling to their homeland to bury a loved one.

She slammed the last book shut, and hopped down from her bed. She didn't take the time to put the books away, but left the room in a mad rush.

"Johnny! Young Blood! Come on!" she shouted as she dashed toward the front door. "It's time to go. I have all I need. We're going to St. Genevieve. I've a wire to send to Washington!"

"A wire?" Johnny asked, running out of his room. Young Blood came close behind him, clutching his marble.

"I don't have time to explain," Dede said, rushing outside and swinging herself into her saddle.

As she rode off in the lead, Dede ran over everything in her mind. She would need to make a valid, logical argument in order to prove to the Secretary of the Interior, the man in charge of treaty rights, that she knew what she was talking about. She smiled when she thought of how amazed he would be when he realized just how much knowledge she did have about everything that had to do with the Ponca. Yes, oh, yes. Before daybreak tomorrow Thunder Heart and his people would surely be free to go on to the Black Hills. She knew it. She had faith in herself that she could make it happen.

"Ross, be with me, guide me," she whispered, gazing heavenward. "Oh, if only you were here to do the arguing for me."

But she knew that if Ross were there, she wouldn't have even known Thunder Heart. She fought back the tears that always came with remembering things as they had been, and as they might have been. She had been so blessed to know Ross. And now she was wonderfully blessed to be loved by such a man as Thunder Heart.

"I will make things right, my love," she whispered. In her mind's eye she saw Thunder Heart standing before her, his love for her evident in the way he looked at her, and the way he reached out for her, to hold her, to kiss her . . .

"Mama, we're almost there," Johnny said, bringing her out of her reverie. He edged his pony closer to hers. "Can you truly do it? Can you save the Ponca?"

"All I can do is try my hardest," Dede said, smiling back at Johnny as he grinned from ear to ear. He fell back a ways and rode with his friend, jabbering away about what was happening and about what they hoped would happen.

"Lord, please give me the strength to do this," Dede whispered, looking heavenward.

The small group finally got to town. As they approached the telegraph office, Dede's heart pounded. She could feel eyes on her and the children, especially since they were all dressed in Indian attire.

She ignored the rude stares of the townspeople and paid no heed to some racial slurs shouted at them. She simply went on to the telegraph office and explained what she wanted to do.

"You can't just wire the Secretary of the Interior like that," the man in his black hat and fustian suit said, his eyes raking slowly over her and then the children, who stood wide-eyed at her side.

"I'm a citizen of the United States and it is my right to wire anyone I choose. I wish to send this telegram to the Secretary of the Interior," she said, shoving her written note through the small window toward the thin, unfriendly man.

He sighed heavily, snatched the note, then reached out a hand, palm side up. "Payment first, and then I send wires," he said, smiling wickedly as she took coins from the pocket of her dress and slapped them down on the counter.

Hands on her hips in indignation, she watched the man finally send the telegram, then waited anxiously for a reply.

When there wasn't an immediate response, her hopes fell that she would be able to reach the important man in Washington. Then her heart skipped a beat when the telegraph machine suddenly began tapping out its message.

"I'll be gum," the telegraph officer said, reading the wire out loud to Dede. "It says here that he already knows about the problem, that the White House has been receiving wires from angry citizens who have seen the law officers escorting the Indians back toward St. Genevieve. The people are actually sympathizing with the Indians, especially as they learn about why they are riding together toward their homeland. It seems the people are seething with indignation at this latest evidence of the government's cruelty toward the red man. They are demanding their release."

"Well?" Dede asked anxiously. "Are they going to listen to the people?"

"It doesn't say," the man replied, shoving the telegram toward Dede so she could read it herself.

"Then send back another wire and ask him," Dede said, pushing more coins toward the man. "I need answers. Now."

She could envision her beloved Thunder Heart being forced along by armed men, his hopes of burying his father at Wind Cave gone.

She was glad, though, that after people along the way saw the wrong being done to the Ponca, they actually took action to do something about it.

She vividly recalled how so many people had

come out of their homes and watched the procession when she was traveling with Thunder Heart. She had wondered then what those people felt, especially when they saw the travois carrying the dead chief.

Now she knew. They were not looking scornfully at them. They had felt empathy. That response gave her some hope for the future . . . that perhaps the white people could be more kind to the redskins!

But she had to see that things were made right for those who were in need now! She read the telegram carefully, then dictated a response to the Secretary of the Interior, demanding the release of the Ponca.

His return wire was an adamant "no." He wrote that the Ponca would be placed behind bars for having left the land they had been assigned to.

So angry she could hardly see straight, and familiar enough with the law to continue arguing the Ponca's case, Dede wired another message to the Secretary of the Interior, telling him that she would apply for a writ of habeas corpus in the federal court in the Ponca's behalf.

He responded, saying that he would deny the prisoners' right to sue out a writ, on the grounds that an Indian was not a person within the meaning of the law.

Stunned by this response, that the Secretary of the Interior could actually say that he didn't consider Indians to be people, Dede sent another heated telegram. This time she said that she would hire an attorney to fight for the Indians' rights.

She asked him if he truly wished to see this taken to court. Did he wish to arouse the anger of everyone across the land who now sympathized with the plight of the red man? She told him that this could cost not only his post at the White House, but the job of the president during the next election. She would put this in all of the newspapers across the country . . . that the president was denying a peaceful Indian tribe the right to bury their dead in their rightful burial grounds.

Nervously, her pulse racing, Dede waited for the next response from Washington. She only hoped that she hadn't gone too far this time, that what she had said would not be seen as a threat, or a cause for her to be arrested.

When the next wire came from Washington, she could hardly believe it. The Secretary of the Interior had backed down! He said that he would wire the sheriff's office and demand the instant release of the Ponca and that he would allow them to go to their burial grounds without further interference. Better yet, he would provide them a safe military escort there.

Stunned, Dede read and reread the wire, then burst into tears as she grabbed Johnny in her arms and swung him around, her laughter mingling with her tears of joy.

"I did it!" she cried. "Oh, Johnny, I actually did it!"

Young Blood reached up for Dede. She knelt and

drew him into her arms. The way he clung to her so desperately made her feel warm with love for him.

"It's truly going to be all right," Dede soothed, as she stroked his thin back. "Sweetie, everything is going to be all right."

Young Blood hugged her one last time, then stepped back and stood proudly at Johnny's side.

"I have one more wire to send, and then we'll ride out and meet Thunder Heart and the posse," she said, brushing the tears from her eyes.

She turned to the telegraph officer, whose face showed how stunned he was over what Dede had achieved today—not only because she was a woman who had the courage of a man but because her knowledge of the law gained the Ponca's release!

"Wire the Secretary of the Interior and tell him to send the telegram for the sheriff here, and I will personally give it to him," Dede instructed, pride shining in her eyes when the man nodded respectfully to her and did as she asked, this time without demanding payment first.

When that wire came, she read it through a blur of tears. Holding it tightly, she ran out and swung herself into her saddle, then raced away with Johnny and Young Blood right behind her.

They didn't even get to the edge of town before they saw the posse bringing in the Ponca. But Dede didn't see the travois upon which lay Chief Seven Drums. Her heart almost stopped for fear of what might have happened to it. Had the white men left it along the road as though it was worthless? And then she saw a horse and wagon coming up far behind the Ponca, and she sighed with relief. The old chief must have been put there by the sheriff to make the travel much faster.

When Dede was able to make out Thunder Heart among the others, she sank her heels into the flanks of her steed and rode off at a hard gallop. She reached him and sidled her horse up next to his, and she told him that things were going to be all right. She felt eyes on her back and she knew whose they were.

She had ignored Bill as she rode past him. And even the sheriff as he looked at her with narrowed, angry eyes.

"Darling, I've taken care of everything," Dede murmured, reaching over to put her arm around Thunder Heart. "But I've something to do to prove it."

Thunder Heart's pulse raced as he saw Dede go to the sheriff and hand him a piece of paper. He watched with much pride in his heart as Dede spoke up in his people's behalf. Then he learned what the paper had said, what it gave him and his people. Their freedom!

"Seems you're free to go," Dan said, approaching Thunder Heart. "This woman here has taken care of everything for you. But you've got to come on to the jail."

"Why?" Dede asked, riding protectively nearer to Thunder Heart. "You know that Thunder Heart and those who ride with him are free to do as they please. They don't have to do anything you say. Especially not go to the jail."

"It's here in black and white how the Indians are to have a military escort on their journey to the Black Hills," the sheriff said, waving the telegram in the air. "And I am going to see that it's done."

"Military escort?" Thunder Heart asked.

"Yes, darling, to make sure nothing like this happens again on your long journey home," Dede answered. She smiled at Johnny as he rode up with Young Blood.

"Isn't Mama amazing?" Johnny asked, beaming as he looked at Thunder Heart. "She used her knowledge of the law to help you, Thunder Heart. I'm so proud of her. Aren't you?"

"Yes, very, very proud," Thunder Heart said, gently touching Dede's cheek. "Thank you, my woman. Thank you from the bottom of my heart."

"Dede, I don't understand any of this . . ."

Bill's voice behind her drew Dede's attention, and she turned to face him.

"No, I'm sure you don't," she said, her voice breaking. "And I'm sorry, Bill, that I was put in the position of having to go against you. You have been so good to me and Johnny. Please know that I will always be grateful."

Bill looked guardedly at Thunder Heart, then at Dede again. "How does he figure in the scheme of things where you are concerned?" he asked. "And

Johnny? What about Johnny? You both are dressed . . . dressed . . . like Indians."

"I'm going to marry Thunder Heart, Bill, and Thunder Heart is going to raise Johnny as his," she said calmly. Then she swung her horse around and rode off with Thunder Heart. He led his people away from the posse, who still sat, slack-jawed, watching them.

"Whew!" Dede said, sighing heavily as she looked from Johnny to Young Blood. "This has been some day, hasn't it, Johnny? Hasn't it, Young Blood?"

"But the best," Johnny said, his eyes twinkling as he smiled up at Dede. "Mama, it's been the most exciting day I can remember."

Dede found Thunder Heart smiling at her. "I love you so," she mouthed.

His nod and the wondrous look in his eyes was all that Dede needed to know that his love for her was as intense.

"Johnny and I will go with you on the rest of your journey," Dede said.

"Young Blood too?" Johnny asked, his eyes begging Dede as she looked over at him.

"Young Blood too—if his parents allow it."

"They will," Young Blood said excitedly.

Suddenly Dede heard a familiar sound behind her. She looked over her shoulder and saw Four Eyes running after Thunder Heart. Thunder Heart stopped, slid out of his saddle, and swept his coyote up into his arms.

Tears glistened in his eyes as he hugged Four Eyes to him. When he and his people were stopped, one of the posse had kicked Four Eyes and left him for dead at the side of the road. Thunder Heart had not been allowed to get him, or check on him.

"You are all right?" Thunder Heart whispered, checking over the coyote. He found only a bit of dried blood on his one side.

"Where has he been?" Dede asked, then was mortified as Thunder Heart explained how badly the coyote had been treated.

She glared over her shoulder at the white men, who were lagging far behind, then her eyes locked with Bill's. Although he looked at her as if he didn't know her, she wondered now if she could have ever known his true side.

"Come, we shall ride onward," Thunder Heart said, still holding Four Eyes in his arms.

He rode briskly into St. Genevieve, knowing that soon all of this would be behind him. He could take Dede as his wife and begin life anew, a proud husband. Surely there was no other woman like his woman!

CHAPTER TWENTY-SIX

The blessed demoiselle leaned out
From the gold bar of heaven;
Her eyes were deeper than the depth
Of waters stilled at even.

—Dante Gabriel Rossetti
(1828–1882)

The long journey to Wind Cave now over and the return trip to Missouri still ahead of them, Dede stood back from Chief Seven Drums' grave and watched as Thunder Heart performed the ceremony of burying his father with tribal honors among his ancestors.

A little food and water was placed with Seven Drums' body, and it was buried in a shallow grave with a peaked roof made of logs erected over it. Before Thunder Heart had covered the log roof with dirt, he painted special designs denoting his Wasabe, Grizzly Bear Clan, on the roof.

Other special insignia, indicating things that his father had loved during his life on earth, also had been painted on the roof.

But even before he had done all of that, before he

had lowered his blanket-wrapped father into the grave, Thunder Heart had placed moccasins made from deer skin on Seven Drums' feet so that he might not lose his way but could go on safely and be recognized by his own people in the spirit world.

The roof was now covered with dirt. Thunder Heart, alone, knelt over the grave. Johnny stood holding Dede's right hand and Young Blood held her left. The warriors who had accompanied the body of their elderly chief to his gravesite stood opposite the grave, their eyes filled with tears of grief for their fallen leader.

It was just becoming dusk. The setting sun was splashing a lovely color of orange along the horizon, outlining Wind Cave. The cave whistled and moaned in the evening breeze a short distance from the Ponca burial ground. The tall shadow of the mountains fell across Thunder Heart as he still knelt quietly over the grave with his head bowed, the last words he would speak to his father not having yet been spoken.

In the far distance Four Eyes howled from high above the burial grounds, where he had gone to sit. His silhouette was vivid against the evening sky as the sun crept lower. Echoing cries from other coyotes gave Dede goose bumps, for it seemed mystical, as if they could communicate somehow with the spirits of the dead.

As Dede waited for Thunder Heart to say aloud his final words to his father, she turned her gaze once more to Wind Cave. She understood now how the name for the cave had been chosen. Air inside the cave was usually of a different temperature than air outside, which caused quite a noticeable draft at the entrance.

She had gone there with Thunder Heart to experience some moments of silence as he communed with those who had gone on to the higher world before him. She had known that in those silent moments he had been with his wife and beloved mother, and perhaps even some favored aunts, uncles, and cousins.

In that place Dede also remembered those loved ones who had passed on before her, feeling them strangely close, even though they had been buried far, far away from this place of mystery and beauty. She realized, somehow, that neither she nor Thunder Heart would ever be jealous of those they had loved in the past. Being at Wind Cave had brought so much of the past into Dede's heart once again and then suddenly had swept it away, leaving her with a feeling of peace she had never known before.

That was when she understood why bringing Chief Seven Drums there for burial was so important to Thunder Heart. She knew now that when Thunder Heart left this place, he would be at peace with the loss of his father and able to begin life anew.

Dede's thoughts were stilled when Thunder Heart began speaking to the grave. He placed a gentle hand on the freshly sown earth above it.

Remembering what Thunder Heart had gone

through to bring his father to his final resting place, the humiliation he must have felt when he was arrested, Dede became choked up with emotion. She listened to the words that she knew were meant for his beloved father to hear before he joined his ancestors.

"My *indadi*, my father, although you are no longer physically among those who walk on earth, you are still living and still will exercise a care over your people and seek to promote their welfare," Thunder Heart said softly. "When your people look heavenward, they will know that you are there, looking back at them and smiling."

Thunder Heart bowed his head, swallowed hard, then once again gazed heavenward. "My *indadi*, when I and those who lovingly accompanied you here are received back among all of our Ponca clan, there will be a mourning feast in your honor. On this occasion, presents will be distributed in your name. There will be much singing, and it will reach high into the sky for you to hear and enjoy."

He paused again, sighed, then spread both hands on the earth before him as he looked at the grave. "My father, I shall always sorely miss you," he whispered, his tears falling onto the fresh earth. "Someday when this son joins you in the high heaven, we will embrace again. Until then I shall carry with me for all time the remembrance of your arms around me and your voice that taught me everything that I know. My sons, your grandsons, will know my voice well, also, for I know from being your son the importance of a father's devotion."

He leaned low and kissed the black earth. "Rest well, *indadi,*" he whispered. "You are home, forevermore."

When he pushed himself up from the grave, Dede eased her hands from the two children's and went to stand beside Thunder Heart. Knowing that he would wish it of her, she knelt at the grave and brushed a soft kiss across the damp earth. She then stood and held Thunder Heart's hand as everyone else gave their own kiss to the fallen chief.

Four Eyes came romping toward Thunder Heart. The chief took a step away from Dede and caught the coyote as he leapt into his open arms.

"It is now time to turn our travels back toward those who await us," he said, looking over his shoulder at Dede. "Come, my woman. We have two celebrations awaiting us. My father's mourning feast, and then our wedding."

Smiling, so glad that Thunder Heart was ready to move on with his life, Dede slid an arm through his and they walked away from the grave. The others followed behind them, while the wind whistled through Wind Cave like voices speaking.

The military escort had left after seeing that Thunder Heart and his entourage arrived safely at the sacred burial place, and Dede felt somewhat apprehensive about the trip back to Missouri. If anyone along the trail resented Indians, Thunder Heart and his few warriors would be a tempting target.

She was anxious to get the trip behind her. Once she did, she would soon be Thunder Heart's wife.

The thought of Bill made her a little uneasy. She would never forget the look on his face when she had told him that she was going to marry Thunder Heart. She hoped that after having time to think about it, and knowing this was what she wanted, he would accept it and not try to do anything to stop it.

She knew that he would be especially uncomfortable about having to explain to everyone his and Dede's relationship—that they had never been married, and why.

But she had made her choice, and it made her radiant to even think of a future with the man she truly loved.

Riding now beneath the moonlight, searching for a place for their campsite, Dede looked over at Thunder Heart. She loved him so much. She adored him.

And after they became man and wife, she hoped that she soon would be with child. She had seen how Thunder Heart treated Johnny, so gentle, so caring.

She could only imagine how wonderful a father he would be to a true son, the same as his own father had been to him . . . treating him with total respect and feeling undying love.

Dede was relieved that the burial was behind them now, and that Thunder Heart had been able to carry out his mission of the heart. Not too many sons would go to that much trouble for their father.

"Your son will be as loving toward you," Dede whispered. Then she shivered, suddenly transported ahead many years in time, when there would be another burial, another son speaking over a grave.

She swallowed hard and looked away from Thunder Heart. She hoped that the disturbing vision wasn't an omen of some sort, warning her about an impending death . . . Thunder Heart's! She could hardly wait now to get these long miles behind her, in case the cavalry might be laying a trap for Thunder Heart's return.

To be sure, none of the soldiers were friendly toward Thunder Heart or those who rode with him to the Black Hills. There had been a keen resentment in their glares. And they had been more than eager to leave Thunder Heart once they had escorted him to the burial place.

Dede looked slowly around her, peering at all of the shadows made by the moon, relieved when they turned out not to be shadows of men, but only trees and bushes.

She edged her horse closer to Thunder Heart's.

"My woman, do I sense that you are afraid?" he asked, reaching over to take one of her hands.

"It's such a long way home," she said. "That's all."

"The days will pass quickly," he assured her, yet she knew by the guarded look in his eyes that he wasn't completely comfortable with the miles stretching out before them either.

"Yes, they will pass quickly," she repeated, but to herself she added, "but not fast enough!"

She smiled shakily at Thunder Heart as he squeezed her hand.

CHAPTER TWENTY-SEVEN

She spoke through the still weather,
Her voice was like the voice the stars
Had when they sang together.

—Dante Gabriel Rossetti
(1828–1882)

Finally back in Missouri and among the Ponca again, the mourning feast now behind them, Dede could hardly contain her excitement of knowing that tomorrow she would become Thunder Heart's wife.

Too often she had thought that it might never happen.

She had worried so much about the long journey home from the Black Hills, about the possibility of tragedy. But they had made the journey without confrontation. It had even become something wonderful as those who traveled with Thunder Heart bonded even more tightly with their new chief.

And now that they were among Thunder Heart's people again, Dede felt as close to Silken Wing as though she were a second mother. Silken Wing was filled with compassionate love, which she willingly shared not only with Dede but also with Johnny.

"Mama, your mind has traveled again," Johnny said, as he sat next to her beside the outdoor fire that they had built a short distance from Thunder Heart's lodge. The stars were bright overhead. The moon was full. An owl hooted in a tree behind the tepee. "You were talking about schooling and explaining things to Young Blood. He wants to know, Mama. He wants to be tutored along with me."

Dede was pulled out of her thoughts by Johnny's voice. She smiled clumsily at him and then gave Young Blood a smile of apology. He sat beside Johnny, attentive to what Dede had been saying, about how she had always tutored Johnny and would resume teaching him the day after the marriage ceremony.

She had felt that talking to the children about school tonight was a good way to pass the evening, to hurry it along, so that tomorrow would arrive more quickly and she would finally become Thunder Heart's wife.

Her special dress was already laid out in the tepee. Silken Wing had sewn it especially for her.

Her heart thumped wildly even now as she thought of the precious moments she would soon share with the man she loved.

Tonight they purposely were being kept apart, for it was the custom that they should not see one another for a full night and day before their marriage ceremony.

It had been a long day. With the children there beside her, surely the night would not seem as long.

"Young Blood, because of the distance from where we lived to the public school in St. Genevieve, I felt it was best that I teach Johnny what he would have learned in a classroom," she began, though still unable to keep her mind from wandering as she spoke.

Bill.

She was stunned that Bill had not shown his face since the day she had fought for the Ponca's rights and had saved them from being arrested. It was strange to her that Bill had done nothing to interfere with her decision to live with the Ponca instead of with him. And she certainly had thought that he would fight to keep Johnny from living the life of an Indian.

She was very glad that he had decided to allow them their choices. But she wouldn't feel truly free of him until after she had spoken her vows with Thunder Heart, which would seal her bond with him forever. Only then would she fully believe that Bill would do nothing to stop her from living with the Ponca.

She could not help but feel somewhat guilty about pushing Bill out of her and Johnny's lives. He had been so good to them. Soon she planned to go to him and try to make things right between them. She so badly wanted him to understand and give her his blessing. But she wouldn't chance approaching him until after the wedding!

"Mama is a good teacher," Johnny said, again drawing Dede back to the present. "Anyway, I always thought so. So did Joel."

"Who is Joel?" Young Blood asked, scooting closer to the fire and rubbing his hands together to ward off the autumn chill.

"Before I met you, he was my best friend," Johnny said, a touch of melancholy in his voice. "But I'm sure he's moved to St. Louis by now. I'll probably never see him again."

"I am your best friend now," Young Blood said, proudly squaring his shoulders. "I will show you everything about the hunt and tell you about how I sought and found my vision."

"Vision?" Johnny asked, curiously. "What is a vision?"

Young Blood cast Dede a questioning look, then said to Johnny, "I shall tell you about visions when it is only you and me talking of such things." Then he shivered, for the breeze had turned into a chilling wind.

Dede noticed how uncomfortable Young Blood was, and even she felt cold. The outdoor fire was not enough to ward off the first hint of winter. "Come inside," she said, pushing herself up. "Let's sit beside the fire in the tepee. There we can resume our talk."

Laughing and playfully shoving at one another, Johnny and Young Blood rushed inside, Dede close behind them.

After she got the entrance flap closed and added

a log to the lodge fire, she sat down on pelts close to the fire pit. "Now we can continue talking of your education," she said. "I'm going to talk to Thunder Heart about possibly tutoring all of the Ponca children." She gazed at Young Blood. "Do you think your friends would like that? Do you think they'd like to learn how to read and write? I can even teach you arithmetic."

"That is a strange sort of word," Young Blood said, cocking his head. "What does it mean?"

"Arithmetic is the study of numbers," Dede answered, smiling to herself at this child's innocence. She did hope that all of the children's parents would approve of her teaching them. The Ponca children would be better prepared for their future if their parents allowed her to teach them, better able to succeed as adults in a world where they would be surrounded by white people who were school-educated.

Thunder Heart was an intelligent man, yet he had never been taught how to read. He did know enough about numbers and how to count to get by.

"Young Blood, do you have the pouch of marbles I gave you?" Johnny asked, his eyes anxious.

Young Blood nodded and plucked the pouch out of his front breeches pocket.

"Shake the marbles out of it," Johnny said, watching while Young Blood did as he asked.

Proudly Dede watched with interest as Johnny did his own form of teaching. As intelligent as he was, and as eager as he was to learn, she could not help but think about how well he would have done in law school. But that was something that would never come to pass, and not only because Bill would not finance it. But because she knew now that her son absolutely did not wish to be a lawyer. It was something that she had wanted for him, but she could accept his choice in life.

She wanted him to be happy. Being happy meant doing what you chose to do, not what someone chose for you to do.

Johnny took four marbles and placed them in a row on the floor mat before him. " There are four marbles now," he said, then slid one away. "And when you take one away, which is called subtraction, you then have only three marbles."

He reached for several more and placed them before him in two rows of four. "And watch how I multiply," he said. Young Blood indeed was watching attentively. "There are two rows of four marbles, which when multiplied together, as you would say two times four, equals eight."

Young Blood's eyes widened. He took the marbles and slid them all together. "Two times four equals eight," he said. "When they are all together, there are eight."

"Yes, that's it," Johnny said excitedly. "You now know something about arithmetic."

"It's fun," Young Blood said, his eyes wide as he looked at Dede. "My friends would enjoy learning such things."

Then Young Blood's eyes wavered. "But the

teaching of the Ponca is very different from how you do it," he said solemnly.

"Tell us about it," Dede said, touching Young Blood's arm with a gentle hand. "We want to learn from you as well. There is so much we need to know about your people."

"Yes, we want to know everything," Johnny said eagerly. "We want to become Ponca, don't we, Mama?"

"Yes, it's very important to us to become as one with your people," Dede answered. "But we know that it will take time, Young Blood, to learn everything."

"My people are also good teachers," Young Blood said, pride in his voice. "Games are used as learning tools. As well as children's activities. Red hay stems are used by little boys as arrows; little girls use cottonwood leaves to make toy tepees and toy moccasins."

He laughed and his eyes gleamed as he looked from Dede to Johnny. "Children have contests to see who can eat the most unripe wild gooseberries without grimacing," he said. "Spiderbean pods are used by little boys to imitate rattles. Wild sweetpea pods are roasted and eaten in sport by children."

He smiled broadly. "Violets are used by children in a game of 'war,'" he said. "The heads of the violets are snapped at opponents."

He paused, then added, "But it is the elderly who take time to teach children so much. Some older man or woman teaches the children how to act and tells them stories about famous people and battles."

"I find all of that so very interesting," Dede said, enjoying hearing the child talk so proudly about how the Ponca children learn from others. "You could be a teacher, Young Blood. Truly you could."

He smiled almost bashfully at Dede, then told them more. "A Ponca child's education begins as soon as she or he is able to imitate and learn adult patterns and behavior," he said. He smiled as he looked from Dede to Johnny. "I recall my very first lesson from my elderly grandmother. She told me to 'Get up at daybreak' and to 'Go to bed with the sun.' "

His smile faded. "Her words were stilled when her frail old body gave way on our long march from our homeland in the Black Hills," he said, his voice breaking.

Johnny placed a gentle hand on his friend's shoulder. He turned quickly toward the closed entrance flap when the soft music of a flute began playing just outside.

Then he turned toward his mother with a slow smile, seeing something in her eyes that was lovely and dreamy. He, as well as she, knew why the flute was being played tonight. Thunder Heart had talked about it one night while they were on their way home from the Black Hills. He had explained to them that the night before a wedding the man would sit just outside his woman's lodge and play the flute for his wife-to-be to prove that his love for her was true and to prove that he would make her a good husband.

But Johnny thought that the music would come later in the night, when he and his mother were in bed. Otherwise, they would never have sat outside as long as they had. That must have had delayed Thunder Heart arriving with his flute music. He looked at his mother as she listened, so happy that she had found happiness again, and with a man who would treat her gently and wonderfully.

"Isn't it beautiful?" Dede said, tears of happiness filling her eyes.

She clasped her hands in her lap as they all sat quietly listening until it stopped. They knew that Thunder Heart had left for a campfire he had built earlier in the evening, where he would spend his final night alone amidst his blankets.

"I wish he could have played all night," Dede said, sighing. Then she laughed good-naturedly. "But he does need his rest tonight. Tomorrow he marries me."

"And you need your rest," Young Blood said, starting to rise to leave.

Dede reached for his hand. "Sweetie, I doubt I shall sleep a wink all night," she said, laughing softly. "I'm too excited. So please stay a while longer. Tell us more about your way of being educated."

"It is simply done," Young Blood said, relaxing again by the fire. "The girls learn from their mothers and other female relatives and friends. Boys learn from their fathers and male relatives and friends. Occasionally some wise elderly man gathers a group of boys together to instruct them. Such a man is called a *wog-aze*."

"I look forward to being instructed by one of your elders," Johnny said excitedly.

"My grandfather is always eager to teach those who wish to listen," Young Blood said, looking from Dede to Johnny. "He sits alone even now in his lodge. Johnny, would you like to go and sit with him and hear his stories?"

Johnny looked anxiously at Dede. "Mama, can I?" he asked. "Would you be too alone if I leave for just a little while?"

Dede patted him gently on the shoulder. "You go ahead," she told him. "You go and enjoy yourself. I have some things to do."

"I'll be back soon," Johnny said, leaning over to kiss her on the cheek.

And then they were gone, but she didn't feel alone. Her heart, her very soul, were so full of Thunder Heart, it was as though he was there, holding her, whispering sweet things in her ear.

"Tomorrow we shall be together forever," she whispered.

She went to the back of the lodge to admire once more the beautifully beaded doeskin dress that Silken Wing had created for her. The skirt of the dress had slits up each side that where heavily fringed. Beautiful new high-topped soft moccasins and knee-length leggings also lay beside the dress, as well as long quilled pendants that she would wear in her hair in the back.

She knew that she would feel like an Indian princess.

"Just one more night," she whispered, again thinking about Bill and the possibility that he might try to stop her.

She gazed heavenward. "Please keep him away for at least one more night," she begged. "Please?"

CHAPTER TWENTY-EIGHT

As I spoke, beneath my feet
The ground-pine curled its pretty wreath,
Running over the club-mossburrs;
I inhaled the violets' breath.

—Ralph Waldo Emerson
(1803–1882)

The wedding vows had been exchanged. Dede could hardly believe that she was finally Thunder Heart's wife, especially since she had expected Bill to arrive at any moment and stop the ceremony. The fact that he hadn't interfered puzzled her, and she only hoped that he wasn't scheming to disrupt her happy life sometime in the future. Her true wish, what she had prayed for, was that he had accepted her decision and was going on with his own life without her.

The whole village had attended Dede and Thunder Heart's wedding. Even those who had only recently recovered from the stomach ailment and were still somewhat weak were outside on this wondrous day of soft, warm breezes, the scents of wildflowers wafting on the wind.

Violets had been plucked from the forest and lay strewn around the spread pelts, on which the new bride and groom now sat, enjoying the music and dancing. The feast had already been shared by everyone. The dancing, and then the games, would conclude the celebration so that the newly married couple could retire to their private lodge to whisper wonderful things to one another as they made love.

Johnny had been invited to stay the rest of the day and night with Young Blood and his family. Glad that Johnny had found such a devoted friend so soon in his new life, Dede had gladly given her permission.

She could hardly wait to be alone with Thunder Heart as his wife.

As the music played—an art at which the Ponca excelled—the dancers performed for their chief and his new bride. Many musical instruments were being played today—different types of drums; gourd, rawhide and deer-hoof rattles; eagle-bone and cedar whistles; and cedar flutes.

Dede greatly admired the dancers' costumes. On their heads were porcupine and deer-hair roach headdresses, with bone-spreaders and plume holders. A single eagle feather stood erect in the headdress at the front. Two plumes fell over the eyes, in front of which were two buckskin thongs. Small pieces of silver were crimped around the thongs at regular intervals, suspended from a German-silver disk.

Their clothes were fancily beaded buckskins. On

the upper bodies of some of the dancers were "choker" necklaces, with a large shell disk in front. The dancers most favored neck disks made from the smooth surface of a pink conch shell, rounded and polished.

Dede's eyes had widened at first when she had seen some of the dancers chewing dried perfumed leaves while dancing. They spit quantities of this substance onto their bodies and costumes from time to time, using the motions of the dance to disguise the act of spitting.

That, as well as many other customs pertaining to dancing, she would learn so that she could participate during the next celebration. She wanted never to disappoint Thunder Heart. The more she could learn, and the sooner, the more he would see that he had been right to take a white woman as his wife.

She glanced over at him as he sat watching the dancers and smiling broadly. Today his copper face shone radiantly beneath the soft rays of the sun. His midnight-dark eyes twinkled with happiness.

Although his shoulders were hidden beneath a beautiful shirt of otter skin with a red cloth collar, she knew well enough their broadness and could even now see the muscles defined against the shirt. His tight buckskin breeches and leggings revealed his powerful thighs. He also wore knee-high moccasins that were elaborately decorated with dyed porcupine quills.

He wore no head ornaments, not even a headband. His jet-black hair fell back from his shoulders in long waves to his waist. Dede loved the way the breeze lifted the ends of his hair and fluttered them. She had to fight the urge to reach over and run her fingers through his hair. Soon she would do that—and many more things that she secretly desired.

When they were alone, oh, how she would show him the depth of her love . . . the serenity of her happiness at being his wife.

The music stopped. The dancers fell back and stood with the other Ponca as they rose from their blankets and pelts.

Thunder Heart stood and reached down for Dede. "It is time for games, and then, my love, it will be our private time," he said huskily. "But I err when I say 'games.' For there will only be one game today, a special one for a special day."

His smile, his voice, made Dede's knees weak with passion. She returned his smile, took his hand, then rose to her feet before him. It was hard not to fling herself into his arms, to kiss him and hold him.

It was hard not to turn to everyone and shout out how happy she was to be among them as their chief's wife. She wanted to declare to them that she would have many sons for this man.

She would give him daughters also. But deep inside she knew that the daughters would be for herself, for she had always wished for a sister to play dolls with and confide her deepest secrets to. A daughter. Yes, one day she would, she hoped, have many.

Walking with Thunder Heart, his people following behind them, Dede held his hand and gazed up at him. "Where are we going?" she asked. "Where is this game to be played?"

"A field has been prepared," Thunder Heart said. "The game is called *tabegasi*, shinny. It is an Indian ball game, somewhat like your people's game called soccer."

"I heard Johnny talking about it," Dede said, glancing over her shoulder. She smiled when she saw Johnny walking and talking excitedly with Young Blood. Others their same age gathered around and chattered as they kept in step with them.

"I believe Young Blood explained in detail to Johnny how the game would be played," she said.

"And Johnny will play it well," Thunder Heart said.

He sidled up closer to Dede and their eyes met as he continued to talk to her about Johnny and the game.

"Wife, earlier today, before anyone else was awake, I took Johnny into the forest and captured a butterfly," he said. "I told him to be gentle with the butterfly and not kill it, but to rub its wings over his heart and ask the butterfly to lend him its grace and swiftness. I told Johnny that if the butterfly was willing to do this, he would run faster today during the ball game than a bird could fly."

"You truly did this for Johnny?" Dede asked softly, filled with such radiant warmth to know that Thunder Heart cared so deeply for her son.

But she knew how much he wanted sons. To him, Johnny was the same as his. She felt so blessed to have found such a loving and gracious man as Thunder Heart, and she knew that Johnny felt the same.

"For the Ponca, as for most Indians, running is a mark of distinction," Thunder Heart explained. "I taught this to Johnny. I even told him that when boys are the age of just learning how to walk and run, their fathers take them naked into a wide, open field, and teach them to chase birds and butterflies, so that their little legs will be trained for running when they become adults."

"As you will take our firstborn son to the open fields?" Dede asked, her eyes wide.

"Yes, as I will take our firstborn *wizige,* our son," Thunder Heart replied, affectionately squeezing her hand. "And I hope that you will join us and watch the fun of it, how tiny legs run through tall grass and how tiny hands learn the skill of catching butterflies and birds."

"I shall want to see it all," Dede said, sighing. "I want to share every moment that I can of what you teach our sons."

"The hunt is reserved solely for the male Ponca," Thunder Heart said, giving her a somewhat apologetic look. "No woman is ever allowed on the hunt."

"Then while you hunt I shall be doing lady things like making jams or pies," Dede said, laughing softly. She sighed again deeply. "But I must confess

. . . I will have problems adapting to cooking in a tepee."

"One day I shall see that a house of logs is built for you," Thunder Heart said, his gaze moving from Dede to the ball field that had been prepared for the upcoming game.

Dede's heart leapt at the thought of having a real home, yet she knew that it didn't truly matter. She would live anywhere and cook on anything in order to be with Thunder Heart.

She noticed how quiet he had become and how he seemed to be concentrating on the ball field, which was now in view a short distance away. She looked at it herself and saw that goalposts about six feet tall had been erected at each end. Offerings of calico had already been tied to each post.

"Something else I did for Johnny was give him a medicine bundle to wear during the game, the same sort of bundle that Young Blood's father and the other fathers gave their sons. The bundles assure swiftness to those who wear them," Thunder Heart said, as he led Dede to a bench at one side of the field. "Come. You will sit with me. Others will stand on each side of the field cheering for those they wish to win."

Again she saw how violets had been strewn on the ground, this time all around the bench that had been set up for the chief and his bride.

She snuggled into a covering of rich pelts, then nestled close to Thunder Heart as the players took their places on the field, halfway between both goal-posts.

Truly interested, and hoping that Johnny could do well enough among those who had surely played this game many times, Dede sat eagerly watching the game unfold.

First an elder handed each player a shinny stick about three feet in length, made of ash, with a slight bend at the end.

A ball was then brought to the elder who seemed to be in charge of the game. The ball was made of deerskin stuffed with horsehair. It had an interesting design on it, a yellow cross with a red square where the arms of the cross intersected. It was flanked on either side by a design of crossed shinny sticks.

Thunder Heart saw Dede looking curiously at the ball and leaned down closer to her. "The ball represents the earth and is mystically painted as such," he said softly. "Until recently, the game of shinny was more like a religious observation, and certain rituals had to be performed in connection with it. The game had an appointed ritual custodian who was responsible for arranging for its play at a proper time. This custodian used to keep the sacred ball and would always announce the dates of the games. But now the game is played purely for pleasure, on the most special of occasions."

"Like weddings," Dede said, smiling at Thunder Heart.

"Yes, like weddings," he said, chuckling.

Again their eyes went to the ball field, but Thunder Heart continued to talk to her. "The game is started at a point halfway between the goalposts," he said. "Watch how the elder draws a cross on the ground, representing the four winds, and places the ball on it."

The game commenced as the captains of each side raised their sticks above the ball three times. The fourth time they attempted to drive the ball into the opponents' territory.

Dede's eyes widened and she watched Johnny with concern when she saw how fast and furious the game was played. Often a player of one team would mistake an opponent's head for the ball.

Each time a team worked the ball to its opponents' goalpost, one point was scored. The play continued until a team scored four goals. That team won.

Dede was proud that Johnny was on the winning team, but it worried her when she saw a trickle of blood streaming from a slight gash at the right side of his head.

"Do not fret over such a small wound as that," Thunder Heart reassured as he saw her alarmed expression. "Do you not recall how your son's bite from the turtle healed? What you see today is much less serious than that bite."

"Yes, I know," Dede said, swallowing hard. "But . . ."

Thunder Heart interrupted her. "Let him be a boy who will soon be a man," he said.

Dede smiled weakly up at him and nodded. The games of the Ponca were definitely much rougher than Johnny's games of marbles. It would take time, but she would conquer the fears that she suffered with each new thing Johnny tried that seemed threatening to her. She didn't want her son to look like a sissy in the eyes of the other boys.

"My wife, it is time now to separate ourselves from the others," Thunder Heart said. He placed a finger beneath her chin and tilted it up so that her eyes looked into his. "My wife. Do you not hear how good that sounds coming from my lips?"

"It sounds wonderful," Dede said, her pulse racing as he helped her from the bench. They began walking away from the field, and everyone turned and watched them.

Their moment of quiet was interrupted when Johnny came running up to Dede. He stepped into her path and stopped her, his eyes wide and eager as he gazed up at her. "Mama, I want to do something special," he blurted out. "Please allow it?"

Dede frowned. "What are you talking about?" she asked. "What do you want me to allow? You're spending the night with Young Blood. I've already given you permission to do that."

"No, it's not that," Johnny said, pleading with his dark eyes. "Mama, you know about visions, how boys even younger than me go and seek them?"

Dede felt the color draining from her face, afraid to hear what Johnny was going to say next. She could tell by his behavior that he was going to ask her if he could seek his own vision! And if he did ask that, what on earth could she say?

Thunder Heart had just told her how she should allow her son to do things that would make him a man. In the Indians' eyes, a boy going on his vision quest was what turned him into a man. And she knew enough about vision quests to know that the child who sought his vision would go out alone and stay several days without food and water. She doubted she could agree to that, yet how could she say no if she really wanted her son to be accepted by those his own age. Seeking his vision would quickly accomplish that.

"Mama, I want to do a vision quest," Johnny said excitedly. "Young Blood explained how it is done. I'm old enough. And I'm strong enough. Please say yes. This is something I can do while you and Thunder Heart have time alone as newlyweds."

"Johnny, I don't know," Dede hesitated. "It's . . ."

"It is something that all boys do," Thunder Heart said softly, meeting Dede's eyes. "Wife, this will strengthen your son's ties with those his age. And it is not something that you should fear. Although he will go to an isolated hilltop to fast and pray for four days and nights, he will be visited by an elder who will bring him food and water each evening. So you see, he will not starve, and he will not be alone the full time."

"Mama, a Ponca boy secures his first *xube,* which means supernatural power, on his vision quest," Johnny explained. "His face is darkened with ash so that all will recognize his holy errand. If this boy is arduous and a bit lucky besides, the spirit of some bird or animal will appear to him and grant him power."

"Supernatural?" Dede gasped, paling. "You will be doing something that is considered supernatural?"

"That is only a term used to describe the mystic qualities of the vision quest," Thunder Heart said, gently placing his hands on Dede's shoulders. "Allow it, wife. Allow Johnny to go and have ash placed on his face. Allow him to go and seek his vision."

Dede knew that she must agree to this, even though it frightened her to death. If she did not, she would seem distrustful of the Ponca customs.

She smiled weakly at Thunder Heart, then slipped away from him and turned to Johnny.

Kneeling before him, she swept him into her arms. "Be careful," she whispered, refraining from touching the small wound on his head, knowing that worse could happen to him while he was alone. "And if you get afraid, you will not look like a sissy if you come home before your vision quest is over. You will wait perhaps another year, until you are older, and try again."

"I will succeed the first time," Johnny said. An excitement in his voice that she had never heard before told her that this was something he must be allowed to do.

"Yes, I know," she murmured. "But still, Johnny, be careful."

She didn't want to tell him that it was Bill who concerned her. He might be spying on them even now, waiting for the right moment to get back at them for having abandoned him. If Bill saw Johnny out there all alone, oh, Lord, what would he do?

No. She couldn't let herself think of such things. She had no choice but to let Johnny go, and pray that he would be all right.

Johnny gave Dede one last hug, then squirmed free of her embrace. He ran over to Young Blood. "Come on," he said, pulling on Young Blood's hand. "You said your father would prepare me. Let's go. I'm ready."

He stopped, smiled at Thunder Heart and Dede over his shoulder, then ran on away from them, his laughter following along after him.

Her heart thumping wildly within her chest, Dede watched him go. She turned quickly to Thunder Heart when she realized just how quietly he was watching her.

At once she understood that the look he was giving her wasn't because of her behavior about Johnny, but because she had, for a moment, forgotten that she was a new bride with a new husband eager to take her to their lodge.

"Husband, let's go home," she said, forcing herself to brush all thoughts of Johnny from her mind. At this moment her husband should have all her attention. They had waited forever to be able to be married. Nothing should shadow these first moments.

Smiling from ear to ear, his own doubts about his woman briskly pushed away, Thunder Heart reached down and swept Dede up into his arms. He trotted back toward the village. When they arrived at their lodge, and the entrance flap was securely tied shut, Dede stood before Thunder Heart and slowly undressed him.

"I have waited forever for this precious moment," Dede said, tears of pure joy shining in her eyes. "My husband. I can now truly say that you are my husband."

"And that is for always, my wife," Thunder Heart said huskily as the last piece of his clothing fell to the floor beside him.

Dede fell to her knees and gently slid his feet out of his moccasins, then slowly ran her fingers up the inside of his legs. She smiled wickedly up at him when she heard his sharp intake of breath as she cupped his manhood in the palm of her hand.

"I want to make you happier than you've ever been," she murmured, slowly moving her hand on him, feeling him grow thick and long in her eager fingers.

Thunder Heart held his head back, his eyes closed in a building ecstasy. Dede's fingers were like a magical, silken wand around his spreading heat. He gritted his teeth as the pleasure mounted, and he moaned sensually when he felt the warmth of her lips on him, and then the sweep of her tongue.

His hips moved gently.

His fingers wove through her hair.

Not wanting to reach the ultimate release without her, he reached down and placed his hands on her waist and led her to stand before him.

Almost meditatively he disrobed her, his tongue taking slow swipes of her flesh as her skin came free of her clothes. When he bent low and sucked one of her nipples into his mouth, his tongue lapping it hungrily, Dede's knees almost buckled.

Sensing this, Thunder Heart swept his arms around her and gently laid her down on the bed of pelts and blankets on the floor beside the slow-burning fire. As he kissed her he finished disrobing her and then worshiped her body with his lips and his tongue.

Breathless, on fire for Thunder Heart, Dede reached out for him and brought him on top of her. Smiling seductively up at him, she slid a hand downward and led him inside her, then closed her eyes in rapture as he began his rhythmic thrusts.

Her breath quickened when his mouth seized hers in another fiery kiss, his hands sliding down her slim, sensuous body. His fingers fluttered across her flat belly, and then down to where her heat was centered. He smoothed a finger over her swollen nub, flicking, then rubbing, as his strokes within her continued, the curl of heat growing within him.

"I love you," he whispered huskily against her lips. "My wife . . . my wife . . ."

"My husband," she whispered back.

Her world melted away, her senses reeling in drunken pleasure. Twining her arms around his neck, she sought his mouth in a wildness and desperation. She was clinging and floating as he drove in swiftly and surely. As his hands molded her breasts, she leaned into him.

Then he gathered her into his arms and held her fiercely as he felt the fever of his passion cresting.

He breathed hard as he stopped for a moment and then lunged deeply inside her again. He kissed her with urgency as his body quaked and quivered, the ultimate bliss overwhelming him.

Dede clung to him, her own release something wonderful and sweet as it swept through her in hot currents of pleasure.

Afterward, they lay together quietly. Then Dede let out a giggle, for she heard Four Eyes whining outside the entrance flap. He had been gone since late last night. Finally he was home again and must be exhausted after a long night of gallivanting around.

Still naked, Dede crawled to the entrance flap and untied it. Opening the flap only wide enough for the coyote to get through, she watched him scamper in, then collapse, soon fast asleep beside the lodge fire.

"Seems he has found his own mate," Thunder Heart said, leaning over to pet the coyote's tangled fur.

"And it looks like he had quite a night of it," Dede laughed, untangling some of the worst witch's knots and removing some cockleburs from his fur.

"That's what lies ahead of us," Thunder Heart said, taking Dede's hand and drawing her close to him. "We will make love, rest, make love again, rest, make love again."

"Oh, we will, will we?" Dede giggled, snuggling close.

"Only if you wish to," Thunder Heart said, placing a finger beneath her chin, lifting it so that their eyes met and held.

"Need you ask?" Dede said, smiling when she saw how that question caused his eyes to gleam.

With a groan he pulled her against him. He gathered her close and swept her beneath him.

As he thrust himself inside her and began his rhythmic movements all over again, he gave her an all-consuming kiss.

She was overwhelmed with surges of ecstasy.

CHAPTER TWENTY-NINE

Continuous as the stars that shine
And twinkle on the Milky Way,
That stretched in never-ending line.

—William Wordsworth
(1770–1850)

Dede kept watching the bluff where Johnny had gone on his vision quest. It had been three days and two nights now, and even though the elder who took him food and drink reported that he was all right, Dede couldn't relax in her son's absence.

He was used to eating more than one meal a day, and he was used to sleeping where it was warm and safe.

As the sun lowered in the sky, marking the third night Johnny was to be gone, Dede found it very hard to concentrate on tanning her family's garments for the long winter months ahead. Although limited to hunting grounds on the land allotted them by the United States government, the recent hunt had gone well. Dede had seen Thunder Heart's pride in what he had brought home, and the meat had already been prepared and stored.

Tanning the hides was a slower process, especially since Dede was learning how it was done as she went along. Proud to say, she already had produced several beautifully tanned garments. Some of the skins were even colored in various ways, depending on the type of twigs used in the fires during the smoking process.

On her knees, Dede forced herself to ignore the way the shadows were lengthening in the forest as the sun moved lower and lower in the sky. She processed one more hide that Thunder Heart had laid out for her.

He was with his warriors in the council house, deeply involved in meetings that included talks of how they might persuade the United States government to let them join the other Ponca people in Nebraska.

The government must see that having all the Ponca in one place, instead of scattered here and there, would make it easier for them to watch—that word "watch" like a thorn in the Ponca's sides.

The Ponca felt as though they were being treated like children by the white people. Every move they made seemed to be observed by one or more whites, the news spreading to Washington by way of telegram if those who disliked redskins thought the Ponca were stepping out of line again, as they had when they had set out for their ancestral burial grounds in the Black Hills.

Dede had listened to Thunder Heart and his closest friends discuss how they might approach the whites for permission to leave for Nebraska as soon as the ice cracked in the rivers. Spring would be the perfect time for them to travel, keeping them away from both the hottest and the coldest months of the year.

Dede had begun to figure out in her own mind how she could speak on behalf of the Ponca again.

"If only I had more of the lawbooks with me," she whispered to herself. She again tried to concentrate on what she was doing so that she could show off the end result to her husband.

"Husband," she whispered, the very sound of that word like pure honey as it feathered across her lips.

Yes, she was married now, and she was well into learning the ways of a Ponca wife. Beef stew was simmering over her lodge fire, and a persimmon pie lay cooling on a small table that Thunder Heart had brought to her for use during her "kitchen time."

Of course it was only large enough to place one item on it at a time. And it was so short-legged, she had to use it as she sat on the matted floor beside it.

She smiled at her husband's promise to build her a log cabin soon, before the blustery winds came with their cold, clutching claws. She remembered with fondness how she had gone with him one day as he sat on a hillside studying a log cabin that sat only a short distance across the border line of his people's land. She could see his mind working, calculating how the stone chimney would be built, and how the logs would be set together with mortar made from clay that he could get along the Mississippi River.

But, for now, she had much to do. So again, she tried to concentrate on the tanning. First she spread the fresh green hide out on the ground and staked it down. With an elkhorn tool, she scraped off pieces of meat and fat that were still stuck to the hide. After that, the hide would be left to dry, then turned over so she could scrape the hair from the other side. This hide would be used to make moccasin soles, parfleche bags, and other heavier pieces.

The piece of hide now left to dry, Dede went to another one that she had been working on as well. This one was going to be made into buckskin by rubbing bone grease—marrow from the bone—into it.

She threw herself into preparing it and when that was done, she rubbed a sandstone, also called a pumice stone, over the hide to make it soft and of an even thickness.

Stopping to glance up at the bluff again, where her Johnny was, she noticed once more how quickly it was growing dark. She grimaced at the thought of Johnny being away from her for another full night.

"I must put it out of my mind," she argued to herself, going to a pit that she had dug earlier a little way from her tepee. She had measured carefully, to make sure the fire pit was the same size as the hide that she would smoke over it.

She now busied herself by making a fire in the pit. After it was burning low and even, she stretched the hide over the fire and staked it down to the ground. She would leave it there until the fire burned itself out. She was told that this process would assure that the skin would be waterproof. If she had wanted to make a robe, she would have left the fur on the hide.

Bone-tired and weary from the long day of work, Dede almost fell into the tepee. She stretched out on her back beside the fire. "I'll go and bathe later," she whispered, her eyes growing heavy with the need for rest.

Yes, she would take a short nap, and then she would bathe before her husband came home for the evening meal.

"If only Johnny were here," she whispered.

She fell into a deep sleep, but not a restful one. As the fire snapped and crackled in the fire pit beside her, her dreams took her to the bluff where Johnny was supposed to be awaiting his vision.

What she found there, instead of Johnny, made her cry out in her sleep. She found feathers from an eagle strewn across Johnny's blanket. She found several wolves lurking nearby, their icy gray eyes peering at her through the darkness. But Johnny was nowhere in sight. Except for the blanket that he had taken with him, nothing of his was there.

It became dark and eerie as the moon was hidden behind dark, rolling clouds. Lightning began to move in lurid zigzags across the velvet backdrop of sky. Thunder boomed so hard it shook the ground beneath Dede. In her dream, Dede desperately cried Johnny's name. And as the wind began blowing in thrashing gusts, threatening to toss her off the high bluff to the ground far below, she fell down on the blanket of feathers and clung to tufts of grass on each side.

Sobbing so hard that her body shook, Dede was brought out of her dream, which had turned into a hideous nightmare. Inhaling deep, ragged, frightened breaths, she sat bolt upright and looked all around her.

Then she realized that it wasn't storming outside. Everything was calm.

Except for her heart and her frantic thoughts.

She hated to believe that the nightmare would be an omen of some kind. But why else would she have such a dreadful dream? *Fear does that to you,* she tried to reassure herself. *Being afraid for Johnny made her dream that.*

Still shaken by the experience, Dede went to the entrance flap and shoved it aside. While she had slept, it had grown pitch-black outside. Some women still worked with the hides by the light of huge outdoor fires.

She glanced toward the council house. Through the open doorway and small side windows she could see the fire's glow and knew that her husband was still in conference with his warriors.

Again the nightmare flashed through her consciousness.

She stepped on outside, moved briskly to the back of the tepee, and looked up at the bluff. She so badly wanted to shout out Johnny's name. But she knew that everyone would hear her. Especially Thunder Heart.

He had encouraged her to relax. He had said that she should just let things happen for her son . . . let him experience what all young braves experienced before him. It was something they all had to do in order to become a warrior of courage and insight.

"I must have faith that Johnny will be all right," she told herself. Her insides tightened when she saw far in the distance a jagged streak of lightning, followed by a faraway rumble of thunder.

Was her dream going to come to pass? Had she been forewarned that something was going to happen to Johnny?

She glanced heavenward. Although there was still much activity at the village, she knew that it must be close to the midnight hour. If so, Johnny should be well asleep by now and resting before his last night of fasting and seeking his vision.

"If I can only wait that long . . ." she whispered, returning to her lodge for clean garments so she could go to the river to bathe.

Always worried that Bill might be lurking about, Dede went inside the tepee and not only grabbed soap, washcloth, and clean clothes, but a pistol as well. She made sure it was loaded.

Then she left the lodge and ran through the darkness toward the river. Before she even reached it, she froze in place at the sound of wolves howling far above her.

Scarcely breathing, afraid to see if those wolves were up on the bluff where Johnny was supposed to be peacefully sleeping, she waited a moment. She inhaled a deep breath of courage, then swung around. She dropped everything and gasped with horror when she saw silhouettes of wolves high above her—yes, on the bluff.

"Where . . . is . . . Johnny?" she gasped, paling at the thought of the wolves having harmed him.

Her heart pounding, so afraid for Johnny that she felt ill, Dede grabbed the pistol in one hand, lifted the hem of her fringed buckskin skirt with the other, and broke into a mad run.

When she reached the slope of land that led upward to the bluff, she slipped and slid and had to grab hold of trees that jutted out from the hillside. She finally made it to where the land straightened out toward the bluff.

"Please, God, let Johnny be all right," she prayed. She saw the wolves, but no signs of Johnny . . . except for the lone blanket that he had taken with him.

Fear clutched her heart, and she stopped and stared at the wolves, then again at the blanket. She slowly looked around her for any signs of her son, or signs of him having been attacked by the beasts.

She recalled the feathers strewn across the blanket in her nightmare. The feathers could have represented blood! Johnny's blood! But thankfully the moon's glow revealed nothing like that to Dede, not even any signs of a struggle or an attack by the wolves.

It was as though he had disappeared into thin air!

"What . . . am I to do?" she gulped. A stark cold sliced through her when she thought of what might have happened to her son.

"Bill!" she cried, her eyes going wild. "Oh, Lord, could it be?"

She gazed down at the village, where the fire's glow was still bright in the council house. Thunder Heart had explained to her that when he was in council with his warriors he was not to be disturbed.

She had no choice but to go out on her own to find her son!

She scrambled down the side of the hill and went to the corral to get her horse, then stopped dead still when she saw a figure standing in the dark.

She slowly raised the pistol and aimed at the faceless person, the moon now behind a cloud, its light momentarily gone.

"Speak or I'll shoot," she said, her voice thin with fear.

CHAPTER THIRTY

Like a high-born maiden
In a palace tower,
Soothing her love-laden
Soul in secret hour.

—Percy Bysshe Shelley
(1792–1822)

As the clouds slipped away from the moon, revealing the face of the stranger, Dede gasped and took a shaky step away from him.

"Bill?" she said, her voice raspy. "Lord, Bill, what are you doing here in the middle of the night, unless . . ."

"Dede, please lower the gun to your side," Bill said, interrupting her. "I'm not here to cause trouble. I've come because of Johnny."

"What about Johnny?" Dede asked guardedly, still holding the pistol aimed at Bill. If her worst fears had come to pass, he might already have taken Johnny.

And the reason Bill had been able to get this close to the village was because all of the warriors were in council with Thunder Heart. They had even drawn sentries away from their posts so that everyone would be able to take part in the council, a council that was being used to map out plans for their future . . . a future they hoped to spend in Nebraska, not in Missouri, where they seemed penned in like animals.

"Dede, Johnny is at my house," Bill said. "What on earth did you think by . . ."

"Johnny is . . . at your house?" Dede interrupted. A coldness crept through her veins now that she knew where her son was. In what she now considered her enemy's house!

"Oh, Lord, Bill, what have you done?" she asked, her voice breaking. "Why couldn't you just let things be? I'm happy with Thunder Heart. So was Johnny. Why would you even want us to be a part of your life? Especially knowing that is not what we want."

"Dede, will you just listen?" Bill asked, his voice drawn. He took a step toward her, then stopped abruptly when she gestured daringly with the pistol.

"Bill, you are the one who is going to listen," Dede said tightly. "I don't know how you managed to get Johnny to your house, but by God, if it was by force, I'll see that you are arrested for kidnapping."

"Good Lord, listen to what I have to say," Bill insisted, desperation in his voice. He hung his head and kneaded his brow, then gave her a pleading look. "Dede, I didn't force anything on Johnny. He showed up at my doorstep tonight, confused, afraid, and crying. Should I have slammed the door in his face? Should I have acted as though I don't know him, as though I don't care? You know that you and Johnny have become very important to me. Damn it, I'd never do anything to harm either of you."

Dede slowly lowered the firearm to her side, trembling as she went over in her mind what Bill had said. The thought of Johnny going to his house, crying, totally confused her. She knew how much her son had wanted to make this vision quest. Why on earth would he abandon it—and especially why would he go to Bill instead of to her?

"Johnny became afraid," Bill said solemnly. "And because he felt as though he would look like a sissy to his Indian friends, he came to me. He didn't want the Ponca to know that he was too afraid to stay one more night alone on the bluff. And he didn't know how to tell Thunder Heart. He's afraid that he'll look like a baby and a coward."

"Good Lord," Dede said, paling. Her heart ached as she thought of the desperation Johnny must have felt to have gone to Bill instead of to her and Thunder Heart. Now she knew that too much emphasis had been placed on him achieving his vision quest.

She knew that Young Blood waited even now to hear all about Johnny's adventure, to see what his vision had brought him those nights he had spent on the bluff.

"When Johnny fell asleep in his bed, in his own bed, not on some savage pelts and blankets in a tepee, I asked a neighbor to watch him and decided to come and tell you what had happened, to talk some sense into your head," Bill said, taking another step toward Dede. "Yes, I know that your infatuation with the Indian warrior has blinded you to what you should want out of life for both you and your son. Tonight proved the wrong in what you are doing . . . in what you are forcing on your son. He's been reduced to a child of three, Dede, so ashamed of not succeeding at what the Indians pushed on him."

"No one pushed anything on him," Dede quickly corrected. "This was something that he wanted to do with all of his heart. And it's sad that he felt ashamed of not being able to do it. But after Thunder Heart talks to him and explains that not every young brave succeeds in a vision quest the first time and that it is nothing to be ashamed of, Johnny will be all right about things."

"You still don't see how wrong all of this is," Bill said, his eyes sweeping slowly over her, noting her buckskin and moccasins. His jaw tightened. "The child came to my door with tear-streaked black ash on his face. He was dressed in buckskins and moccasins. And his hair has grown long past his shoulders. Lord, Dede, you've almost changed him into an Indian. Surely you don't want that for Johnny. Where are those plans for him to attend college and become an attorney? He can't do anything like that if he stays among the Ponca. He'll just grow up having to listen to insults from white people who will call him a savage, a half-breed. Lord, some people will even think his father *is* a savage."

"Quit calling the Ponca savages," Dede said through clenched teeth, her spine stiff as she glared at Bill. "And I don't care how you assume things should be. It is *my* life. It is Johnny's. I'm going to go and get him, Bill. I'm going to bring him home."

"Home?" Bill stammered. "How can you call this place . . . home?"

"Because it is," Dede said stubbornly. She lifted her chin proudly. "I am married to a proud Ponca Indian chief. And I hope to give him many sons and daughters."

His lips parted and Bill stared openly at Dede. "You're married to Thunder Heart?" he gasped, then slowly hung his head and sighed. "All right," he mumbled. "I understand. And . . . I'll do nothing else to try and talk you out of what you so obviously want."

He jerked his head up and gazed at her with a softness in his eyes. "Come on with me," he said, reaching a hand out for Dede. "Let's go to my house. You can gather up all that you want to make life easier for you here among the Indians. Perhaps somewhere down the road, when Johnny sees that life as an Indian isn't enough, he might want to study law after all. And if that ever happens, I'll still be there for him. I'll pay his way to college." He swallowed hard. "And if you ever want for a thing, I'll be there for you. I care, Dede. I shall always care."

"I don't know what to say," Dede whispered, truly stunned by Bill's change of heart. "You would do that for me and Johnny, after . . . after . . . ?"

"After you practically made a fool of me?" Bill interrupted. "Yes, my friends are having a field day with this, Dede. But I'm just ignoring them. It will all pass. In time I'll be able to look them square in the eye again."

"I'm sorry you've been humiliated by what I've done," Dede said, going to Bill, gently touching his whiskered cheek. "I never wanted that for you."

"Well, sometimes in life one doesn't have choices, now does one?" he said, his eyes locked with hers. He reached up and took her hand. Lovingly he held it, then eased it away and slid his hands into his pants pockets.

"I've got to go and tell Thunder Heart what's happened," Dede said, glancing toward the council house. Although it was way past midnight now, the warriors were still discussing their future.

"Thunder Heart and his people hate living in Missouri, don't they?" Bill suddenly blurted out.

"Yes, they hate it," Dede answered, taking a deep, quavering breath. "And my husband is trying to figure out a way to get permission to go to Nebraska, to join the others. But I doubt the government will agree. I imagine we'll be here for many years to come, even though white people don't want the Ponca here any more than the Ponca want to stay."

"I can do something about that," Bill said, squaring his shoulders proudly. "I've got connections in Washington. If the Ponca really wish to join those who are in Nebraska, perhaps I can persuade the president to let that happen."

For a moment Dede only stared at him, seeing him as that man she had always known before she had overheard his plan to raid the Ponca.

But as she thought about that, and about how he seemed ready to do anything to rid this land of the Indians, she saw his offer as a selfish maneuver. If he could persuade the president to allow the Ponca to relocate to Nebraska, wouldn't that free up the land for Bill and his friends?

Although she suspected that was the true reason he was offering to help the Ponca, she didn't voice this aloud. Just the fact that he might be able to help the Ponca's cause was enough. If Thunder Heart's people got what they wanted, who cared what Bill's motive for helping them achieve it was?

"Whatever you can do would be greatly appreciated," she said. But before he could reply, Bill and Dede found themselves surrounded by several warriors, their firearms drawn and aimed at Bill. They had obviously heard their voices and had come stealthily like panthers through the night to save her. They must have thought that Bill was there for all of the wrong reasons.

Thunder Heart came out of the shadows, a rifle pointed at Bill.

Dede went straight to Thunder Heart. "It's not

what it seems," she told him. "He's not here to harm me. He . . . he came for Johnny's sake."

Thunder Heart kept his rifle steady on Bill, yet gazed questioningly into Dede's eyes. "What do you mean?" he asked, his voice drawn.

"Please tell your warriors to go on to their lodges," Dede said, giving them all a nervous glance. "Everything is all right here. Truly it is."

Thunder Heart searched her face for a moment longer, frowned at Bill, then nodded at his warriors. "Go to your lodges," he ordered. "If my wife says things are all right here, you are no longer needed."

They nodded in response, then left.

Bill stood stiffly as Dede hurriedly told Thunder Heart what had happened. She closely watched her husband's reaction to the news that Johnny had felt too ashamed to come to them tonight, but instead went to Bill.

When she saw compassion enter his eyes instead of anger she knew that he, in his gentle way, understood and would not hold Johnny's weakness against him.

"Johnny has no need to feel badly over not being able to stay the four full nights and days as he awaited his vision," Thunder Heart said, lowering his rifle to his side. "Many young braves must go a second time. They are not always ready for their visions. Nor is the vision ready to come to them. I will go to Johnny and explain this to him. I will assure him that he can come back into my people's village without shame."

He sighed heavily and looked at Bill, then peered deeply into Dede's eyes. "But it is not a good thing that he felt as though it was best to go to this man to confess his feelings instead of coming to us," he said quietly.

"It was shame and humiliation that sent him to Bill's, it wasn't because he didn't love us enough," Dede said. "After tonight, when he has time to think about it, he will know that he should always trust our love enough to come to us."

"I think we'd better hurry back to the house before Johnny awakens," Bill said. "It would be best if you were there to explain things to him the minute he wakes up. When it all comes back to him as he first awakens, the shame might be twofold."

"Yes, let's go," Dede said, rushing toward her horse. "If I am there to console him, and Thunder Heart is there to explain, I believe things will be all right."

As they all rode away from the Indian village, they saw that the lightning that had been far away a short time ago had come closer. Dark clouds were scudding across the moon. The wind was much more brisk, bringing with it a sudden autumn coolness.

Dede was glad when they were finally at Bill's house, she and Thunder Heart on each side of Johnny's bed. As they watched him sleep, she reached over and took Thunder Heart's hand and smiled at him. She had much to tell him. Bill was going to help his people get permission to return to

Nebraska. It would not take many weeks and months of deliberation with the white government as Thunder Heart had expected.

But they still would have to wait out winter and begin the long journey next spring.

That is, if Bill succeeded.

She could hardly wait to see Thunder Heart's realization that Bill was not such a bad man after all. Perhaps his reason for helping the Ponca was greed for their land, but maybe it was feeling guilty for stealing their weapons, their horses, and their pride.

If Bill helped them now, it would wipe the slate clean. He would be forgiven for his past evil deeds.

Bill came to the door, the candles in the wall sconces casting off enough light for Dede and Thunder Heart to see his outline there. When they saw what he held in his hand, Dede gasped in wonder.

Thunder Heart stiffened when he saw his bow, and he recalled the many hours he had spent carving the figures into it and the way it had been stolen from his lodge. He quickly looked up at Bill. As streaks of lightning flashed into the room through the window above the bed, Bill held out the bow to Thunder Heart.

"I'm sorry I took it, and also the quiver of arrows," Bill said quietly, so that he would not awaken Johnny who still rested peacefully. He stepped farther into the room. He held it closer to Thunder Heart. "Please take it."

Thunder Heart walked around the bed and stopped only a few inches from Bill. He gazed intently into the man's eyes, seeing a true measure of guilt. He took the bow, nodding a quiet thank-you to the white man who had so heartlessly taken it from his lodge.

Tears came to Dede's eyes as she watched Thunder Heart caress the carved figures on his bow. She could see such pride in his eyes. She had heard him say more than once that an Indian's bow became a part of the warrior's soul, that the hours spent making it made that so.

"Mama?"

Johnny's voice drew Dede's eyes quickly to him. "Oh, Johnny," she said, bending low to sweep him into her arms.

As he lifted his arms to put them around her neck, she could feel the desperation of his hug.

"Mama, I let Thunder Heart down," Johnny sobbed. "I . . . I . . . became afraid. There were so many wolves! They chased Four Eyes away, then I ran away. I couldn't finish my vision quest. I'm such a baby. My friends will look at me with pity in their eyes."

Thunder Heart slid the string of his bow over his shoulder, then knelt on the other side of the bed, opposite Dede. He reached out and gently touched Johnny's cheek as the boy eased out of his mother's arms.

"My son, no one will see you as a coward," he said. "Did Young Blood not tell you that it took him four times of fasting to finally be blessed with his vision?"

"Truly?" Johnny asked, his eyes widening. "No. He didn't tell me."

"It was not because he was too ashamed to tell you, it just did not seem important. It was not something that he was ashamed of," Thunder Heart said softly.

He took one of Johnny's hands and gently held it. "The time you spent alone on the bluff was a time of learning, as much as it would have been had you been blessed with a vision. A young boy does not become a man from just one experience. It takes many. And so you have had your first Ponca experience. There will be many more."

"I didn't want to disappoint you," Johnny said, fighting back the urge to cry. "You are your people's chief. You are now my father. I was afraid that if I failed you, I would set a bad example."

"My son, do not worry about such things. Both your mother and I are so proud of you," Thunder Heart said, drawing Johnny into his arms. "And even though you did not experience a vision as you had hoped to, you will still be given an Indian name that you will carry with you into adulthood. At that time, you can adopt another name, should you choose to. Since it was the snapping turtle incident that brought you into the lives of the Ponca, you will now be called Snapping Turtle."

"Snapping Turtle," Johnny repeated, his eyes wide. "That is a good name. Like the jaws of the snapping turtle, the name is powerful! I love it. Thank you, Thunder Heart. Thank you!"

Dede's eyes filled with tears as she watched her son and her husband bond, perhaps becoming even closer than they would have if Johnny had achieved his vision quest.

She glanced over at Bill and saw that even he was touched by this scene of father and son.

Suddenly everything seemed right.

She felt as though her family was complete, for she had never wanted Bill out of her life, and now he was again a part of it!

CHAPTER THIRTY-ONE

O wild west wind, those breath of autumn's beings,
Thou, from whose unseen presence the leaves dead
Are driven, like ghosts, from an enchanter fleeing.

—Percy Bysshe Shelley
(1792–1822)

Thunder Heart's people were now where they felt they belonged. Although they weren't at their homeland in the Black Hills, they were with the other Ponca, whole once again.

True to his word, Bill had managed to persuade the government to allow all of the Ponca people to be together in Nebraska.

Warm beneath blankets on her bed, Dede winced and grabbed her abdomen. She had not managed the long journey well, for just before leaving with her husband and his people, she had discovered that she was with child. She had had no trouble at all with her first pregnancy, so she had not been concerned about the trip.

But with this one, after they were only a few days out of St. Genevieve, she had begun suffering cramps, as though she might involuntarily lose the child she wanted so much.

But she hadn't told Thunder Heart about how she felt. If she had, it would have delayed his people's journey to Nebraska, and she hadn't wanted to be responsible for that. The Ponca had waited too long to gather together as one after having been sent from their homes in the Black Hills.

So each day, as she had sometimes walked, and sometimes ridden her horse, Dede prayed. And with each added day came hope that she might win the battle with a body that was trying to fail her.

At night, when they would stop and rest, and she lay cuddled next to Thunder Heart amidst their blankets, she silently prayed that their child would last until they reached Nebraska. If that could happen, Dede just might be able to carry the child full term.

They had made only one side trip on their journey to Nebraska. Dede had stopped to see her Aunt Mae. When she arrived, she discovered that her aunt had been buried the day before. Although it saddened Dede, she knew that Aunt Mae would have preferred being in her grave to continuing to live as a shell of the woman that she had once been . . . someone who knew nothing or no one, passing her lonely days in her rocking chair.

After that one stop, they made it to Nebraska without mishap.

It was now the eighth month of Dede's pregnancy. She spent most of her time in bed, and she was so proud of the two-room cabin that Thunder Heart and his warriors had built for her and her family. She no longer kept her health problems secret from anyone, for she knew the risk of not having total bed rest the last several weeks of her pregnancy. Back in Missouri, she had often accompanied her physician father as he visited women who were having the same sort of problems with their pregnancies. She remembered how her father urged them to stay in bed the last two months.

If only Dede could last one more month, then surely the child would be healthy.

But she hated lying there and watching the women come and go as they cleaned and cooked for her family. She could hardly wait to get back on her feet and be the sole person in her brand-new kitchen, surrounded by the pots and pans, the lovely china and silverware, that Bill had allowed her to take from his home.

She smiled as she recalled how he had said that they were more hers than his, since she had been the one to cook delicious food for him.

Now she wondered who was caring for him. When she envisioned him in his home, she saw him lonely and sad. She now understood just how much he had depended on her and Johnny's presence in his life. She hoped he would find a woman who could fill the vacant spaces in his heart. He had mourned his wife for too long as it was.

"No, please . . ." Dede gasped as she clutched at

her abdomen, the cramps attacking the very core of her being.

Sweat poured from her brow.

As the pains worsened, she closed her eyes and gritted her teeth.

She tried hard to concentrate on something else, on the rain-making ceremony that was taking place outside in the middle of the village. It was autumn now. It had been a hot, dry summer, and small fires had been started by lightning. The water level in the rivers and streams was low.

As she fought her pain she envisioned the rain-making process. First the Ponca rolled up bunches of redgrass, the sort used in building earth lodges. Then they made fires with the redgrass, dampened more redgrass, and put it on top. This formed a gas, and as it exploded, rain would be made and brought from the sky. Throughout it, prayers were offered.

A soft voice brought Dede's eyes open, and she found herself gazing into the beautiful face of a woman who was perhaps around forty years old. But neither the age nor the loveliness of the woman's face, was what caused Dede to momentarily forget her pain.

It was the fact that the woman's skin was white and her hair blond, with only a few wisps of gray, yet she was dressed in full Indian attire.

"Who . . . are . . . you?" Dede managed to ask, again very aware of the discomfort she was in as the pains continued to stab her abdomen. "I've never seen you before, and I thought I had met everyone who lived among the Ponca when . . . when . . . we arrived and celebrated being together."

"I was at the celebration, but I did not join the dancers or make myself known to those who came from Missouri, because, as you see, I am not truly Ponca," Song of the Moon explained. "When I saw you, and saw that you were also white, I was tempted to come and talk with you, but just then your husband whisked you away into a lodge. I was told later that you were having trouble with your pregnancy. I did not want to interfere by coming to you with small talk."

"Why are you here now?" Dede panted out, as the pains sliced through her abdomen.

"I hope that I can help you," Song of the Moon said, slowly pulling the blanket off Dede. "While among the Navaho, I helped bring many children into the world."

"Navaho?" Dede asked, watching the woman as she now lifted Dede's gown and began carefully pressing her fingers here and there along her abdomen. "Did you say you lived among the Navaho?"

"Yes, until I managed to run away and was rescued by a group of Ponca warriors," Song of the Moon said softly. "I have since lived among them. Also my son."

"Your son?" Dede asked, gritting her teeth as the pains worsened.

"Yes, my son, who was born after I was kidnapped by the Navaho," Song of the Moon said, her fingers now down at the lower part of Dede's abdomen, again softly pressing in. "I was pregnant when I was abducted. Thank God they allowed me to keep my child when he was born. I had feared they would kill him because he was white. But the Navaho warrior who took me as his wife saw that the child was spared. He, in fact, raised the child, even grew to love him. I escaped when Winter Hawk was five. He is now fifteen and the image of his true father, who was white."

At the mention of her son's age, Dede began to wonder. Although she was finding it hard to think past her pains, something about this woman's story brought Bill to her mind. When Bill's wife had been abducted, he had blamed it on the Navaho. He had said that his wife was pregnant at the time. And wouldn't the child now be the age of this woman's son?

Dede doubted her own conclusions. The chances of ever running into Bill's wife—the chances of her even being alive—were almost nonexistent.

Yet Dede could not let this rest until she absolutely knew who the woman was, where she had come from, and—most of all—who her husband had been at the time of her abduction.

"You say your Indian name is Song of the Moon," Dede managed between heaving breaths. "What . . . was . . . your original name? The one that you were born with?"

Dede vividly remembered Bill talking about his wife and calling her Julia.

His wonderful Julia.

His beautiful Julia with the golden hair.

Julia, with the soft voice and gentle hands.

"Julia," Song of the Moon said matter-of-factly. "My birth name is Julia Adams. My married name was Martin. But I have gone by the Indian name for so long now it wouldn't seem natural to be called Julia. And it makes it easier for me to live among the Ponca if I am called by an Indian name."

Dede's eyes widened.

At this moment of discovery she actually could not feel the pain that seconds ago had been devastating.

Lord, oh, Lord, she had found Bill's long-lost wife! She couldn't believe it! She couldn't stop staring! She must have heard wrong. The pain must have confused her.

"Did you say your name was . . ."

Song of the Moon interrupted. "Julia," she said. "Julia Martin."

Song of the Moon slid her hands away from Dede, her eyes wide as she caught the look of wonder in Dede's eyes . . . a look that told Song of the Moon that this woman somehow knew her, or at least had heard of her.

"How do you know me?" Song of the Moon asked guardedly. "I can tell that you recognized my name. How could you?"

"If you are Julia Martin, yes, I know of you," Dede said, again feeling pain, closing her eyes and panting as she waited for the latest wave to pass.

When she opened her eyes, she reached a hand out to Song of the Moon's face. "Bill has talked about you so often to me and Johnny," she murmured. Tears spilled from her eyes, not from the pain, but from the joy of having found the woman Bill loved with all of his heart. The woman he still mourned.

Song of the Moon's face drained of its color.

She took an unsteady step away from Dede's bed. "You . . . know . . . my Bill?" she gasped in disbelief. Dede's nod encouraged her to go on. "You know where he lives? When I was abducted I lived at the fort with him. Bill never talked much about where he was from, so when I escaped from the Navaho I had no idea where to find him. And . . . and . . . the fort was no longer there, so there was no one to ask. I have lived with the Ponca people a content woman. So has my son, whose true name is William Joseph, after his father."

"It's so unbelievable," Dede said, again closely studying this woman's features. It was easy to see how Bill could still see her in his mind's eye, for she was more than beautiful. There was something ethereal about her.

"How do you know Bill?" Song of the Moon asked, settling down on a chair beside Dede's bed. She didn't think Dede needed to be prepared just yet for delivery. The pains were still quite long intervals apart.

And Dede had one full month left in her pregnancy. It would be best if the pains could somehow be stopped. Perhaps talking to her might get her mind off the pain enough to make her relax, which sometimes stopped premature labor.

Dede began to tell her about her marriage to Ross, the birth of her child, and then the death of her husband. She explained about how she and Johnny had lived with her father, and then after he had died, how she had lived with Bill, though not as man and wife.

"He stayed true to you even though he doubted he would ever see you again," Dede said. She reached out a hand and twined her fingers around Song of the Moon's. "He lives just outside of St. Genevieve, Missouri. He has a grand house just waiting for a woman to share it with him. He owns much land and is a very wealthy man. He will be so proud to know that he fathered a son."

"And you say that he never forgot me?" Song of the Moon asked, wiping tears from her eyes. "Even though he had to know that an Indian warrior claimed me as his, that . . . that . . . I would have shared a bed of blankets . . . and even more with an Indian warrior?"

"It was not your choice to do any of those things," Dede said. The pain returned, getting worse and coming closer together now. She knew that she would not get through this day without giving birth to a child.

She prayed that it would be well enough formed to live, that it had not been damaged in any way, that it would have ten fingers and ten toes.

"I have never forgotten my Bill," Song of the Moon said. She winced when she saw the intensity of Dede's pain now.

"You must hurry to the nearest town and send Bill a telegram that you are alive and . . . and . . . that he has a son. Julia, wire him at St. Genevieve. Tell . . . him . . ." Dede stammered, then inhaled sharply. "Lord, I believe it's time! The baby! It has shifted lower!"

"I'll go for the others who are prepared to help you," Song of the Moon said as she scrambled to her feet.

"And then go and wire Bill," Dede encouraged. "He will be so happy to know."

"I won't leave you until I know that you and the child are all right," Song of the Moon said over her shoulder as she hurried toward the door. "Then, after the child is born, I shall also have that news to share with Bill. I'm sure he is anxious to know about how you come through the delivery . . . and if it is a boy or a girl."

Dede was deeply touched that this woman, who was a total stranger to her, would think of Dede first, her own self second.

And then everything but the pain and the safety of the child was swept from Dede's mind. Silken Wing came rushing into the cabin, several women following closely behind her.

"It will be all right," Silken Wing reassured her, placing hides for the birthing beneath Dede. "Soon you will give your husband a child."

"Johnny," Dede breathed out as Silken Wing gently removed her gown. "Where . . . is . . . Johnny?"

"He is just outside the cabin with Thunder Heart," Silken Wing replied. "They both comfort each other as they wait for the child to experience its first cry. Then they will come in and celebrate the birth with you."

"I hope the child will be all right," Dede said, wincing at another pain. "I've prayed and prayed."

Lightning Eyes, the Grizzly Bear Clan's shaman, was standing just outside the bedroom door chanting and shaking his rattles as the women bustled about preparing for the birth.

When Song of the Moon came back into the room and stood on the left side of the bed, opposite Silken Wing, Dede reached out a hand for her.

"Song of the Moon . . . Julia . . . I am so happy for you," Dede said, then closed her eyes, again suffering an onslaught of pain.

"You must now get in your kneeling position," Song of the Moon encouraged, her hands on Dede. With Silken Wing she helped Dede kneel. In that position she would give birth in the Ponca fashion.

The pains seemed to be tearing her apart, and Dede fought to keep her mind elsewhere . . . on her beloved husband, who waited anxiously to learn that she came through the childbirth all right, and who longed to hold his child in his arms for the first time.

She thought of Johnny and how she would make sure he would not feel less important in her and

Thunder Heart's lives, even though a baby would be taking so much of everyone's attention.

She managed a smile when she envisioned Bill reading the telegram that would tell him of a wife who still was alive and who still loved him.

And then there was Bill's son! Oh, how she wished she could be with Bill when he realized that he had fathered a son!

Soon too there would be news of Dede and Thunder Heart's newborn child!

Tears came to Dede's eyes when she thought about how terribly she had suffered during her pregnancy. But she knew she would forget all of the pain once she held her child in her arms and felt the tiny lips suckling at her breast.

"It is time!" Silken Wing cried, sounding to Dede as if she were talking from somewhere deep in a tunnel. The last pain had taken Dede away to a place where she now felt nothing but a serene joy, knowing that it was nearly over and soon she would have her child in her arms.

This peaceful state kept her from worrying any longer about the condition of her child. Somehow she knew that the baby would be all right and that it would be a daughter!

"Megan," she whispered to herself. "Megan Sunshine."

Yes, Megan after Dede's beloved mother, and Sunshine because that was what this daughter would bring into her family's lives.

"It is a girl!" Dede heard Song of the Moon cry out. "And she is fat and healthy!"

"Look how long her fingers are," Silken Wing cooed. "And look at her beautiful copper skin and long black eyelashes."

The pain magically eased and Dede once again became aware of everything around her. She allowed herself to be slowly turned onto her back while the blood-soaked hide was pulled out from beneath her.

Some of the women bathed her with soft cloths, while others quickly cleansed the child. Dede gazed rapturously at her daughter, then welcomed her when Silken Wing placed her in her arms.

Dede had been told that her child's umbilical cord would be placed in a buckskin amulet especially made to preserve it. These fetishes were usually made in the shape of a horned toad for boys, symbolizing endurance and longevity, and in the shape of a turtle for girls, representing fertility.

In earlier times, children would wear such fetishes until puberty. But now the amulets were wrapped in cloth, and placed in a small wicker chest, and stored where they would be safe.

Dede had also been instructed that the down of cattail was used as a talcum for babies, as a padding for cradleboards, and in quilting baby wraps.

She was anxious to know if she would have a good enough supply of milk to breast-feed her baby. If not, she knew to eat skeletonweed stems in order to increase the flow.

Song of the Moon settled a blanket over Dede as she studied her daughter and marveled at how beautiful and how perfect she was.

She looked adoringly up at Thunder Heart as he came and knelt beside the bed, and Johnny arrived soon after to kneel on the other side.

"She's so perfect," Dede murmured as she handed the child to Thunder Heart.

Johnny went to Thunder Heart's side and gazed with tears in his eyes at his sister.

"Do you want to hold her?" Thunder Heart asked the boy, smiling at him.

When Johnny nodded eagerly, Thunder Heart eased the naked child into her brother's arms. "Little sister, I will always protect you," Johnny promised, slowly rocking the baby back and forth in his arms. "No harm will ever come to you as long as I have breath in my lungs."

Thunder Heart and Dede gazed at one another and smiled. Out of the corner of her eye, Dede saw Song of the Moon slip silently out of the cabin. She smiled to herself when she heard a horse and buggy leaving the village, knowing that a woman was going to send word to a man whose life would once again be worth living.

She reached for Thunder Heart's hand. "I've something wonderful to tell you about that woman who just left the cabin," she said, thinking that this day had turned out perfect in all ways.

Everyone grew quiet with wonder when a great bolt of lightning was followed by an enormous rumble of thunder . . . and rain began to fall, slow and wonderful rain pattering across the scorched land!

CHAPTER THIRTY-TWO

Announced by all the trumpets of the sky,
Arrives the snow, and driving o'er the fields
Seems nowhere to alight; the whited air
Hides hills and woods, the river, and the heaven.

—Ralph Waldo Emerson
(1803–1882)

According to the telegram stating when he would arrive, Bill was now considerably overdue. Snow had come early in Nebraska. Tall drifts lay around all of the lodges. The howling wind incessantly whirled the snow around and around like pure white miniature tornadoes.

But all of the Ponca people were warm in their lodges. Dede was keeping herself busy making jam from the last of the wild berries, picked before the sudden bad weather, which had brought a killing frost.

Song of the Moon, whom Dede usually called Julia, was melting paraffin over Dede's fancy new wood-burning kitchen cookstove. As Dede finished each jar of jam, Julia slowly poured the paraffin over the top to securely seal the jam inside.

Dede tried not to let Julia see her concern for Bill, because she knew that Julia was already suffering in her own silent way. It was best left unsaid that everyone thought that Bill had gotten lost in the blizzard, or had died from exposure, having not been dressed well enough for such a drastic change in the weather.

In her apron, which had at one time been her mother's, and the buckskin dress, warm and wonderful against her skin, Dede thought of the changes in her cooking habits and what she had learned from both Silken Wing and Song of the Moon.

Dede actually now craved the delicious drinks made from various plants. Elderberry blossoms dipped into hot water was her favorite, next to Indian tea made from redroot.

Dede kept a good supply of tipsina bulbs, which to her were prairie turnips, for use in soups. Bunches of other herbs for use in soups and beverages were dried on her porch during the summer. She was proud of her garden, where she grew maize, beans, squash, pumpkins, gourds, and, for her husband's pipe, tobacco. She was also proud of how she had learned to use milkweed sprouts and wild flaxseed to season her soups.

She smiled as she thought of a practice that had at first abhorred her, but now seemed quite useful. From Silken Wing she had learned how rodents collected wild beans and stored them in their burrows. These beans, called "mousebeans," made a delicious meal.

But her favorite of all the foods that she had discovered as the wife of a Ponca chief was a dessert made from wild honey mixed with nuts.

Dede smiled as she looked over at the cradle. Her beloved daughter was already familiar with honey. At times, Dede let her suck small portions of honey from her fingertips.

Ah, what a delight the child was for her mother, father, and big brother. Megan Sunshine rarely cried. Even now she lay awake, her dark eyes alert, her sweet cooing sounds serenading Dede's heart like a beautiful song.

Dede would never forget the trials and tribulations of bringing Megan Sunshine safely into the world. It was something she did not allow herself to think about, or she might start worrying about the child that she was now carrying, only four weeks along inside her womb. So far, there was no sign of trouble. She prayed diligently each morning and night that this pregnancy would be different.

She wanted to be able to care for her children and her husband all the way through her pregnancy without asking for help. She loved them all so much that she truly enjoyed doing for them. If someone else were there, caring for them, she would feel cheated.

"I'm going to check on our men," Dede said, smiling over at Julia. "I'll be only a minute."

When Julia smiled faintly back at her, Dede knew that she was thinking about her own man, and wondering if she would ever see him again.

Dede rested a gentle hand on Julia's arm. "I understand what you are going through," she comforted. "Have faith, Julia, that Bill is all right. Surely God would not have brought him back into your life again only to take him away. Just you wait and see. I expect that before the sun sets today you will hear a dog team pulling a sled into the village. On that sled will be your husband."

"Husband," Julia repeated, easing away from Dede to stare out a window at the blinding snow. "For so long, through the years, I ached to be with my husband again. I had lost all hope."

She turned tear-filled eyes to Dede. "I feel that same sinking feeling inside my stomach today as I felt then," she said, a sob catching in her throat.

Dede went to her and drew her into her arms. "Wish him here," she said. "Wish hard and he will arrive safely into your arms."

"I believe my wishes are useless," Julia said, stepping away from her. "I believe they were used up long ago."

"There is always hope until proved wrong," Dede said, then glanced toward the door that led into the living room. She smiled when she heard her husband's voice. He was speaking to three attentive young men, Four Eyes asleep near the fire.

She looked at Julia again. "I'll be only a minute," she said, then stepped just outside the kitchen door. As she watched her husband, her heart filled with a joy she could not define, it was so overwhelming and wonderful. She could never feel more blessed, as now. She hoped the same for Julia and Bill. But only time would tell if that was possible.

She heard Johnny refer to Thunder Heart as *Indadi,* "Father," as he always did now. It made her heart swell with pride to know that her husband and son had such an endearing, respectful love for one another. She smiled as Johnny asked him a question. The boy was so attentive to everything Thunder Heart taught him.

"*Indadi,* what sort of wood did you say was the most prized, yet not available now for making bows?" Johnny asked as he sat with Thunder Heart, learning the art of making bows.

Young Blood and Winter Hawk were there also, sitting on blankets spread out before a roaring fire.

"Osage orange, or bois d'arc, is prized as bow wood," Thunder Heart said. "But our bows can also be made of rough dogwood or Juneberry shoots. Seasoned ashwood, the same wood we use for our tri-feathered arrows with their beveled stone points, is the most favored."

"I like the shorter bow," Young Blood said, looking over at Johnny, whom he now referred to as Snapping Turtle. "Four feet in length is better for me."

"I like the six-foot bow myself," Winter Hawk said. "It fits me better than the shorter ones."

"I seem to get more speed from the shorter one," Johnny said, casting a smile toward his mother when he caught her standing in the muted shadows of the room. Then he smiled at Thunder Heart.

"And, as you have taught me, *Indadi*, my bow is always unstrung when not in use."

"A bow lasts much longer if cared for in that way," Thunder Heart said, addressing Johnny, yet looking past him and smiling at his wife.

He was jubilant that she was with child again, yet he could not help but be somewhat apprehensive. Should she have the same trouble with this pregnancy as the last, he would not want her to carry any more babies inside her body. She was far more valuable to him than his being able to brag about having many sons and daughters. She was like a precious star, always shining brilliantly, spreading her radiance to everyone who was near her. She did not know it yet, but he had chosen an Indian name for her . . . Proud Star. He was waiting for just the right moment to tell her and see if she approved.

"I like how the Ponca bow is rounded on the outer surface and flat on the inner one," Johnny said. His father was lost momentarily in thoughts of his wife, as evidenced in the way he gazed at her, saying everything he felt in the depths of his dark eyes. It made Johnny feel warm and good inside to see such love between his mother and father. And he was so proud of his sister he could pop!

He didn't tell his parents, but he was very worried that his mother was with child again. He was there to do everything for her that she might not be able to do, though. He would even learn to cook and wash dishes if he had to.

He would do anything for his mother, for she was

always there for everyone, doing for them. She was a woman with a big, gentle heart, adored and respected by all who knew her.

"I also like how the top of the bow is pointed so that it can be used as a crude spear in an emergency," Johnny continued. "And it's easier for me to use the Ponca bow because the bottom is cut off straight with a slightly greater bend above the grip than below it . . ."

He stopped talking immediately when he heard the sound of several dogs yapping in the distance. That had to mean a dog sled was arriving at the village. And if so, it might be . . .

"Bill?" Julia said, rushing out of the kitchen when she heard the same noise outside. She untied her apron and tossed it aside as she ran to the door. "Oh, God, please let it be Bill."

Dede hurried to Thunder Heart. He rose and took her hand and walked with her toward the door, which now stood wide open. Snow blew inside, the draft cold and blustery as it swept into the cabin.

He left Dede long enough to get a bearskin cape from a peg on the wall. He put it gently around her shoulders, then slid the hood protectively up over her head.

"Do not step out into the snow without boots," Thunder Heart said, grabbing her hand, stopping her. "You can watch from here. If it is Bill, he will soon come into the cabin."

Four Eyes came up beside them, barking, the sled

dogs barking back at him. Dede's heart thumped wildly as she watched the dog sled getting closer. Only one man was standing on it, too bundled up to reveal who he was.

Then she heard Bill's voice as he shouted Julia's name and watched as Julia ran to meet him through the snow, crying. Dede sighed heavily, relieved that it was Bill, and that he was safe, after all.

Bill drew the dog sled to a quick stop as Julia came up beside it. He grabbed a blanket and hurried off the sled and wrapped it around them both. Then he hugged the blanket more snugly against her and kissed her over and over again.

"It's so wonderful," Dede said, tears flooding her eyes. "That man has loved her for so long. No one would have ever believed it possible that they would be together again."

"*Inaha*, Mother, I'm just as anxious as anyone to see Bill again, but the snow is blowing over everything," Johnny said, now always using the Ponca word when he spoke to his mother. He came to take her by an elbow, to lead her away from the door. "Bill will come inside with Julia. Please step away from the door. We've got to make sure you don't get a chill."

Deeply touched by her son's attentiveness, Dede smiled and moved away from the door, as did Thunder Heart. After Johnny closed the door, Dede took off the cape and hung it back on the peg. She went and stood over the fire to get warm again, but whirled around, eyes wide, when she heard the door open. Bill, his arm around Julia, swept her into the cabin.

"Dede," he said, going to her, drawing her into his arms. "It's so good to see you."

"I'm so glad that you're safe," Dede said, clinging to him. When she saw how eager Johnny was to give Bill a hug, she stepped away.

She stood beside Thunder Heart as Johnny and Bill hugged and laughed and talked. Julia stood in front of the fire, basking in its warmth, as well as the nearness of the man she had been denied for so long.

Julia's heart leapt when she looked over at Winter Hawk. In the excitement he had been momentarily forgotten. And to Bill, his son might be the most important person of all during these moments of joy and reunion. Shrugging the blanket off her shoulders, Julia took Winter Hawk's hand and led him closer to Bill.

When Bill saw the young brave and saw the boy's resemblance to himself, he stepped away from Johnny and with a sob of joy went to Winter Hawk. He desperately hugged him. "My son," he said, his voice breaking. "Oh, God, my son."

Although Winter Hawk had never known his father, except for everything his mother had told him, the young man clung to him. "Father," he sobbed. "It is really you? You are really here?"

"Yes, and I will never be apart from you again," Bill said, choked with emotion.

Eager for Bill to meet Megan Sunshine, Dede

started to go for her, then stopped, for now was not the time. She did not want to interfere just yet in this special family reunion that had been delayed for far too long.

Johnny stepped up beside Dede and took her hand. Dede, in turn, took Thunder Heart's as he stood on her other side. Several months ago, when Bill had been full of hate, she would have never thought it possible for them all to come together as friends. And that he found his wife was just the icing on the cake! What could make it more perfect other than Dede delivering another healthy child?

"I'm here to stay," Bill said, as he drew his wife and child into his arms, one on each side of him. "I've sold my home and land. I've liquidated everything except what you see on that sled out there. I'm going to make my home here, among the Ponca."

He paused and gave Thunder Heart a questioning look. "That is, if I am welcome," he said.

Thunder Heart broke away from Dede and Johnny. He went to Bill and placed his hands on his shoulders. "You are as one with us already," he said in a serious tone. He smiled and almost fell over backward when Bill suddenly lunged into him with an exuberant hug.

Dede covered a sob of happiness behind a hand. Now was the time for her to show off her daughter to a man she knew would adore her.

She went to the kitchen and took the baby from the cradle, then carried her little bundle of joy out to the living room and stood where Bill could see her.

Bill gasped and broke quickly away from Thunder Heart. Teary-eyed, he went and gently took Megan Sunshine from Dede's arms. Dede pulled the blanket back from her face so that Bill could see her features.

At that moment, a warning shot through Dede. She hadn't even thought about the color of her daughter's skin, or about how seeing it might affect Bill's feelings for her. There just might still be a trace of prejudice in him.

But when she saw his eyes light up and heard his delighted laugh, when he touched Megan Sunshine gently on her copper cheek, Dede sighed and knew that Bill had gotten past those old feelings of prejudice. She knew now that he would be able to live peacefully among the Ponca.

Megan Sunshine began to cry and Dede took her from Bill. Suddenly a great burst of thunder stopped her in her tracks. Everyone grew quiet and stared out the window to see the snow turn to rain and then to ice.

Dede shivered, for she realized that if Bill hadn't arrived when he had, he would probably have never made it. Ice storms were the most deadly of all storms.

She knew that Julia was thinking the same thing. It was there in how she suddenly went and desperately hugged Bill.

"It is time for a hot cup of coffee for everyone," Dede said, carrying the baby toward the kitchen.

"And some of that freshly made jam on biscuits

would taste mighty good, *Inaha*," Johnny said, coming to take his baby sister from her arms.

"Now, how did you know that I made a batch of biscuits earlier?" Dede asked, giving Johnny a smile as she went to the oven and pulled them out.

"How did I know?" Johnny asked, slowly rocking his sister back and forth in his arms. "Because I know you, *Inaha*, so very, very well."

"And you also smelled them cooking, didn't you?" Dede teased back, now making a fresh pot of coffee.

"Well, yes, that too," Johnny said with a giggle.

After setting the coffeepot on the burner of the stove, Dede tousled Johnny's hair affectionately. "My son," she murmured. "Do you know how much I love you?"

"Just a little," Johnny said, leaning toward her as she brushed a soft kiss across his cheek.

Thunder Heart stood at the door and watched his wife and son and their loving affection for one another. In his lifetime, he had never been as content. He could even truly accept the white man among his people without reservation. The white man had proved he could be trusted. Thunder Heart's people would not even be in Nebraska now were it not for Bill Martin!

Yes, for now all was well, but he could never forget that changes could come as unexpectedly as the ice storm had arrived. At this wonderful moment, though, he would not allow himself to think of such things!

CHAPTER THIRTY-THREE

Now the heart is so full
That a drop overfills it,
We are happy now because God wills it.

—James Russell Lowell
(1819–1891)

A full year had passed since Bill had struggled through the blustery storm to the Ponca village. It was another snowy night, but everyone was safe and warm in their lodges.

Ready for bed, Dede and Thunder Heart were making their final rounds in their cabin before retiring to their warm blankets. When Dede had given birth to two healthy children only moments apart, and she and Thunder Heart became parents of beautiful twins, he and his warriors had added two rooms to their log cabin.

One room was for Johnny's privacy, since he had now achieved his vision quest, which made him feel as though he was a man. The other room was for Megan Sunshine, whose exit from Thunder Heart and Dede's room made space for the twins' cradles.

In one lay a daughter with white skin, in the other a son with copper skin. Their chosen names . . . Dancing Water and Red Leaf.

Dede adored her new home, the smell of the freshly cut cedar, the cobblestone fireplace, the skin-covered home-made chairs, the tanned hides laying on the hardwood floors. Beautiful kerosene lamps sat on tables that also had been made by her husband. She had embroidered pretty designs on her kitchen towels made of flour sacks.

But the most prized of her new possessions were her babies. Both had already suckled from their mother's breast that night, which should last them until the wee hours of the morning and give Thunder Heart and Dede some moments of privacy.

Now Dede started to go on past Johnny's closed bedroom door, thinking that she and Thunder Heart might disturb his sleep. But she stopped when she saw traces of lamplight shining beneath the door.

She gave Thunder Heart a quizzical look, then turned back to the door and tapped lightly on it. "Johnny?" she asked, and waited for him to open the door.

When he did, the lamplight revealed to her why he was not asleep yet. Her eyes widened and she took quick steps to his bed, which was covered by several of Ross's lawbooks. Four Eyes lay among them.

She picked one up and then turned to Johnny. "What are you doing with these?" she asked softly. "Why are they in bed with you at this late hour?"

She went to him with the book. "Johnny, were you reading this?"

"I read them every night," Johnny said, gently taking the book from his mother. "I've made a decision, *Inaha*. I'm going to be a lawyer after all."

Dede was taken aback by this. She stared disbelievingly at Johnny. He had always rejected any notion of becoming a lawyer like his true father.

She wanted to contain her own excitement so that Johnny wouldn't see how glad she was that he had made this choice. If he decided against it again later she didn't want him to feel pressured by knowing how much it would mean to her. The part of her that would always love Ross wanted her son to be somewhat like him.

Now, since Johnny had lived among the Ponca, he seemed more Indian than white in his everyday ways. And that brought worry into Dede's heart, for if Johnny went to law school looking and behaving like an Indian, wouldn't he run into trouble with his white classmates?

If so, would he be able to look past such prejudices and still succeed at what he had chosen to do with his life?

"When did you decide this?" Dede asked, thinking that Bill had somehow been talking to him about law school again. Bill had always wanted Johnny to be a lawyer and had been willing to pay his way. In fact, he still had the money that it would take for Johnny to attend school.

"Johnny, was it Bill who persuaded you to become a lawyer?" she blurted out before Johnny had the chance to answer her.

"It has nothing to do with Bill," Johnny replied, smiling up at her. "It's because of you, and because of me. I know how you have longed for me to be a lawyer. And only a short while ago I decided that's what I also want."

"That's so wonderful," Dede said, glad that Thunder Heart slid his arm around her waist. That small gesture of love proved that he was happy for what was happening tonight, that he approved of Johnny's choice instead of resenting him for wanting something that would take him away from his family and his people for many years. It just proved to her once again that her husband was a very special man, one with unlimited compassion.

"*Inaha*, so much of my decision came because you are such a good teacher," Johnny said in a rush of words. "The way you tutor the Ponca children every day in the new school made me hunger for a higher education."

His eyes lit up when he looked quickly from Dede to Thunder Heart. "And I have the best news," he gushed. "Young Blood and Winter Hawk are going to attend law school with me. All of us want to learn everything we can to defend the rights of all Indians. It is clear every day how lawyers for our people are needed. Isn't it wonderful, Mother and Father, that my best friends in the world are going with me to law school?"

By the way Thunder Heart's arm tightened

around Dede's waist, she knew that he was not all that happy about losing three young men at once from their fold. Yet he knew that this was what they wanted, and he did not wish to interfere in a future that could be bright for them all. So he said nothing, only smiled and nodded.

"Bill said that after selling off most of his things back in Missouri he has enough money to send all three of us to school," Johnny said, even more excited now. "He's such a good man, isn't he?"

Dede could not help but think back to that day when she had been on the bluff and had seen Bill and his friends ride into the Ponca village and steal their weapons and horses. When she thought of the hate that had driven the men to do such evil against an innocent people, she tried her best to block it from her mind. Bill had changed.

She knew that he felt guilty when he thought of what he had done that day and of how he later had tried to get the Ponca arrested for taking Seven Drums to the Black Hills for burial.

"What are you thinking about?" Johnny asked, breaking into her reverie.

Dede smiled awkwardly. She slipped away from Thunder Heart and went to Johnny and hugged him. "I'm thinking about you and how proud I am of you," she murmured.

"*Inaha*, when I become a famous lawyer, I'll be able to make sure nothing happens to my brother and sisters, or to any of the Ponca people," he said.

"And won't my brother and sisters be proud of their older brother?"

"As everyone who knows you will be proud," Dede said, raking her fingers through his long black hair.

She stepped away from him and returned to Thunder Heart. She twined her fingers through his. "I think we should let this young man study his lawbooks, don't you, darling?" she asked, gazing lovingly up at her husband.

"My *wizige*, my son, I love you and I am glad that you have made a choice that will make you happy," Thunder Heart said. "It is good of Bill to spread his wealth among my young men. He is a good man."

"Yes, and he regrets all the things he did when he was guided by vengeance," Johnny said, sighing.

"We know that. It's good to have him here among us," Thunder Heart said softly.

"Johnny, don't stay up too much longer," Dede said over her shoulder as she and Thunder Heart turned to walk toward the door. "We mustn't use too much kerosene at once. With the weather so bad, it might be hard to get into town to get a fresh supply."

"I'm going to bed now," Johnny said, already picking the books up from his bed. "I'll study tomorrow after school."

"You teaching our children means a lot to them all," Thunder Heart said as he closed the door behind them. "All children yearn for wisdom and all of the Ponca children have brighter futures because of your teaching."

"I love teaching them," she said. "They are all such eager students."

They went into their bedroom where a lamp glowed faintly on their bedside table. It gave off enough light by which to see the babies sleeping in their twin cradles, their faces wondrously contented.

Dede turned to Thunder Heart. "We are so lucky," she whispered. "And how I do love you so."

He bent low and blew out the fire on the wick. He reached over to her and slid her nightgown up over her head and tossed it aside over a chair.

She, in turn, disrobed him.

The fire in the fireplace out in the living room gave off enough warmth that they did not have to immediately pull the covers up as they climbed onto the bed.

But to make sure that Dede would not be chilled, Thunder Heart blanketed her with his body. His lips came down onto hers, and he gave her a meltingly hot, passionate kiss.

Dede's head swam with pleasure as Thunder Heart's hands moved slowly over her, caressing her, touching her, lifting her into clouds of rapture.

And when he nudged her legs apart with his knee, and she felt his manhood probing where she was wet and ready for him, Dede sucked in a wild breath of ecstasy. He pushed himself deeply inside her and began his rhythmic thrusts.

Thunder Heart whispered into her ear. "My Proud Star, how I love you," he said, holding her endearingly close.

"As I love you," she whispered back, adoring her Indian name.

And as their children peacefully slept and the snow blew in swirls against their bedroom window, Dede twined her arms around Thunder Heart's neck and rode with him again to the bright, hot stars!

Dear Reader:

I hope you enjoyed *Thunder Heart*. The next book in my Signet Indian Series, which I am writing exclusively for NAL, is *Sun Hawk*, about the Ojibwa Indians during the time when Minnesota was only a wilderness. You will find much intrigue, romance, and adventure in this novel. I hope you will buy *Sun Hawk* and enjoy reading it as much as I enjoyed writing about the interesting customs and lives of the Ojibwa.

For those of you who are collecting all of the books in my Signet Indian Series and want to read more about them, you can send for my latest newsletter (autographed), photograph, and bookmark. Write to:

Cassie Edwards
6709 N. Country Club Road
Mattoon, IL 61938

For a prompt reply, please send a self-addressed, stamped, legal-size envelope.

Or visit my web site at www.cassieedwards.com.

Thank you from the bottom of my heart for your support of my Signet Indian Series. I love researching and writing about our country's beloved Native Americans.

Cassie Edwards